"Lynette has another hit on her hands. *Target Acquired* grabs hold with non-stop action and doesn't let go."

Dani Pettrey, bestselling author of *One Wrong Move*

"Lynette Eason's fans will not be disappointed. Kenzie is a strong heroine readers can root for, and the twists and turns of the plot will keep them on the edge of their seats until the last chapter."

Janice Cantore, author of *Code of Courage* and *One Final Target*

Praise for *Double Take*

"*Double Take* is Lynette Eason at her best, and readers are sure to be captivated. Smart plotting, action-packed suspense, well-developed characters, and sweet romance made this a truly enjoyable reading experience for me, and I devoured it in one sitting."

Reading Is My Superpower

"It's time to get out your calendar and clear your schedule. Lynette Eason's *Double Take* is sure to cause you not to give a second glance at any other commitments until this riveting new story is 100 percent complete. I thoroughly enjoyed the characters, the banter, and the suspense."

Jaime Jo Wright, ECPA bestselling author
of *The Vanishing at Castle Moreau*

"*Double Take* is phenomenal and had my heart racing from the moment I started reading. Brilliant plot. Incredible story. Proof again of Lynette Eason's prowess that keeps her at the top!"

Kimberley Woodhouse, bestselling and award-winning author
of *26 Below*, *The Heart's Choice*, and *A Mark of Grace*

"This book should come with a warning: do not start unless you've got plenty of time to finish! *Double Take* kept me up turning pages and wondering what would happen next. It's a heart-stopping ride from start to finish."

Kathleen Y'Barbo, *Publishers Weekly* bestselling author of *The Black Midnight*, *Dog Days of Summer*, and The Bayou Nouvelle series

TARGET
ACQUIRED

BOOKS BY LYNETTE EASON

LAKE CITY HEROES ▪ 2

TARGET ACQUIRED

LYNETTE EASON

Revell

a division of Baker Publishing Group
Grand Rapids, Michigan

Published by Revell
a division of Baker Publishing Group
Grand Rapids, Michigan
RevellBooks.com

Printed in the United States of America

Library of Congress Cataloging-in-Publication Data
Names: Eason, Lynette, author.
Title: Target acquired / Lynette Eason.
Description: Grand Rapids, Michigan : Revell, a division of Baker Publishing
    Group, 2024. | Series: Lake City heroes ; 2
Identifiers: LCCN 2024006047 | ISBN 9780800741204 (paperback) | ISBN
    9780800745844 (casebound) | ISBN 9781493445516 (ebook)
Subjects: LCGFT: Christian fiction. | Thrillers (Fiction) | Romance fiction. | Novels.
Classification: LCC PS3605.A79 T37 2024 | DDC 813/.6—dc23/eng/20240213
LC record available at https://lccn.loc.gov/2024006047

This book is a work of fiction. Names, characters, places, and incidents are the product of the author's imagination or are used fictitiously. Any resemblance to actual events, locales, or persons, living or dead, is coincidental.

Cover photography by Rekha Garton, Arcangel

Baker Publishing Group publications use paper produced from sustainable forestry practices and postconsumer waste whenever possible.

24 25 26 27 28 29 30   7 6 5 4 3 2 1

Dedicated to my amazing family.
I love you all to infinity and back. xoxo

CAST OF CHARACTERS

Kenzie King—SWAT medic and the newest member of Lake City's SWAT team

Ben King—Kenzie's father and former chief of police for Lake City

Paul King—Kenzie's oldest brother

Kash King—Kenzie's second-oldest brother

Logan King—Kenzie's youngest brother, detective with Lake City Police

Betsy King—Kenzie's paternal grandmother and best friend to Eliza Crane

Dr. George King—Kenzie's paternal grandfather, former head physician at the Lake City State Hospital

Cole Garrison—SWAT team leader and detective with Lake City Police Department

Mariah—Cole's younger sister

Riley Marie—Cole's niece

Addison (Addy)—Cole's older sister

Eliza Crane Garrison—Cole's grandmother

William Garrison—Cole's grandfather

Bart Crane—Eliza's father

Additional SWAT

Judson Hill—commander

James Cross, also Cole's partner on the police force (read his story in *Double Take!*)

Sampson Greene

Otis—Sampson's Belgian Malinois K-9

Cowboy McEntire

Scott Butler

Buzz Crenshaw

Max Mann, aka Magic Man

...

Lainie Jackson—emergency department physician assistant (read her story in *Double Take!*)

Jesslyn McCormick—fire marshal

Kristine Duncan—air marshal

Stephanie Cross—sister to James Cross

Oscar Woodruff—Lake City police officer

Harold Woodruff—Oscar's father; contemporary of Kenzie's father, Ben King

Stephen Woodruff—Harold's father, Oscar's grandfather

PROLOGUE

LAKE CITY STATE HOSPITAL
LAKE CITY, NC
A BRANCH OF THE DOROTHEA DIX HOSPITAL
JULY 1947

"Is she coming today?" Eliza Crane asked the nurse standing just inside the small room. Her name was Nurse Alice. Nurse Alice with no last name. She wore a white uniform with a white hat, white stockings, and white shoes. Her expression was just as pale, and she looked every one of her confessed forty-three years—especially sporting that gray streak down the side of her otherwise dark hair. There was no kindness in her green eyes, but no malice either. More of a weariness that Eliza could relate to. "Please, is Betsy coming today?"

Eliza sat on the hospital bed, her back against the wall, knees drawn to her chest to ward off the chill of the room in spite of it being a bright summer July day. When was the last time she'd been warm? She couldn't remember.

"Not sure, Eliza," the woman said, planting her hands on her hips. "If she does, I'll come get you."

"Can you ring her and tell her I need her to come? She's only been allowed to come once and I need to see her."

11

"The phone lines are down, but you have an appointment with the new doctor in an hour, so you need to get dressed and make yourself presentable." She waved to the garments thrown over the changing screen in the corner.

"New doctor?" Eliza shook her head, still in shock that her long dark brown curls were no longer there. They had been chopped off to make the lice easier to get rid of. Leave it to her to be stuck with a licey roommate her first night in this miserable place. Thankfully, the woman had been removed on her second day and no one had taken her place. "No. I don't want to see a doctor, I want to go home." But as soon as the words left her lips, her heart cried a denial. She did *not* want to go home.

But she didn't want to stay here either. She walked to the changing screen, pulled the clothes down, and began to dress. Why did the thought of home fill her with such dread? And where was William? As her fiancé, shouldn't he be allowed to see her? But he hadn't come. At least no one had told her he had.

"That's not possible," Nurse Alice said. "Dr. King's reviewing your chart as we speak, so get ready."

"I thought the doctor's name was Rinaldo." The one she'd been scheduled to see, but her appointment had been cancelled.

"It was, but he had a heart attack and died the day after you got here. I can't believe they found a new doctor so quickly. They're not exactly lined up to work here, you know." Her matter-of-fact words weren't mean; she was just overworked like everyone else in the overcrowded mental hospital.

Eliza still wasn't sure how she'd wound up here. The first few days were fuzzy, the itchy lice incident more clear than anything else. Today, her mind seemed to be working despite the pain in her head. She rubbed the knot on the side of it, wondering how she'd gotten it. Then she glanced at the bandages on her wrists. She'd taken a pair of shears and . . . and what? Why couldn't she remember what happened next? The pain in her head increased.

"Eliza. Come on!"

Eliza bit her lip on a whimper and stepped around the screen. "I don't want to be here."

Alice sighed, a glint of pity showing for the first time in her gaze. "Your father put you here for a reason. The only way you'll get to go home is if you get better."

"But, what's wrong with me?" she whispered.

"You tried to kill yourself. That's what's wrong with you, and the doctor needs to determine if you're still a danger to yourself."

Eliza blinked. She'd tried to kill herself? Why? An argument echoed in the recesses of her mind—raised voices, harsh demands. She pressed her hands over her ears and focused, but she couldn't quite grasp the topic of the shouting match and pull it forward. "I didn't. I wouldn't."

"But you did." Finally her face softened a little more. "You'll like Dr. King. He's very forward thinking when it comes to ways to help patients like you. He likes to talk a lot, ask questions, and get to know you. He said patients need to know that someone is not only listening but hearing."

Well, that didn't sound so bad.

"Who was screaming all night long? Such wretched screaming. My ears are still ringing with it."

"It's just the way of this place. You'll learn to ignore it." Nurse Alice snagged a cup from the cart just outside the door, and Eliza let the memory—and the screaming—go. The woman thrust the cup with two little pills at her, along with another matching cup that held about two ounces of water. "Swallow."

Eliza did as told. She really did want to get better, and her father promised her this place would help her. But . . . better from what? And she didn't trust her father anymore. She hadn't for a long time. So—

"I have two more patients to see," Nurse Alice said. "Be ready when I get back." And then she was gone, the door snicking locked behind her.

Tears leaked from Eliza's eyes. She was only twenty-two. She'd barely begun to live and already it felt like her life was over. She looked at her wrists once more. They didn't hurt any longer and she decided one of the pills must be some kind of painkiller. Probably the one that made her want to sleep the hours away. She frowned. Why give her that before her meeting with the doctor? It was going to be all she could do to stay awake.

With a sigh, she lifted the mattress and pulled out her journal along with the ink pen Betsy had managed to sneak her. If Nurse Alice found the pen, she'd take it. Because if Eliza truly wanted to kill herself, she could find a way to do so with the writing instrument.

But Eliza didn't want to die. She wanted to live. She desperately wanted to live. She pressed the pen to the paper and wrote until the door rattled when a key slid into the lock. Pushing the haze of the drugs aside, she stuffed the book and pen back into her hiding place, then slipped into her black slippers just as Alice stepped inside.

"The dose of pain medicine was lower this time so you wouldn't be so sleepy. Can you walk?"

So that's why she'd been able to form coherent sentences for her journal. "Yes. I think so."

"Then let's go. Dr. King is reported to be kind but can't abide tardiness."

"I'm ready when you are."

ONE

PRESENT DAY
WEDNESDAY, OCTOBER 15

SWAT medic Kenzie King grabbed her firearm and medical kit, then aimed her steps toward Dolly, the TK-4 tactical vehicle. With Commander Judson Hill's quick briefing still playing in their heads, she and the other unit members moved with focused precision.

Outside, snowflakes dusted her and she blinked. Lake City, North Carolina, didn't see tons of the white stuff this early in the season, but the mid-October temps had dropped last night, and the weatherman's predictions had come true. Thankfully, it wasn't supposed to freeze and should be gone almost before it touched the ground. Next week would find the temperatures in the midsixties.

She'd been on the job almost six months, so this was her first fall with SWAT, but she'd lived in Lake City all her life. Long enough to learn the weather could be as unpredictable as her schedule. Which was fine. Growing up with her father as the chief of police for the first fourteen years of her life, she was used to rolling with change. They made plans, her dad changed them. Constantly. Didn't mean she liked it, but she could turn on a dime without blinking or whining. It helped that the majority of their missions were planned right down to the very last detail as opposed to the "hurry up and save lives" missions like this one.

Kenzie climbed into the vehicle, and Sampson Greene eyed her with that flat look she could never read, then turned his gaze to his phone. No doubt checking to see if there were any new or developing details about the situation they were walking into. His K-9, a seventy-five-pound Belgian Malinois named Otis, settled at his feet, ears flicking back and forth, tension running through his sleek, well-muscled frame.

Buzz Crenshaw, driver and sniper, climbed behind the wheel while Sergeant Cowboy McEntire checked his weapon in the passenger seat. Cowboy had been an explosive ordnance specialist in the Army before getting out and joining the team. He shot her a glance when she dropped onto the bench that lined the vehicle's wall. "You good, King?" he asked her.

She bit her lip on her initial response, hating that snarky was her "go-to" these days. Cowboy filled in as SWAT team leader when Cole Garrison wasn't there, which was fine. He did a good job with the role, and he didn't mean anything by the question. And yet he hadn't asked any of the others if *they* were good. *"You catch more flies with honey, sweetheart. Remember that."*

"I'm just fine."

Her grandmother was right as usual. Kenzie was getting worn down by all the hazing that had been going on since she'd joined the unit. But that was her secret. No way would she let it show.

"How's the ED treating you?"

As of last month, she worked shifts at the hospital emergency department when she wasn't working with SWAT, because renovating a house was expensive. "Fine."

"You really gotta quit being so talkative," Cowboy said over his shoulder.

"I'll work on that."

Kenzie shifted her medical kit out of the way of her feet and checked her weapon before sliding it into her holster. She might be the medic, but she'd been through all the training required to be a part of the SWAT team.

"All right, people," Buzz called out, "we're headed to the West Hampton part of town. Update just came in. Three hostages instead of two, still just one gunman. No known fatalities or injuries as of this moment. Garrison's meeting us there."

And just the mention of his name tightened her gut and caused her palms to sweat. A reaction that made her want to bang her head against a wall because of the confusion it ignited. Instead, she clamped her hands together and ran through the plan once more. As the team medic, she'd wait in a safe zone and pray her services weren't needed. Nine times out of ten, the incident resolved peacefully, but there was always the chance this call would be the *one*.

Officer Scott Butler climbed in and slammed the door. His gaze met Kenzie's and his lip curled just before he took the seat next to her. She refused to cringe as his hip butted against hers, rationalizing that it was a tight fit and couldn't be helped. She just wished he didn't hate her simply because she was a woman on the team.

"Rolling!" Buzz cranked Dolly, pressed the gas, and spun the wheel.

Butler rolled with the sharp turn and slammed into her, shoving her against Greene, who shot her a hard look but shifted, creating a fraction more space for her. James Cross sat across from her and frowned, started to say something, then stopped when Kenzie narrowed her eyes at him, daring him to voice his thoughts.

Determined to ignore them all, she righted herself and refused to let Butler get to her. No one had come right out and said it, but she had a feeling he was jealous of her position and acting out his frustrations like a three-year-old. He had medical training and felt like he could do the job as medic just as well as—if not better than—she could.

He couldn't. She had MD after her name. He didn't. Which, she suspected, played into his need to prove something to his other teammates. Some ego thing.

Or it could be something entirely different. Who knew?

She was clueless and wasn't sure whether she should ask him or not. She just kept hoping when he didn't get a response out of her, he'd eventually let it go and get over it. Hopefully soon. *Please, God, soon.*

Five and a half months in and she was still hoping.

Her gear was hot despite the cold weather, and Dolly's air-conditioning hadn't reached into the back yet, so sweat slid down the groove along her spine.

"All right," Buzz said. "Get ready."

Finally, they rolled through the police barricade and to a stop at the edge of the convenience store parking lot. Kenzie checked the pistol at her hip and grabbed her medical kit, maneuvering it to the middle of the vehicle where she could snap it open in a moment's notice.

The men stood behind the protection of the SWAT vehicle, and Cole—she only referred to him as Garrison in front of the unit—exited his 4Runner, dressed in his gear, to join them. Kenzie couldn't help but wonder where he'd been. Probably working one of the many cases he juggled in addition to his duties with SWAT.

And then it was time to focus. She listened as they ran through the plan once more if the negotiator on scene couldn't talk the armed man down.

Two gunshots sounded. Glass shattered. Screams from inside the store echoed. Kenzie jumped out of the vehicle, her feet hitting the asphalt as the men swarmed toward the store, each heading for their area of responsibility, or AOR. Kenzie hung back but positioned herself so she could watch everything go down, listening for calls for help. The comms in her ear spit information nonstop as the members stayed in touch, giving by-the-second updates.

Cole's orders came through and she visualized their movements through the store.

"Stay safe," she whispered. "Please stay safe."

SERGEANT COLE GARRISON relished his role on SWAT when he wasn't working as a detective with the Lake City Police Department. And right now, he was trying to stop a shooter who seemed content to put bullets through windows and inventory before he escalated to people.

Cole and the team had entered through the back of the store in silence and stood next to the candy aisle, out of sight of the convex mirror above the checkout counter ten yards ahead. A woman and young child huddled next to the freezer in the corner. Cole raised a finger to his lips in the universal sign for silence. The woman— probably the kid's mother—nodded and pulled the child closer.

If he waved them out the back door, the noise could cause the shooter to turn and then they'd all be up the proverbial creek. They'd managed to stay out of sight of the worker at the checkout, but if he took his eyes off the gun pointed at him, he might spot them. They needed to act before that happened.

The man with the weapon stood at the counter, his back to Cole and the team, gun held at arm's length on the quivering teen at the cash register. "I said get him out here! Tell him to come face me like a man!"

"I tried, Kev! You heard me. He won't come out of the office!"

The shooter and the worker knew each other. Good. Maybe. Especially if they were friends once upon a time. Might make it less easy to shoot the worker.

"He got me fired and he won't even face me?" Kev scoffed. "Typical. What a coward!" He paused and rubbed his free hand down his face while the hand with the gun never wavered. Then he gave his head a slight shake and flicked the weapon toward the exit. "You've always been nice to me. I got no beef with you. Get out of here."

The teen behind the counter darted around the side and bolted toward the door that led to the parking lot.

James had his weapon up and ready to fire. He nodded to Cole that he had a shot, but Cole balled his fist and held it up—the signal for everyone to freeze. If the shooter was going to let people go, he wasn't going to interfere with the process. "Let's see how this is going to play out," he said, his voice one decibel above silent.

Greene signaled Otis to the floor. The dog lay on his stomach but was ready to spring with the force of a catapult should the moment come. He kept his eyes on his handler while his ears twitched.

The guy with the gun aimed himself and his weapon toward the office. "Leo! You're dead, man! Stacy left me and it's all your fault!"

Cole signaled Greene, who gestured to Otis.

The dog launched toward the suspect. The guy turned just as Otis clamped his jaws around the forearm of the hand holding the weapon.

A scream ripped from the man's throat and he pivoted, weapon still clutched in his hand, barrel aimed at the team.

"Everyone down!" Cole's shout echoed as the weapon barked and the team dropped.

Greene slammed the shooter to the ground with a command for Otis to release. Within seconds, he had the man in cuffs. "Clear!"

As one, the unit rose to their feet and moved in—all except Cowboy. He lay on the tile, gloved hand clutching his head while blood flowed between his fingers.

"Cowboy!" Cole darted to his teammate, hand reaching for his radio. "Kenzie, get in here! Officer down!"

Almost before he'd finished the order, she was through the door and at Cowboy's side. "Cowboy, let me see it," she said, her voice low, calm, the eye in the middle of the storm.

Even Cole thought his blood pressure might have lowered a fraction. He nodded when she gently tugged Cowboy's hand from the side of his head.

"How bad is it?" The man's voice sounded like he had gravel in his throat.

"Well, you're conscious, so that's a good sign."

Cole glanced at the others, who'd cleared the rest of the store. The suspect had already been led outside where he would enjoy the view from the back seat of a patrol car.

The manager stepped out of the back with Butler at his side. Had to be the man named Leo. "He was going to kill me! You heard him, right? You're going to put him away for life, right?"

"The justice system will take care of him," Butler said. He rolled his eyes at Cole.

Cole frowned. The manager had just lived through a pretty terrifying ordeal. Granted, some might consider him a coward, but not everyone reacted well when they were afraid. He could have compassion for the guy. He stepped forward and placed a hand on Leo's shoulder. "Take some time to regroup, all right? See a counselor if you need to. Even though it ended without anyone seriously hurt"—including Cowboy, he prayed—"it's going to have a lasting effect on you."

Leo met his gaze and nodded. "Right. You're right. Thank you. I . . ." He swallowed. "I'm sorry I wasn't more brave, I just . . . I didn't know how or what . . . I knew he hated me because I fired him, but he was late all the time, didn't show up and never called to let me know, and I just . . . never mind." He dropped his chin to his chest and headed out the door.

"Coward," Butler muttered.

"Hey, he was terrified. You and I wouldn't have reacted that way, but we've had training. Don't judge him."

Butler raised a brow. "Whatever you say, Sarge." He trotted away and Cole shook his head. The guy was young, true, but he had a hardness about him that Cole didn't much care for. Only the fact that he did his job and did it well allowed Cole to let some things slide.

He hurried to find Kenzie and Cowboy and spotted them still on the floor, although Cowboy was sitting up, leaning against a display of chips. Kenzie had her back to Cole and was working around Cowboy's head.

"How is he?" Cole asked.

She glanced up at him, her brow furrowed. "It's more than just a graze, but . . . I'm not exactly sure. I think it was a fragment that penetrated the skin, but not the bone."

"You're saying I got a bullet fragment between my skull and skin?" Cowboy asked.

"Yeah." She shot him a small smile, but Cole could see the concern in her eyes.

Cowboy blinked. "So, get it out."

She gave a short, choked laugh that sounded more like a cough. "Not here. That's going to require some surgery." She glanced back at Cole. "He'll need to be monitored for a concussion too. He was out for a few seconds. If I were his doctor, I'd order a CT scan and keep him overnight."

"Shouldn't have told you I lost consciousness for a fraction of a second," Cowboy said. "I'm fine."

"Only because the bullet didn't hit something before it hit your head," Cole muttered. "Ambulance is outside. Let's go."

"Aw, man, I—"

"That's an order."

Cowboy snapped his lips shut and nodded. Then winced.

"You'd make me do the same if the roles were reversed," Cole said, his voice softer.

"No I wouldn't. I'd never treat you like that." The whine in his voice was unmistakable and Cole smothered a laugh.

"Liar. Get out of here. You're done until you get that piece of bullet out of your head and the surgeon—or Kenzie—releases you." He helped the man to his feet and noticed he swayed before catching his balance.

"Dizzy?" Kenzie asked.

"Uh, yeah, maybe. A little."

She stepped up and gripped his arm. Cole caught the look she shot him and nodded. They weren't going to let him walk out under his own power.

Once Cowboy was safely in the ambulance with two paramedics hovering over him, Cole looked at Kenzie. Beautiful Kenzie King, who took his breath away and pulled all his protective instincts to the surface. Instincts he had to stuff down into the deepest corners of his heart. "Good work."

She flashed him a tight smile. "Thanks. I just gotta grab my stuff, then I'll be ready to roll."

She hurried back inside the store, and Cole turned to find James watching him. James Cross, his best friend and partner. A man who knew him better than just about anyone. "What?"

"Didn't say anything."

"Didn't have to. What are you thinking?"

"What do you think I'm thinking?"

Cole scowled. "I don't know, but you're wrong."

"If you don't know what I'm thinking, how do you know I'm wrong?"

"Shut up."

James' low chuckles followed him all the way to Dolly.

TWO

Kenzie sometimes accompanied her "battlefield patients" to the hospital and sometimes she just patched them up on scene and let the paramedics escort them. Today, she was at the hospital. The wounded one was a team member, and she was going to be there for him no matter what he—or anyone else—thought about her position with the unit. She knew she belonged. One day they'd see it too. She hoped.

Cole and the others would be right behind her as soon as they could get away from the scene.

She walked into the ED and spotted Lainie Jackson, who was speaking to one of the doctors at the nurses' station. Lainie and Kenzie had met during an incident much like the one that had injured Cowboy. Only Kenzie had been the one grazed by a stray bullet. Lainie had kept watch over Kenzie throughout her short hospital visit. Friendly, concerned, intent—and eyes shadowed with secrets and pain.

Like her own, no doubt.

She shook herself and walked to Cowboy's room and knocked. She'd speak to him first, then get out of the way so the others could have a turn when they arrived.

"Come in."

She pushed open the door and stepped inside, then leaned against the wall. The man in the bed was not a happy camper. He scowled at her. "This isn't necessary."

She shrugged. "A bullet—going very fast, I might add—hit you in the head. You could have a concussion."

"I don't."

"If you haven't seen the doctor, I can examine you and tell you for sure."

"Go away."

His mild tone brought a smile to her lips, and she pressed them together to hide it. But he was verbally sparring with her like he would any other member of the team, and that did more for her morale than anything she could possibly think of.

"You got there fast," he said, his voice low.

"I heard the shots and Garrison's shout. I knew someone had been hit."

He eyed her. "Like really fast."

"Just doing my job."

His eyes stayed glued on hers. "Right."

The door opened behind her and she turned. Cole. Her heart did *not* skip a beat, because that simply wasn't allowed.

"Hey," he said. "How's he doing?"

"I'm right here," Cowboy said, the growl in his throat unmistakable. "You can ask me, you know."

"Yeah, but you won't tell me the truth, so I'm not wasting my breath."

Cowboy huffed. "Hey now."

Kenzie snickered, then tried to cover it with a cough. "He'll be all right. I'm sure he has a headache, he just won't admit it. Probably a mild concussion. He's on medical leave until he gets the all clear."

"Now wait a minute—"

Once again the door opened and Lainie stepped into the room. She raised a brow at them. "Getting kind of crowded in here, isn't it?"

"I was just leaving," Kenzie said. She turned to go.

"Hey, King." Cowboy's voice was subdued, but it stopped her. She glanced back and he met her gaze. "For real. Thanks."

She smiled. "Of course."

Cole gave her a sharp nod and a thumbs-up. "Hang around for a sec, will you?"

"Sure. I'll just go give the guys an update." They'd be pacing holes in the waiting room floor.

She left them alone and detoured to the nurses' station where she found Dr. Allison Lambe reviewing a chart. Allison had become a fun-loving friend Kenzie was always glad to run into. The woman's dark eyes lifted to meet Kenzie's. "Hey there. How's it going?"

"Just another day in the life of a SWAT medic. How's it going for you?"

"Dr. Lambe!" a nurse called from the hallway. "Need you in room 3, please."

Allison lifted a brow. "Just another day in the life of a trauma doctor."

Kenzie laughed. "See you later."

Allison hurried off two seconds before Cole stepped out of Cowboy's room and walked over to her. "The guys okay?"

"I stopped to talk to Allison for a moment," she told him, "so I haven't been out to the waiting room yet."

He pulled his phone from his pocket. "I'll text Greene and Hill and let them know he's going to be fine. Lainie said he needed a few stitches and a couple of days of rest."

"I'm sure that went over well."

When he finished tapping and looked back up at her, Kenzie did her best to focus on her thoughts and not his blue eyes. "Concussion?"

"A mild one. Everything you said, she confirmed. She made a point to emphasize how much worse it could have been and he did the right thing by coming in to get checked out."

"That sounds like Lainie. I'll bet he didn't agree, though."

"Not in the least." He nodded to the door. "You ready to start your time off?"

She glanced at him and shrugged. "Sure."

"Big plans?"

Why was he asking? He'd never shown much interest in what she did with her off hours before. "Nothing huge. It's been a while since my days off here in the ED and SWAT coincided, so I plan to take advantage of that. I'm going to run a few miles and put in some time at the gym, a contractor is coming to repair part of the ceiling in the guest bathroom, but other than that, I don't have anything pressing."

"Other than—" He laughed. "You're not going to the get-together tomorrow night at the lake house?"

"What get-together?"

He narrowed his eyes. "When's the last time you checked your text messages?"

"Um . . ." When *was* the last time? "Sometime this morning, I think. Early."

"Check the group text."

She pulled out her phone and scanned the screen as they reached the exit. "Wow, thirty-two missed texts. I'll have to catch up on all that, but yes, if that's the plan, then I'll be there."

"Good. I think a firepit and s'mores were mentioned."

When they stepped into the waiting room, the other team members stood, their concern palpable. Butler stood to the side, his phone pressed to his ear, a frown on his face. When he saw them, he said a few more words, then hung up.

Cole stepped away from her, distancing himself in a subtle action, all friendly camaraderie from just seconds before stripped away, leaving a hard-faced leader. "He's going to be all right," he told the team, "but he's got a slight concussion. They did remove the bullet fragment, which surprisingly did very little damage. Thanks to Kenzie's quick actions, the trauma was much less than it could have been."

All eyes shifted to her and she thought she could detect a slight thawing in their gazes. For a fraction of a second anyway.

"Good job, Kenzie," Greene muttered.

The others looked at him, then back to her and nodded, murmuring their thanks—including Butler, even though his frown deepened.

James gave her a thumbs-up. "You did everything right."

She shot them a tight smile. "Just doing my job, but I'm very glad it wasn't any worse and he's going to be fine." She pulled in a deep breath and snagged her phone from the clip on her belt. "Now, assuming you all want to stay here with Cowboy, I've got to call an Uber. I need to get back to headquarters and get my car."

Cole shook his head. "We're all ready to leave now." He glanced at his phone. "Cowboy's here for the night. His brother's in town and headed this way. I'll just go tell him to behave himself and see y'all at Dolly."

"Well, I've got a friend who's supposed to be coming to get me," Butler said. "Personal errand." He glanced at his watch and frowned. "If he ever gets here. I'll meet you later at headquarters when I'm done."

Cole gave him a thumbs-up while Kenzie processed Cole's statement. He could have just waved her on and let her get the Uber, but he'd made a point to include her in the trip back to headquarters.

Interesting. She shrugged. "Okay."

"Be there in a few."

While he headed back to Cowboy's room, Kenzie followed the guys outside and down the sidewalk.

The hospital entrance sat at the top of a U-shaped drive with brick pillars holding up the roof of the porte cochere that offered protection just outside the entrance. Across from that was the larger hospital parking area. The SWAT vehicle was parked outside the porte cochere—leaving the area under the roof and the entrance clear for any emergency vehicles that might need it—and appeared to be generating a lot of interest from a group of teenagers. Two young ladies eyed her and the others as they approached. One broke away from the group and walked closer to Kenzie. "You're on SWAT?"

Kenzie smiled. "I am."

"Whoa. That's cool." She grinned and silver glistened from her teeth.

"Daaaang," one of the boys said, then gave a low whistle. "They let girls on SWAT now?"

The girl who had spoken to Kenzie popped the guy in the head. Not hard, but not exactly gentle either. "Shut up, JJ. You're revealing what a moron you are."

"Hey!" JJ rubbed the back of his head and glared at the girl. "That was a little harsh, don't you think?"

She rolled her eyes at Kenzie. "Brothers are such a pain."

"I can relate." Boy, could she. "But just to be clear, they don't *let* anyone on SWAT," Kenzie said. "You earn it, it's yours. I had to work for it like the other guys on this team." She'd worked for it all right. She narrowed her eyes at the pouting sibling. "Hard work. Just like anything in life worth having. Set a goal and go after it."

"Good for you," the sister said. Apparently, the siblings were the only ones in the group interested in talking. "I admire that."

"Come on, Missy, let's go." The disgruntled brother pulled on his sister's bicep.

Kenzie fist-bumped Missy and shook her head. Then noticed Cross, Greene, and Crenshaw watching her. Even Otis studied her with his intelligent dark brown eyes. Unable to discern what any of them were thinking thanks to their poker faces, she simply held out a hand to indicate they should get in. She sure didn't expect any special privileges just because she was a woman, and they didn't bother to argue. Greene and Otis went first, then Buzz slipped behind the wheel.

Cross stopped and motioned for her to get in, but she held his gaze and tilted her head, indicating he should go first. She would *not* accept special treatment on the job. A flicker of a smile crossed his lips, and he climbed in.

She turned to follow and, out of the corner of her eye, caught Cole coming out of the building.

An engine revved behind her, then roared as the driver gunned the gas. She swiveled, intending to motion for the driver to slow down, only to see the car closing in on her.

"Kenzie! Move!"

Cole's warning shout came at the same time she spun and dove into Dolly, landing partially inside on the hard floor. A hand on her arm jerked her the rest of the way in. A split second later, the vehicle whipped past and the wind buffeted her. Otis barked. For a moment, she lay there, trying to process what had almost happened. The hand squeezed and she looked up into Greene's black eyes. His skin looked a couple of shades paler. "You okay?" Cross and Crenshaw also looked shaken.

"Yeah." She sucked in a breath and took a quick physical inventory. "I think so. Yeah."

She sat up, noting the throbbing in her left hip. She grimaced. She'd have a bruise there soon, but she was alive. Barely.

COLE STEPPED UP TO HER, his gaze locking on hers, relief catching his breath in his lungs at seeing her in one piece. "You're okay."

She pushed strands of hair from her face and shuddered. "I am. You get the plate?"

"No. I didn't." He'd been too busy trying to make sure Kenzie got out of the way. "But we'll get it off the hospital security footage. That guy needs a lesson on how to drive in a parking lot."

"How to drive period," Greene muttered.

Otis nudged her and she scratched his ears while her eyes stayed on Cole's. He cleared his throat, finally got his pulse under control, and ran a hand down his cheek. "All right, everyone, back to headquarters. We'll deal with him later." Like personally.

Twenty minutes later, they pulled into the headquarters parking lot and unloaded.

Kenzie headed for the locker room and Buzz stepped up to Cole. "She did good today."

"Yeah. She did." He eyed the man's frown. "But?"

Buzz sighed. "This ain't a TV show, man, where everyone has to be PC with character roles and representation. I do understand that times are different now, and I don't have a problem with women following their calling or even being on SWAT, but on the flip side, this is real stuff and her presence is causing division for the team. We're just not the same since she joined." He held up a hand and Cole tightened his lips against the words ready to spill. "Don't get me wrong. I admire the heck out of her. She's worked hard. Harder than some of us have ever worked. She's had to. But . . . some of the guys aren't happy she's here and it's causing issues."

"I know."

Buzz's eyes never left Cole's and the man nodded. Slowly. "Yeah, I reckon you do." He shifted. "Truth is, we're torn. Butler's been with us for a couple of years now, and we feel like we need to be loyal to him even if we don't necessarily agree with him."

"I get it. Give her time to win him over."

"It's been almost six months."

"Five and change." Okay, so that was almost six months. "But unless she volunteers to leave, she's here for the duration and the guys are just going to have to accept it."

Kenzie stepped out of the locker room, dressed in black jeans, a white T-shirt, and running shoes. Her straight dark hair hung slightly below her shoulders. Her brown eyes were shadowed, but her face glowed with the shine of health and a good scrub.

She slung a backpack over her left shoulder and headed for the exit. Butler walked into the area from the kitchen, saw Kenzie, rolled his eyes, and did a one-eighty to head back into the room.

Cole curled his fingers into fists before he realized what he was doing. "Thought he had a personal errand to run," he muttered.

"Guess it was a quick one," Buzz said with a raised brow aimed at Cole's fists, then walked away.

Cole bit back a groan. "Hey, Kenzie, wait."

She stopped at the door and turned. "Yeah?"

"Looks like we have the same days off this week. Want some company on the run tomorrow?"

She blinked at him like a deer caught in the headlights. He wanted to squirm, but more than that, he wanted to know where those words came from and how they managed to exit his mouth. He'd been doing his best to keep his distance from Kenzie, to maintain a professional relationship *only*, and now he'd just jumped feet first into awkward—and definitely stepped over the professional line. But . . . he had a slight sketch of a plan running around in his head and this was part of it.

"Um . . . sure," she said. "I guess."

Well, that was enthusiastic. "I just thought . . ." He needed to shut his mouth before he shoved his foot all the way down. "Aw, dang, Kenzie, I'll be straight with you. I keep thinking my being so professional and . . . cool . . . in front of the guys is causing them to do the same. Maybe if we start hanging out some, the other guys will follow suit."

She chewed her bottom lip like she did occasionally when she was deep in thought—or confused. Then she gave a small shrug. "If it'll help the team, then sure. Meet me at my house around eight o'clock?"

"See you then."

She studied him a tad longer, then turned and slipped out the door.

Cole dropped his chin to his chest and closed his eyes, wishing he could reverse time and have a do-over of the last ten minutes.

"Hey."

He snapped his head up and turned to see Greene watching him. "Yeah?"

"That car that almost flattened Kenzie. It was a Honda, right? Kind of beat up? Silver?"

"Sounds right. Why?"

Greene frowned. "Thought I saw it on Fifth Street after we turned into the parking lot. The gate shut and the car kind of paused before driving off."

"You're saying it followed us?"

"Naw, not saying that, just saying I caught a glimpse of a car that looked like the one from the hospital and thought I'd mention it."

"Right. Thanks. I'll get hospital security to see if they can get me a plate. Maybe we can get one off the camera outside here too and see if they match."

Greene nodded, then crossed his arms. "You know, Butler is convinced she doesn't belong on this team."

"Commander Hill thinks otherwise."

The man nodded again but kept anything else he might have to say to himself and walked away. Cole let out a low breath.

So, now he'd head upstairs to the desk he rode as a detective when he wasn't in SWAT HQ. He had cases to study, reports to write, phone calls to make, and leads to chase down.

Then he'd go running with Kenzie in the morning.

He jogged up the stairs and headed for his desk. James was already seated at his and looked up when Cole dropped into the chair.

"You okay?" his partner asked.

"Yeah. Just still a little freaked about the car that almost hit Kenzie. I want a plate." He called the hospital, gave the information he needed, the time of day the incident occurred, and the location. Then left his email address and hung up.

"Hey, I keep meaning to ask you how Riley's doing," James said. "You donate blood for her, don't you?"

Riley Marie, Cole's little four-year-old niece currently battling a bout of anemia. "I do." He often did. "She's been in the hospital the last couple of days, but Mariah texted me and said she might get to go home later if her counts are good."

"Tough thing for a kid to have to deal with."

"Yeah. Tough on the parents too. But having someone who loves her with the same blood type is a good thing." His sister, Mariah, and her husband, Greg, were strong in their faith and their love for their adopted daughter. Cole just wished they could get Riley stabilized so she could have a normal life. But until then, she'd have the support system she needed and all the love she could tolerate. Including his

O negative blood type. Neither Riley's parents nor any of her siblings had O negative blood. He was Riley's donor and happy to do so.

James checked his phone. "Kenzie still hasn't responded about coming to the lake house. Did you talk to her about it?"

"I asked. She said she'd be there." Cole tapped the keys while he spoke and pulled up the cameras that would allow him to see the perimeter of the building and finally found what had captured Butler's attention.

The beat-up silver Honda. He leaned in, then tapped the screen. "There."

"What?" James looked up.

"That car outside the hospital that came real close to turning Kenzie into a human pancake?"

"Yeah." His partner's jaw tightened. "I was already in Dolly. Couldn't do a thing to help her."

"I know. Anyway, Greene said he thought he saw the same car outside the precinct, so I pulled up the footage and there it is."

"What's it doing?"

"Nothing. It stopped for a second while the gate closed, then drove away. Fast. And when I pause it, the picture's too blurry to get a plate or really identify it, but I agree with Greene. It looks similar to the one from the hospital."

James raised a brow. "I can see you thinking."

Cole shrugged. "It's probably nothing, but I wanted to try and find the driver."

"What about the hospital security?"

Cole checked his screen. "Nothing yet. One of the security guys—Jared—said he'd send it to me if he found something." He blew out a low breath. "I'm going running with Kenzie in the morning."

This time James sat up and gave him his full attention. "That so? Why?"

"Because I told her I would."

"Why would you do that?"

Cole rolled his eyes at his partner. "Shut up."

"You opened the door, man."

"Just trying to . . . figure out a way to right a wrong."

James turned serious. "How so?"

Cole paused, then sighed. "When Kenzie made the team, I knew there were going to be mixed feelings. There were a lot of really good applicants, but honestly, Kenzie was the best of the lot. Even better than Logan, who I would have welcomed to the team with open arms. But . . . when faced with the evidence of his sister's skills, I couldn't protest."

"But you wanted to?"

"Maybe. A little. Just because I knew the conflict it was going to cause. They weren't going to see her stellar scores or her physical abilities or her medical degree. All they were going to see is that she's a woman. A rather small woman compared to us. And I was right. But . . . they're right too. Their concerns are valid."

"Yeah. Sometimes brute strength comes in handy."

"Exactly. And while she's strong and in excellent physical shape, she'll never be as strong as any male on this team."

"There's always one," James said.

Cole blinked. "What?"

"On any team, there's always going to be one who's not quite as strong as the others. Male or female. If Kenzie wasn't on the team, one could argue that Buzz is the weakest—even though he's stronger than the average man. One could also argue that Kenzie is stronger than the average woman." He snorted. "She's actually probably stronger than the average man as well, thanks to all the training she does."

Okay, that was true. "Yeah, but in our situation—and I'm talking our situation only—a male team member is still going to be stronger than most females. And in Kenzie's case, she's the weakest."

"I'm not saying you're wrong. But Kenzie's smart. She'll rely more on brains than brawn. And as team leader, you're going to use wisdom and not put her in a situation where strength is the solution. You'll pick someone else."

Again, true. "I've been praying about what to do with this situation, and it was almost like God gave me a light-bulb moment earlier, so I acted on it, but I'd be lying if I said I wasn't worried about her. And the team." And what the guys would think about him spending personal time with Kenzie.

James nodded. "I'm more worried about the guys having her back if she needs it."

Cole pursed his lips and narrowed his eyes. "I think they'll have her back, but I think they'll resent having to have it."

"Meaning they'll be mad for having to protect her whether it's a situation of her making or not?"

"Exactly."

"As long as she—and everyone else—walks away alive."

Cole sighed. "Yeah. As long as."

THREE

Kenzie's phone rang just as she turned out of the SWAT parking lot. She tapped the screen. "Hey there."

"Hello. Are you done for the day?" Amelia Watson's voice came through the speakers and Kenzie sighed. Amelia was dating Kenzie's second-oldest brother, Kash, and while Kenzie liked her okay, the woman wasn't her first choice for an after-work conversation buddy.

"On my way home now," she said.

"Kash and I are having a little dinner party next Friday night. We were wondering if you'd like to join us."

A dinner party? Since when did her brother do dinner parties? "Uh—"

"It's for his job. His boss and his boss's son are going to be in town and Kash thought it would be a good gesture." Kash worked for an investment firm, and even Kenzie would admit he was a genius with all things numbers. He made a lot of money and had a lot of happy, wealthy clients.

"Kash did? Or you did?"

"Well, I didn't figure it would hurt to put the offer out there. Kash thought it was a brilliant idea." The smile in the woman's voice surprised her. Maybe Kenzie needed to give Amelia more of a chance than she had. She'd be the first to admit she'd made assumptions about her character simply because she was dating Kash. Her brother only went out with snooty women who had money. And Amelia definitely had money.

"I don't know, Amelia, dinner parties aren't exactly my forte. I'm not sure I'd know how to act." Especially one where her brother was half of the host team. He thought she should have gone into a different line of work.

Amelia scoffed. "I happen to know that your grandmother taught you how to act like a lady should the need arise. So, I'm asking you to come and do her proud."

Well, how could she say no to that?

"No." The word came out easier than expected. "I really don't think—"

"Please?"

Kenzie bit off an exasperated sigh. "Let me check my schedule. I need to see if I'm working." She didn't *think* she was on the schedule, but maybe she could trade with someone. "Do I need to bring a plus-one?" Kenzie wasn't sure what part of her brain decided to ask that, but she needed to find a shutoff switch for it.

"Do you have one to bring?"

"Um . . ."

"That's what I thought. Then no, I'll take care of everything. All you have to do is show up."

Why didn't she like the sound of that? Kenzie glanced in the rearview mirror and frowned. The person behind her was following awfully close. She tried to get a look at the driver, but the windshield was too grimy to make out anything other than the shape of a man. She sped up a little and relaxed a fraction when the car turned off.

"Makenzie?" Amelia asked.

"Yeah, sorry. I'm here." She'd given up asking the woman to call her Kenzie. Apparently Amelia didn't do nicknames.

"So, you'll check your schedule?"

She sighed. The woman was a pit bull. "Sure, Amelia. I'll check it. And don't set me up with anyone. I'll bring someone."

"Who?"

"Does it matter? Just a guy I know." What was she doing? *Stop talking and stop now!*

"Okay. Be at my house at seven o'clock sharp. We'll dine at 7:30."

So they'd be dining fashionably late. Was that even a thing?

"Got it. Seven o'clock. Next Friday night. Hold on a sec, who else is going to be there?"

"Just the family."

So, that meant Logan and Paul too? She opened her mouth to ask.

"See you then," Amelia said and hung up.

Kenzie blinked. Wait a minute. Had she just agreed to be there? Yes. Yes, she had and she'd promised to bring a date. She was an idiot.

Too tired to worry about it at the moment, she pulled into her garage and shut the door. It didn't take long to get inside her house and breathe in the scents that said she was home. Vanilla and lavender along with a hint of pine cleaner.

Grandma Betsy had finally decided it was time to move to an assisted-living home and signed her house over to Kenzie. "Lock, stock, and barrel, it's yours," she'd said and handed her the keys. No one had been more surprised than Kenzie, but she'd been beyond grateful and had moved in as soon as possible.

Not that she didn't love her three brothers and her father, but there came a point when a girl needed her own space. And she'd been way overdue.

Her father.

Now there was a subject worthy of a multitude of therapy sessions. A former chief of police, he'd been known as The Dictator. TD for short. And then the accident—

But no . . . she wouldn't think about that. Not tonight.

Shortly after her two older brothers, Paul and Kash, had moved out of the family home, she did the same. Her youngest sibling, Logan, still lived with their dad. Their mother was dead.

As always, the arc of pain swept through her when she thought about her mother. It had been twenty years, but some days it seemed like yesterday.

Kenzie placed her weapon and purse on the counter, then headed to her bedroom while she dialed Lainie's cell.

"Hello?"

Lainie's sweet voice was a balm to Kenzie's battered nerves. "Hey, are you still at work?"

"Still here for the next five minutes or so."

"I just wanted to check on Cowboy."

"Your SWAT buddy."

Kenzie smiled. "Yeah. His last name is McEntire, but everyone calls him Cowboy because of his Texas accent and penchant for boots and Stetsons when he's off duty." She paused. "And the fact that no one knows his first name."

"I did notice the accent. And he's doing all right. Last time I looked in on him, he was sleeping."

"Sleep is good. You going to bust him out of there tomorrow?"

"As long as nothing changes overnight, that's the plan. And I'm only telling you that because he cleared me talking to anyone on the SWAT team who called and asked."

"Good to know. You don't happen to have his first name on the chart, do you?"

"Um . . . says Cowboy."

"What does his driver's license say?"

Lainie laughed. "You'll have to ask him that."

Near her window, a shadow caught Kenzie's attention and she walked closer. The blinds were open to filter the last rays of the sun before it sank below the horizon. However, she had some time before sunset. She peered out the window. A glance to the left and right didn't reveal anything to cause alarm, but she shut the blinds anyway.

"Kenz?"

"I'm here. Sorry, got distracted."

"You okay?"

"Sure. Fine. It's been a long day, so I think I'm going to crawl into a hot bubble bath, binge a few episodes of something, and crash."

"You're coming to the lake house Friday, right?"

"Uh . . . this Friday? I thought that was tomorrow. Thursday night."

"And if you scroll down the text messages, you'll see we had to change it to Friday. Stephanie has to host an emergency baby shower for a friend there tomorrow night. The other hostess came down with the flu or something."

"Okay. So Friday. This Friday." Which Friday had she inadvertently promised to attend Amelia and Kash's shindig? Next Friday, right? Or— "Cole mentioned something about it, but . . ."

"When are you going to start reading your texts?"

"I saw them."

"You *saw* them but didn't *read* them. You're the absolute worst when it comes to communicating by text, my friend."

"I know. I'll catch up before I go to bed, I promise."

"It's not necessarily a bad thing that you don't have your nose in your phone all the time."

"I hate the thing, to be honest. But I know it's a necessary evil."

"You're hilarious. Get some sleep and we'll talk later. Night."

"Night." Kenzie hung up. She might not have much interest in her personal phone, but her work phone was different. She checked it regularly and kept it turned on with the volume up at all times.

She dug her personal phone out of her purse and tapped the screen. She scrolled through the messages and a wave of gratitude swept over her. It hadn't been that long ago she'd been doing nothing but working, focusing on her goal of finishing medical school and getting on SWAT, knowing the obstacles she would face if she ever found herself on Lake City's all-male team. She'd been lonely and tired and had thought of quitting more than once. Then, thanks to a bullet graze, she'd been sent to the hospital where Lainie had walked into her life and befriended her within seconds.

And brought her into this circle of friends without hesitation. In addition to Lainie, there was Jesslyn McCormick, a fire marshal, and Kristine Duncan, an air marshal. And, of course, Stephanie Cross, Lainie's best friend since childhood. Jesslyn, Lainie, Kristine, Allison, and Steph had a special relationship, but they'd all pulled Kenzie into the midst, making her feel welcome without the slightest hint of awkward.

At the time, Kenzie hadn't realized Cole was a part of that group, and when she'd discovered it, she almost pulled away but couldn't quite bring herself to give up her newfound community. A community that she'd craved for as long as she could remember.

Just thinking about Cole made her antsy. His on-again, off-again attitude was about to drive her up the proverbial wall. Today he'd been more on than off. And offering to go running with her? What was he *really* up to? His explanation about trying to set an example for the guys made sense, but she wasn't sure she believed it.

Not that Cole had ever lied to her before. That she knew of anyway.

She was too tired to think about it. The call with Lainie had perked her up a bit, but that was long gone, and now she wanted nothing more than to crash. She didn't even have the energy for that bubble bath. After a quick supper of leftover chicken pot pie, she changed into sweats and an old T-shirt, then turned on the gas logs—best upgrade she'd done to the house thus far—curled up on the couch, and aimed the remote at the flat-screen on the wall.

Unfortunately, not even Tom Cruise and his top gun flying abilities could keep her mind from reliving the day. The moment she'd rushed in to find Cowboy's head drenched with his blood, to the moment in the hospital where she felt—if only for a moment—that she belonged with the unit. And then almost getting flattened by the car with the careless driver.

She might not always read her texts in a timely manner, but she had no problem sending one when it suited her purpose. She pulled up Cole's number.

Any news on who the car belonged to?

Just got the answer. The plate didn't belong to
the vehicle. The owner didn't even realize it was
gone. So, no way to trace the one that nearly ran
you down.

His response was almost instantaneous. She shook her head. Did all of her friends stay glued to their phone? Three little dots said he had more information coming.

I'll be honest. That whole incident makes me a
little nervous. Like there's more to it than just a
random close call.

You think he WANTED to run me over?

I don't know, but it sure looked like it.

Right.

Anything else weird been going on for you?

Like someone trying to turn me into roadkill? No.

Well, that's good.

I'm restless, though. I'm going to go get in a
workout and hope that takes the edge off. See you
in the morning.

Night, King.

Kenzie stared at the words for a brief second before swinging her legs over the side of the couch and standing. Why was he being so nice all of a sudden? Not that he was ever *mean*, but . . .

She went into a stretching routine and, once she had the kinks out, headed to the kitchen and down the stairs to her basement, skipping the one that squeaked out of childhood habit.

Some might consider the area creepy with the concrete floors, dim lighting, and drafty head-height windows that needed to be replaced, but she'd played hide-and-seek in this place from an early age—especially when she wanted to get away from her brothers—and found the space her safe zone.

She'd set it up as a home gym and made her way to it several times during the week—or when she knew there was no reason to try sleeping. Kenzie walked to the nearest window to assess whether the tape was holding fast. Her grandmother had done nothing to the house before her transfer to the assisted living home, but over the past two years, Kenzie had started with the big stuff.

New roof, new HVAC system, new hardwood floors, and new electrical wiring. The windows had to wait, so she'd taped them up. Not exactly HGTV worthy, but it did the trick. Sort of. "Okay, windows next," she muttered.

She walked to the punching bag and turned it until the worn and wrinkled picture faced her. She'd punched it a lot but could still make out the face.

A noise near the window to her left spun her attention from the bag, and she froze at the sight of a pair of booted feet facing her on the other side of the glass.

COLE GRIPPED THE STEERING WHEEL of his 4Runner and aimed the vehicle toward Kenzie's home. He couldn't get the whole incident with the car trying to run her down out of his head, and the word *why* kept spinning in his mind. If the person had been aiming for Kenzie, *why*? If the person had followed them back to HQ, *why*?

And then the haunting question "Would he try again?" was right there with every breath he took.

The exchange of text messages had eased his anxiety somewhat, but still . . .

He'd just ride by. Check on her. Then he sighed. Never before had he been compelled to go by one of his unit members' houses.

Then again, none of them had ever been deliberately targeted like Kenzie had.

44

His phone rang and his heart plummeted. Mariah. He tapped the screen. "Hey, brat, what's up?"

"I have a little girl who wants to say hello to you. She insisted on calling to let you know she was going home."

"Well, put my favorite four-year-old on."

Less than a second later, Riley said, "Hi, Unca Cole. I'm better and I'm on da way home."

"I'm so glad, little soldier. I'm going to try and see you soon, okay?"

"Thank you for giving me your Cole-y juice."

Cole's throat tightened unexpectedly. He'd give her the moon if it would make her better. "Anytime. You can have it all."

She giggled. "Nuh-uh. You need most of it."

He smiled. "What are you going to watch when you get home?"

"VeggieTales. Bob and Larry."

Most would think VeggieTales was outdated, but as far as he and his sister were concerned, it was timeless. Riley thought so too. "Okay, kiddo, you tell your mama to let me know when you're up for an ice cream date and we'll get some chocolate and strawberry swirl."

"Yay! Bye, Unca Cole. I love you."

"Love you too, sweet girl." She hung up without passing the phone to Mariah, and he went back to worrying about Kenzie.

Okay, that was it.

He blew out a harsh sigh and wished he could just ignore the little voice urging him to make sure she was okay. But he couldn't. He voice-dialed her number and waited.

Voicemail.

He hung up. Tried again.

He sighed, slapped his phone onto the magnet attached to the dash, and pressed the gas a little harder.

FOUR

Kenzie paused in the middle of the steps trying to remember where she'd left her phone. On the end table upstairs next to the remote? Probably.

Her pulse thundered and her gaze went back to the boots at her window. They had moved away a few seconds ago, and Kenzie had darted for the stairs. Only, she paused when the boots returned and one lifted to press against the glass. Testing to see how sturdy it was?

The end of a crowbar appeared for a brief moment before it settled against the window. Did he not realize she was in the room? Or did he just not care?

She ran the rest of the way up the stairs. The door leading to the basement didn't lock, but she shut it anyway. She grabbed her gun, checked the magazine, and then bolted into the den, aiming her steps toward her phone.

Her fingers curled around it and she dialed 911. While it rang, she slipped her feet into the tennis shoes she'd worn home from headquarters.

"What's your emergency?"

"Someone's breaking into my house. I'm a cop and I'm armed and I don't know if this guy has a friend with him." She gave her badge number and returned to the entrance to the kitchen to watch the basement door.

"I have a unit on the way."

"Tell the responding officers I have a basement. The guy was right outside the window that's just above ground level. If he opens it, he can slide in—assuming he's average sized. Can you also alert Detective Cole Garrison?" She rattled off his number.

"Yes ma'am." She heard keys clicking in the background. "Do you know if the intruder is armed?"

"I didn't see a weapon other than a crowbar, but I'm going on the assumption he is and he might not be alone."

"Of course. Where are you? Can you get out of the house?"

"I can, but I'm not sure if he's inside or out now, so I'm staying in at the moment. If he comes through my basement window, there's only one way to access the rest of the house and I've got my weapon pointed at it."

"Detective Garrison was actually nearby. He's pulling onto your street now."

Kenzie backed toward the great room, keeping eyes on the basement door, phone pressed to her ear, weapon aimed. Her ears strained for any hint of sound or movement from below, but all was quiet.

Until a footfall hit the squeaky stair in the middle.

Okay, then. He was inside.

Kenzie darted for the front door, flipped the deadbolt, and twisted the knob.

Only to come face-to-face with Cole, who had his weapon drawn. Relief flashed on his features for a fraction of a second before he stepped back. "You reported an intruder?"

Kenzie ended the 911 call. "Coming up my basement stairs. I ran instead of confronting him. Because *him* might be a *them*." She wasn't ashamed of that.

"Smart."

"But now that I have backup, you ready?"

He hesitated, almost said something, then nodded as he stepped inside. Kenzie steadied herself. This was just like any other situation where she would be going after a burglar. She held her weapon ready and Cole shut the door behind him. They walked toward her basement stairs. Everything looked exactly like she'd just left it. "I'm going to clear this floor," she said. "Keep an eye on the basement, will you?"

"Got it."

Blue lights came into view and bounced through the front door and off the walls. She heard Cole updating dispatch to pass along their current situation to the arriving officers. She ignored them and checked the utility room, her primary bedroom, bath, and closet, then made her way back into the kitchen, where Cole nodded that he still had the basement door covered. It didn't take her long to clear the other two bedrooms, bath, and office, and she walked to the basement stairs.

They were clear. She started down.

"Right behind you," Cole whispered.

"Skip the step 1 do."

"Got it."

She continued down the stairs until she had a full view of the room. And the legs hanging inside her window to the thigh. "Police! Stay there!"

The legs withdrew and the window swung closed. Of course he ignored her.

Cole disappeared up the stairs, speaking into his phone, reporting the intruder at the back of the house and ordering officers on the scene to go after him.

Kenzie darted for the window when a gloved hand reappeared holding a weapon. He fired and she dove sideways, crashing into the punching bag. Another bullet slapped into the floor beside her.

"Kenzie!"

Cole's shout came from above and she rolled behind her exercise bike. "I'm good!"

She peered around the wheel, weapon aimed, but the hand and

48

the gun were gone. Kenzie shot to her feet and darted for the stairs. Cole was already halfway down and she waved him back up. "I'm fine. Go! He's running!"

Cole went. Kenzie followed him up and stopped in the kitchen long enough to grab a powerful flashlight from the drawer next to her oven, then bolted out of the house. She noted the officers fanning out and beginning their search.

The neighborhood was heavily wooded with mature trees, big yards, a few wooden fences, and tons of places to hide should one be fleeing the scene of a crime. She ran toward the back of her home, her flashlight beam on high. While the others searched for the intruder, she scanned the ground around the window.

It had been trampled, but she couldn't see any distinguishing footprints. However, she was able to follow the trampled grass to the edge of her property.

Cole came up beside her. "What is it?"

"He hopped the fence."

"Easy enough to do. It's a low one." He listened to the Bluetooth in his ear, then looked at her. "Chopper is on the way. As are the dogs. Officers are going door to door telling residents to stay inside and locked up."

"It'll be too late."

"Yeah, I think you're right."

HE HATED THAT SHE WAS RIGHT, but he was coming to find out that she usually was. About a lot of things. He followed her into the house, still thinking about her. She was a natural cop and her medical skills were top-notch. He'd welcomed her into the unit with cool reservation, but he'd admit it hadn't taken him long to figure out she was special, a real asset to the unit. He just didn't know how to convince the other guys of that fact without it looking like he was protecting her or giving her special treatment.

Which wouldn't go over well with Kenzie *or* the others. Regardless, for the moment, whoever had gotten in her house was gone.

And Kenzie was pacing.

A helicopter roared overhead and a spotlight swept over the house, illuminating everything for a brief moment. She spun to face him. "What the heck is going on, Cole?"

He shook his head. "I wish I had an answer for you."

She pressed her lips together, then blew out a low breath as she dropped onto the couch and crossed her arms. "I might be able to say the car thing at the hospital was an accident. A reckless driver. But tonight was no accident. Obviously."

"But are the two incidents connected. That's what you're wondering, right?"

"Of course."

"Yeah. Me too."

She stood.

"Where you going?"

"To work a crime scene."

She headed for the basement door and he snagged her bicep in a gentle but firm grasp. "Uh, we're going to have to let the crime scene unit work the crime scene."

"We're trained."

"This is a conflict of interest, Kenzie, you know that."

He thought she might explode right there, but after a few seconds, she groaned, pulled from his grip, and stomped back to flop onto the couch.

To pout?

She leaned forward and dropped her head into her hands. "I know. You're right."

No. Kenzie wasn't one to pout. He sat beside her. "Sorry."

"It's okay," she mumbled, her face still in her palms.

"No, it's not, but it will be." He was tempted to slide an arm across her shoulders and the feeling spurred him to his feet. He couldn't make gestures like that. Not with her. Could he? No. It wasn't against the law or anything, but he was still her supervisor and it just wouldn't be right. But he could still be her friend.

She looked up just as a knock sounded on the front door and a young woman in a crime scene unit vest stepped inside. "Kenzie?"

Kenzie stood. "Hey, Sarah."

Sarah Beckworth, the CSU leader. "Hey, Cole."

He nodded. "Thanks for coming so quickly."

"Absolutely." She looked at Kenzie. "All right if I head down to your basement?"

"Of course."

"Mitch is outside working the area around the window, hoping for a footprint or something."

"And hopefully, a handprint," Kenzie said. "He had his legs in the window and probably braced his hands in the grass as he pulled himself through." She paused. "I saw his hand when he shot through the window. Pretty sure he had gloves on."

Sarah radioed the information to Mitch.

Cole followed Kenzie and Sarah through the kitchen to the basement stairs. Kenzie placed a hand on the woman's arm. "He came up the stairs. About halfway. I heard the step creak. Cole got here about that time, and the guy went back down and was climbing out the window when we got down there. He'd pushed a trunk up against the wall so he could reach it."

"In other words, check the stairs for anything?"

"Exactly."

"Got it." She paused a moment to slip on the little blue booties to protect the scene from any outside trace material. "Why don't you two stay put? If I need anything, I'll holler."

Kenzie hesitated, then nodded. "Fine."

Sarah paused. "Saw Logan outside."

"Guess he heard the call," Kenzie said.

Cole rubbed his chin and tried to read her expression. She was pretty good at hiding her feelings when she wanted to, but he'd known her a while and could pick out the wariness in her eyes. She turned on her heel, and Cole followed her back into the den, where she took her spot on the couch again.

He settled into the recliner. "You and Logan okay?" She and her brother had applied for the same position on SWAT. She'd gotten it.

"We're fine."

"You sure? Doesn't sound like it."

"Well, we are. He made detective about the same time I was offered this position, so we're fine. He'll probably come check on me in a few." She sighed and rubbed her head.

Sympathy made him decide to let it go. For now. "It might be a while before Sarah's back up here."

She eyed him. "I'm aware."

"Right."

A small groan escaped her. "I'm sorry. I don't mean to be snippy."

"You have every reason to be. I can handle it."

"I know you can, but that doesn't mean I should take my frustrations out on you." She leaned back and closed her eyes, and Cole decided this would be a good time to keep his mouth shut. "You can leave, you know," she said. "No need to babysit me."

"I don't consider it babysitting. You'd do it for me."

She cracked an eye at him. "What makes you think that?"

"Instinct."

"Hm. Maybe." The eye shut again.

No maybe about it. He had no doubts. "Why don't you rest? Try to sleep."

"With CSU downstairs?"

"Why not? You got anything better to do?"

"Go find an intruder?"

"Besides that."

"Nope." She paused. "It was just him working alone?"

"Looks like it."

"I should have confronted him."

"You did the smart thing. You had no idea how many people were involved."

"Right." She drew in a deep breath and let it out.

"Adrenaline crashes are real. You know that. Let yourself ride it."

"I couldn't sleep if you threatened me."

He grunted. "There's been enough of that. At least close your eyes."

"They are closed."

He chuckled and she opened her eyes to scowl at him, then her lids lowered once more.

Moments later, he noted her even breathing and almost imperceptible snores. A part of him wanted to record her so he could tease her later, but the other part warned him she wouldn't appreciate that. They didn't have that kind of relationship. Yet. He shook off that last thought.

Forty-five minutes later, after her brother had indeed checked on her and said not to wake her, footsteps on the basement stairs pulled Cole out of the chair and he met Sarah in the kitchen. "All done?"

"We are."

"Find the bullets?"

"One. And one of the casings. Ballistics will have to weigh in, but the headstamp says it's a 9mm." She hesitated, then motioned him to follow her. They walked back down the steps, and she pointed to the bullet hole that had gone through the punching bag to wedge itself in the wall. "Dug that one out." She pointed to the gouged cement floor. "Can't find the second bullet. It may have disintegrated. We found some fragments that probably belong to it. Didn't get anything off the steps, but under the window, there was some loose change that we bagged. Could have fallen out of the intruder's pocket as he was squirming his way through the window. Assuming it doesn't belong to Kenzie."

"It doesn't."

Cole turned at Kenzie's voice. He hadn't heard her come down.

She stepped off the bottom step and walked over to them, tucking her phone into her back pocket. "It's not mine."

"Then we'll have the lab analyze it and see if they can get a fingerprint off of it," Sarah said. "Granted, even if they do, it might not belong to the intruder."

"It's worth a shot," Cole murmured. Sarah raised a brow and he grimaced. "No pun intended."

He thought Kenzie might have snorted, but when he looked at her, she just shook her head and walked back up the steps.

"Thanks, Sarah."

"Sure thing."

Cole followed Kenzie and found her at the sink looking out the window. "I noticed something down there," he said.

She tilted her head at him, questions in her eyes. "What's that?"

"You have Butler's face on your punching bag."

He suspected she turned away to cover a smirk before she shrugged. "It's my own personal brand of therapy."

He frowned. "He's bugging you that much?"

"Yeah, but don't worry, it doesn't affect my ability to do the job."

"Do I need to—"

"Absolutely not." She didn't raise her voice, but he got the message loud and clear. She'd handle it. And yet . . .

"Kenzie, it's my job to make sure the team functions like a team. If Butler is jeopardizing that, then I need to address it."

She sighed. "I get what you're saying, but I'd rather you didn't. Not yet."

He nodded and leaned against the counter. "Will you tell me if he crosses a line?"

She glanced at him, then back at the officers still outside. "How do I know where the line is?"

He studied her a moment, then shook his head. "You'll know."

FIVE

Would she? It worried her that she wasn't sure. Kenzie lay in bed, eyes on the ceiling, unable to sleep. Because of the intruder, yeah, but mostly because Cole was on her couch. She should have sent him home. Had in fact told him to *go* home and he'd asked her if she was comfortable staying alone.

Ugh. She'd dug out a pillow and blankets, pressed them into his arms, and pointed out the guest bathroom. Once he was taken care of, she wound her way to her room where she lay in tangled sheets unable to close her eyes. She could fall asleep on her couch thirty minutes after someone broke into her home and shot at her, but once she was all tucked into bed, she was pulled tighter than a tripwire.

The truth was, she wasn't comfortable.

The other truth was, she could have called someone else.

But Cole was already there, and if she called Lainie or Jesslyn or Kristine or Steph, she would feel like she was . . . infringing. Or imposing. And while in her head she knew they wouldn't see it that way, she still couldn't help hesitating.

She *could* have called one of her brothers, but that was a hard *no way*. She wasn't in the mood for the "told you so's," which would lead right into the smothering, protective helicoptering. Minus Logan, though. Maybe. She couldn't help but wonder and was almost afraid to find out. The fact that he'd checked on her earlier was a positive, though.

Regardless. Cole was definitely the better option.

Maybe.

She groaned and punched her pillow. Too many dumb maybes. She shifted to her side and mentally started going through the steps to clean her weapon. She must have dozed off finally, because the next thing she knew her work alarm was buzzing. She slapped at it and knocked the clock on the floor. She'd forgotten to turn it off the night before.

"Kenzie? You okay?"

At Cole's voice from the hallway, she shot out from under the covers and to her feet. "I'm fine. I knocked my clock off the end table. You still want to go running?"

"I don't exactly have the clothes and shoes for it, but yeah." He was still in the hallway.

"We can run by your place and grab them if you want. I'm just going to get ready. Be out there in a few." She hurried to the bathroom and completed her morning routine in record time. Then found a toothbrush still in the package and met Cole in the den. "Just in case you might need one."

He took it. "Definitely."

"Should have given it to you last night. I'm sorry."

"It's all good. I don't mind the washcloth in an emergency, but a toothbrush is my first choice."

She laughed. "The electrician is coming to repair the primary bathroom wiring and may be here before you're done, so if you hear voices, you know who it is."

"Got it."

As though on cue, the doorbell rang. She headed to answer it, and Cole aimed himself at the half bath off the kitchen.

By the time he emerged, she'd gotten the electrician started, texted her neighbor about checking on the whole situation, and was pacing the floor in front of the mantel. She was tired but wanted answers and prayed a run would help clear her head.

Although now that Cole was in her den, she was having second thoughts. Running with him would not clear her head, it would probably just muddle it more. But he'd offered and she'd agreed, and after yesterday, running with company was probably a smart idea. Safety in numbers and all that, right?

She had no idea why her emotions were all over the place when it came to him, but she thanked the good Lord that because of her brothers, she had lots of practice in keeping a poker face.

He insisted on driving and she didn't bother to protest. Ten minutes later, after a stop at his place, she climbed back into the passenger seat of his 4Runner.

"The park?" he asked.

"Sure."

Once they were on the back road that would take them to Lake City Community Park, Kenzie tried not to give off "I'm uncomfortable" vibes because she really wasn't—even though she was slightly weirded out by the fact she was riding with Cole in a nonprofessional capacity.

He cleared his throat. "So, should we go ahead and address the elephant in the room?"

She blinked at him. "Why?"

He laughed and snorted. "Or we can ignore it."

"Look, Cole, I'm not overthinking this if that's what you're worried about." At least she was trying not to. "Let's just enjoy the day."

He shot her a perplexed look, then shrugged. "Fine by me."

She fell silent for the next couple of miles, then rubbed her nose. "What's the elephant?"

He laughed. A belly laugh that crinkled the corners of his eyes and pulled his dimples out of hiding.

Oh my, he was one good-looking man. Not that she hadn't known that, but . . . sheesh, it shouldn't take *that* much effort to put it out of her mind.

"Just us, I guess. Hanging out together without the company of anyone else. I thought you might be uncomfortable with that."

"Oh, I am."

His laughter filled the vehicle once again, and when it died off, he shot her an amused look. "You're . . . intriguing. I don't remember you being that way from our teen years."

It was her turn to laugh. "That's because you never paid me a bit of attention when we were teens. But the truth is, I'm not really intriguing. Just honest." She cleared her throat. "Yeah, it's weird because I'm never sure what you think of me. At work, I believe you trust me to do my job."

"I do."

"But you've been mostly aloof and distant. Until now." She shrugged. "I'm not trying to read any more into that."

"I'm sorry, I just . . . well, let's just leave it at that. I had my reasons to keep some distance, and while they seemed like good ones at the time, I'm not sure they're good ones anymore. So, I'm sorry."

His contriteness reached her, and once he turned into the park entrance and wound around to the parking lot to stop, she looked him in the eye. "Tell me this. Do you have any resentment that you had to choose me over Logan because I was better qualified to be on the team?"

"No."

His instant response relaxed something inside her. "Okay, good. Now that we have that resolved, I'll say this. While we've known each other forever, I wouldn't call us friends. You hung out with my brothers in the summers when we stayed with my grandmother, and I did my own thing. I'll admit to a teenage crush but was also aware enough that you didn't think twice about me."

"I wouldn't say that," he muttered.

She frowned. "What?"

"Nothing. Go on."

"All you guys talked about was law enforcement, and when you weren't talking about it, you were role-playing it. I just wanted to join in."

He raised a brow. "Is that why you—"

"Joined SWAT? No. Not really. I'm sure that had some influence in my decision to do what I do, but mostly it's because—" She bit her lip, not sure she wanted to get that personal.

"Because?"

"It really doesn't matter."

"It does to me."

He sounded like it really did. "Because of my dad. Because of the way he raised us. From the time my mother died until I put a stop to it, he pitted my brothers and me against each other. There was always some kind of competition to win. Or lose. And, truthfully, because of the smear on his name. It nearly destroyed him, and I had a front-row seat to it. When he learned he was going to be accused of stealing evidence from the evidence room, he nearly lost it."

"So that rumor is true?"

"Yes."

"But charges were never pressed."

"No." She shot him a sideways glance. "But he was never declared innocent either, just that there wasn't enough evidence to bring charges, not because it was proved he didn't do it. The damage was done." The day of the car accident that had left her father with a broken spine and a chip on his shoulder the size of Texas had been the worst day of her life. It had also been the day her mother was ripped from her life at the tender age of fourteen. Her father had run a stop sign and smashed into another vehicle. The other car had been stolen and the driver was never found. "Dad swears he had nothing to do with that missing evidence, that he was framed."

"You believe him?"

She swallowed and looked out the window. "I don't know what to believe. And it kills me to say that." But it was something she'd secretly been investigating since she'd earned access to the database of cases. "I've searched and I just can't find any evidence one way

59

or the other. He ran the stop sign, hit another car, and my mother died. The evidence he supposedly stole was never found, but the man the evidence would have put away for good, Shady Talbot, was released and went on to kill someone. And my father continues to have a black mark on his name."

"I'm so sorry, Kenz."

"I am too, but you know what?" She drew in a deep breath. "Let's leave the past in the past and enjoy the day. What do you say?"

"I say that's a great idea."

They climbed out of his 4Runner, and after stretching, she looked at him. "How many miles? Ten?"

"*Ten?*"

"Too many?"

"You're quite the jokester, aren't you?" She raised a brow and he frowned. "Uh, how many miles do you normally run?"

"Depends on what I feel like at the time." She shrugged. "We don't have to set a number, we can just go until you need to stop."

He blinked. "Until *I* need to—" He chuckled. "That sounds like a challenge."

"Nah, not at all."

"Right."

Kenzie smiled, wondering if she should warn him she'd been training for months for an Olympic triathlon. She smothered a chuckle.

"What's so funny?" he asked.

She gave him her best innocent look. "Nothing."

He narrowed his eyes. "Why do I think that's a lie?"

"Cole. Seriously? What are you worried about?"

"I'm not sure. Something, though." He nodded. "Definitely worried about something."

Kenzie laughed and started off with a slow jog. "Come on. You'll be fine. You're a big bad SWAT man."

He muttered something she missed and didn't bother asking him to repeat it. It was a glorious morning, and if she didn't have the heaviness of the unanswered questions about the break-in at her

60

home and almost being flattened in the hospital parking lot, she'd feel lighter than she had in ages. But it *had* happened and it seemed to be all she could think about. Had the intruder thought she wasn't there? Or just hadn't cared? Well, he'd shot at her, so "just hadn't cared" was probably the answer.

Which was disturbing.

"You're thinking about last night," Cole said.

"I am."

Silence fell. From the corner of her eye, she caught him taking a glance at her. Then he looked back at the path. Then back at her. "That's it?" he finally said.

"Pretty much. Going over the same questions in my head that we already talked about. But let's talk about something different. How are your parents doing?" They still lived next door to her, but she didn't see them for more than a wave most of the time.

"Great. They're visiting my sister Addy and her family in South Carolina and will be back Sunday night."

"That explains why they didn't show up when all the commotion happened last night."

"Yeah, but be prepared for questions once they get home. It will be the talk of the neighborhood."

She sighed. "Already is."

The park trail was two and a half miles of mostly flat land, but there were some slopes at various points, and they were coming up on her favorite. The bridge overlooking the waterfall that crashed into the flowing river. Once they were on the other side of the bridge, they followed the path that would lead them into the shady, wooded area. Moms with jogging strollers rolled past. Young twenty- and thirty- and the occasional older-somethings pounded the asphalt with their dogs at their sides. Kenzie loved Lake City and the small-town feel with all of the big-city amenities when she wanted them.

But not the crime that seemed to be ramping up lately. The fact that they had their own SWAT team and crime lab said a lot about the city. It was forward-thinking, true, but it made her sad that, in many ways, it wasn't the same city she'd grown up in.

Cole turned and ran backward for a moment, facing her. His eyes scanned the area behind them, then he spun like the athlete he was to continue his jog beside her.

"See anything?" she asked.

"No, nothing that worries me."

"Could the two incidents truly be a coincidence?"

"I suppose they could."

"But you don't believe it."

"Having a hard time convincing myself of that, yeah."

"Right."

They fell silent, ticking off the minutes and the distance until Cole finally stopped and rested his hands on his knees.

Kenzie went a little past him, then turned and jogged back to him. "You okay?"

"How many miles have we run?"

She glanced at her smartwatch. "Just under six."

"How many more miles *can* you run?"

She couldn't stop the smile that curved her lips. "Come on, we'll head back to the car."

"You can keep going, can't you?"

"It doesn't matter."

"How far?"

"Cole—"

"How far, Kenzie?"

"I usually do between thirteen and fourteen miles on my days off."

He blinked. "Why?"

She shrugged. "Why not?"

His eyes narrowed. "You're keeping something from me. What is it?"

"Oh, for crying out loud." She chuckled. "I'm training for a tri-athlon, okay?"

"A triathlon? And you didn't think to tell me you could run a hundred miles without stopping for a breath or a drink of water?"

"A hundred is a bit of an exaggeration, don't you think?"

He laughed. Another big laugh that was rare for him. And he'd done it three times this morning. Interesting.

He walked over to the nearest park bench and lowered himself onto it, wiping the sweat from his face with the hem of his shirt.

And continued his obnoxious chuckling.

"Cole? You okay?"

When he finally caught his breath, he looked up. "You got me."

"I wasn't trying to get—" She clamped her lips together, then let a small, reluctant laugh escape. "Okay, maybe a little."

"Well, it's a good thing we've been running in circles and are near the car because I'd never make it back if I had to do six more miles."

She wasn't sure she believed that. "I'm sorry. I should have been straight with you. I've been working up to the longer distances for a while now." She grinned at him and headed toward the car, which was only about a quarter of a mile away. He made it without any trouble, and she raised a brow at him as they exited the walkway to head to his 4Runner. "You could have gone a lot farther."

"What's next? The swim or the bike ride?"

She laughed. "The swim. But not today."

"What now? Food?"

She started to answer when his phone buzzed.

He glanced at the screen. "Well, so much for the day off. I've got a call."

COLE LOOKED AT HER. "You mind the ride to headquarters? We go right past there and it will allow me to ride with the team."

"Of course I don't mind. Let's go." She climbed into the passenger seat, and Cole slipped behind the wheel, putting his phone on Bluetooth.

"Some day off, huh?"

"I'm used to it, just like everyone else."

He shot her a glance as he connected to HQ. She truly didn't look bothered.

Commander Hill's voice came through the speakers. "Hostage situation at an abandoned warehouse."

"Address?" he asked.

"Holmes Street."

"We'll be at HQ in less than five."

"Dolly will be waiting."

He hung up and Kenzie grimaced.

"What?"

She shook her head. "Nothing. Just lots of memories from that part of town from my less-than-stellar high school days. Seems like every call we get is in that vicinity."

"Crime happens everywhere, but never so much as where people are poor and desperate."

"Yeah," she said, her voice low.

"What does your family think about your occupation?"

She raised a brow at him. "I have three brothers, and a father who was the former police chief. What do you think?"

He chuckled. "I know what Logan thinks, what about the rest?"

"The same as Logan. They would prefer it if I had a nice safe job as an accountant or something, but honestly, it doesn't really matter what they want. It's my life and I've chosen my path. They don't get a say in it."

The faint ring of defensiveness didn't escape him. He'd thrown out the question in an attempt at small talk to get to know her a little better and managed to punch a hornet's nest. "I'm sorry." They fell silent a moment while he drove, then he said, "And Paul?" Her oldest brother. "I heard he quit the force about the time your dad was in the accident."

"And my mom was killed."

"Yeah. I'm really sorry about that. I only saw her a few times when y'all visited your grandmother, but I liked your mom a lot."

"I miss her every day. Thank God my grandmother stepped in

and took over. I don't know what I—we—would have done without her. Even though they were mother-in-law and daughter-in-law, they were close."

"Why did Paul quit?" He took a corner with a tight turn and raced toward headquarters. The others were still gathering, and they had time to get there so he could join them in Dolly.

"He was furious at the rumors swirling about Dad," she said. "I know he faced some harassment, but I was fourteen, I'd just lost my mom, and I thought I might lose my dad. I just wanted it all to go away, but the press was relentless with all of us. Paul was twenty-six years old and had been with the department for five years. When another officer, one Paul considered a good friend, nastily wondered if 'the apple didn't fall far from the tree,' that was the last straw. He felt betrayed by people he thought were his friends, his brothers and sisters in uniform. That day, Paul walked out and never went back."

He'd heard some of that but had been so busy with his own career over the last few years that he hadn't kept up. "What's he doing now?"

"Bouncing from job to job. These days he's security for a hotel downtown. He's been there for about a year. Seems to like it okay."

He pulled into the parking lot of headquarters and parked. "To be continued. I have more questions."

"I have clothes and gear in my locker. I'll get changed."

"You don't have to come. Magic Man is on this shift." The team's other medic was Max Mann, but he'd quickly been dubbed Magic Man.

"But you're missing Cowboy. I can fill in. You know I can. I'm a fully trained SWAT officer, Cole. Let me do the job."

He studied her. She was a good officer. Actually, a great one. She'd gotten—and was still getting—a raw deal from the other guys and was handling it like the pro she was. "Fine. Let's go get some bad guys."

She almost smiled. "Let's do that. Give me five minutes."

True to her word, five minutes later, they were both in Dolly, with the rest of the team shooting questioning glances at Kenzie and him as they rolled out toward Holmes.

"Thought this was your day off," Magic Man said, glancing up at Kenzie from checking his weapon.

"It is."

The medic raised a brow, then shrugged. "All right then."

"Don't worry," she said. "I'm not treading on your territory. You do you and I'll do me." She patted the med sling pouch on her lap. "This is just backup."

"Works for me." He hesitated. "If I need help, I'm glad you'll be there."

After that exchange, everyone fell silent, doing their best to mentally prepare for what was to come. Most larger cities had more than one SWAT team. In Lake City, they were it—with a few officers they could call for help if needed. Their days off were staggered enough that getting called to a situation was few and far between. And frankly, Cole had to admit he was a little annoyed at the interruption of his day. He'd been enjoying the time with Kenzie.

Then again, this would give him time to really think about what he was doing. Because enjoying time with Kenzie could have consequences he wasn't sure he was ready to incite.

Dolly swept out of the more affluent area of Lake City and into the less. It was like someone flipped a switch. One moment, you were in a clean, well-kept part of town and the next . . . you weren't.

The old abandoned mental institution coming up on the right, Lake City State Hospital, never failed to send shivers up his spine. His grandmother had been a patient there, and he always wondered about her whenever he passed by the place. Built in the early 1800s, it was finally shut down in the 1990s after numerous allegations of abuse and an investigation led by a bulldog of a reporter. Almost every native of Lake City had a family member who'd once walked those dark halls. The place had been left to rot, although kids sometimes thought they were being cool by partying in the "psycho house."

"That place creeps me out," Mann muttered, as though reading Cole's thoughts.

Kenzie caught Cole's gaze. She knew the story of his grand-mother, Eliza Crane, as well as he did. From everything he'd heard, the woman hadn't been mentally ill at all but was the victim of his sociopathic great-grandfather. Kenzie's paternal grandmother, Betsy King, had been Eliza's best friend, and Kenzie's paternal grandfather had been the doctor who'd saved her life.

"Looks like we know where to have Kenzie's Christmas gifts shipped to once she cracks from the job," Butler joked. "Right, Buzz?"

"Whatever, man."

Butler laughed and shook his head. "Oscar Woodruff and I used to sneak out of his house and walk over to the place to party. His dad never did catch us." He chuckled. "We still laugh at how we outsmarted the chief of police back then." He looked at Kenzie. "Your dad had resigned by then."

Kenzie remained silent and Cole wanted to punch Butler. But then Kenzie would punch him, so that wouldn't help matters. He planned to have a heart-to-heart with Butler in private.

"You and Oscar, huh?" Greene said. "You two still tight?"

"We are. In fact, it should be him on this team, not—"

Cole's glare cut him off.

"As teenagers, you do stupid things," James murmured.

Butler rolled his eyes.

Cole rubbed his. Oscar Woodruff was a good man, having served as a medic in Afghanistan. Now he was a detective with the Lake City Police Department and well-liked by all who knew him.

"My grandfather ran that place for a while," Kenzie said, "im-plementing changes that offered the residents a better life, like humane treatment, decent food, and a clean place to sleep." She lifted her chin a notch. "I'm proud of him and the history my fam-ily has related to that place, the impact they had on caring for the misunderstood and mentally ill. So, say what you want, it doesn't bother me."

"Should have known you'd have ties to the loony bin," Butler said.

"More than one of us have ties to it, and you know it, so lay off." Cole's quiet voice cut through the laughter. "Stay focused, guys."

Kenzie stiffened and lasered a hard look at Cole. He sighed. She didn't want him interfering, but the truth was, he would have done it regardless. They *all* needed to focus.

With the abandoned institution in the rearview mirror, Cole's thoughts turned once more to the situation. He checked his phone. Nothing new. Police were on scene and working to make contact with the hostage taker.

When Dolly pulled to a stop, Cole was the first one out the door and made his way to the officer in charge, Ryan Hollingsworth. They'd worked together before and Cole shook his hand. "Any word?"

"Nothing."

"Who's inside?"

"No idea. That's what's so weird. We got a call that it was a domestic violence situation. A husband holding his wife and two kids hostage, but it's been crickets since we got here. Working on getting eyes in there."

"We're ready to move when you give us the word."

"Have at it."

Cole pressed the comms tighter into his ear. "All right. Let's get some eyes on the situation. Cross, go."

James nodded and followed the command, darting forward, ready to use the small camera to help them get some feedback on the situation. Cole scanned the area once more. Buildings gone the way of the mental institution stood silent and still, windows like eyes that had seen too much of life and had checked out when the junkies checked in.

Usually, the place was a beehive of some kind of illegal activity but was now a ghost town, thanks to the law enforcement presence.

Just in front of James, a window shattered and a grenade rolled to a stop.

"Grenade!" Cole's shout echoed.

But his friend and teammate was already diving behind the cover of a big metal dumpster. Cole threw himself behind the nearest police vehicle and slammed his palms over his ears. Less than a second later, the grenade exploded with a boom that sent debris flying.

SIX

Kenzie and the others had taken cover behind Dolly, thinking the shattering glass was caused by bullets, not an explosive. Her ears were ringing despite the distance they'd been from the blast.

But James . . .

And Cole . . .

She gathered her wits, scrambled to her feet, and darted to the side of the tactical vehicle and scanned the scene. A small crater in the concrete smoked, but no bodies were nearby. "Report in, everyone," she ordered.

"I'm good." James ducked out from behind the dumpster, looking none the worse for wear.

But where was Cole?

"We're going to have to go in." Cole's voice came through her comms as though he heard her silent thought.

She vaguely registered surprise that she could hear through the ringing. "James? You sure you're good? You were closest."

"I'm a little deafened, but all in one piece."

"Thank God," she thought she heard Cole whisper. Then his voice came back louder. "You know the formation. Let's go."

She and the others crept forward, weapons gripped tight, caution in every rigid muscle. Where there was one grenade, there could always be more.

The hostage negotiator was on the megaphone. "Come on, won't you pick up the phone?" They'd tossed one inside and gotten a hand grenade as a thank-you.

While the negotiator kept trying for contact, Cole stepped from behind the police car and fell in with them.

"Don't shoot me!"

The young voice came from inside the building. Cole held up a hand and everyone froze.

Then shots came from across the street.

Greene yelped and spun, but stayed on his feet and turned to fire behind him while he ducked behind an old forklift parked up against the side of the building.

Another spate of pops split the air.

Buzz screamed and went down. Otis barked. The officers behind them hollered and continued to return fire.

"Take cover! Take cover!"

Cole's shout echoed through the chaos, but Buzz was on the ground. Kenzie darted toward the man, grabbed his good arm, and yanked him to his feet with adrenaline-born strength.

Bullets whipped past her, and she expected to feel one find its mark any second, but the officers returning fire must have rattled the shooter enough that he was off his game.

Kenzie shoved Buzz into the warehouse. Butler followed, ducking to the side of the door while Buzz sank to the floor, his hand wrapped around his upper bicep, blood leaking through his fingers. "Man, that stings."

Kenzie went back to the door. "Greene!"

"I'm good! Stay down!"

She hefted her weapon and glanced out the door once more, looking for anyone she could help. A bullet pinged off the metal above her head and she slammed the door.

Buzz grunted and Kenzie swept the area with her gaze. It was

71

quiet. Too quiet even with the chaos still raging outside. "Thought this was a hostage situation," she whispered. "Where's the situation?"

"Yeah." Butler shifted, his weapon aimed at the darkness.

Thanks to the light filtering through the dirty windows above the door and along the wall Buzz leaned against, Kenzie could see about ten feet in front of her. Boxes lay scattered, trash littered the floor. Wooden pallets leaned against the wall, but that was as far as she could see. "Cover us, please," she told Butler. "I need to see to Buzz."

"I got it."

Kenzie dropped next to Buzz. "You okay?"

He quirked a brow at her. "Was counting on you to tell me."

"Someone's in here," Butler said.

Buzz nodded. "I heard him. Sounded like a kid. I'll be all right. Go find him."

More bullets sprayed the side of the building, taking out another window to her right. Kenzie crouched low and aimed her gun into the dark, musty interior of the warehouse, worried about Butler going farther alone. "Who's in here? Call out but stay down!"

The gunfire continued outside, loud pops that came fast and furious along with the answering fire from the cops who had cover. Kenzie thought she heard something not too far from where she stood. Feeling horribly exposed but needing to find who was in there—especially if it was a scared kid—she motioned to Buzz that she was going farther in to cover Butler. She pulled the Maglite from her pocket and aimed it into the darkness, flicking it over the discarded trash, empty beer bottles, evidence of drug use, and more.

James, Cole, and Greene burst in, stopping Kenzie's progress. Greene was tucked under Cole's shoulder, fighting to drag in a breath. He collapsed just inside the door next to Buzz even while he kept his weapon ready to snap up should he need it. Kenzie hurried to Greene, who waved her off.

"Got my vest."

James covered the area in the shadows beyond, while Cole hurried to Buzz, who shook his head. "It's just a flesh wound. I'm fine."

72

"Fine's stretching it."

Buzz stood, his face etched in granite—except she caught the flash of pain in his eyes before he was able to blink it away. "Need to clear this place. There's a kid in here and who knows who else?"

"Stay down," Cole said. "We'll find him."

Preferably before another hand grenade went off.

Buzz hesitated, then sank back to the floor.

Butler stepped toward the darkness. "You sure it was a kid?"

"Sounded like it," Kenzie said. "Voice was still high-pitched and a little cracky." She stood beside Butler to search the black hole with a narrowed gaze. It was useless. With no windows on the back wall, there was nothing to illuminate the inside and the Maglites weren't picking anything up.

"Anyone else hit?" she asked Cole.

"Just Buzz and Greene."

"Lucky us," Greene muttered.

Cole shifted and pressed a finger to his ear. "Where are you, Magic?"

"Pinned down in Dolly," the man said over the comms. "As soon as I can get in there without getting shot, I'll be there."

"Stay put," Cole said. "Don't take any chances. King, stay with Buzz and Greene. Butler, Cross. Clear the back."

As long as her medical expertise was needed, she wouldn't be clearing warehouses. And she was fine with that. Now that she knew the guys had the warehouse covered, Kenzie hurried back to Buzz. She knelt next to him, and he moved his hand so she could get a look. Blood seeped but wasn't spurting. She checked for an exit wound and sighed. "Sorry to tell you this, but you've got a bullet in there."

"So get it out."

"I think we'll let the surgeon handle that."

He huffed. "Just give me a knife and some tweezers."

"As if. Magic Man has the medical supplies, so this is going to be a bit of temporary battlefield medicine I'm practicing here."

"Nothing I haven't been through before."

She knew the big man had done two tours in Afghanistan. "Well, it's not necessary for now." She grabbed her kit and dug inside for gauze and tape. She wrapped the wound, then patted his shoulder. "Stay put for a sec."

The gunfire had stopped, but no one had found the kid in the building. Or any other hostages. Or a hostage taker. And why had the bullets come from *outside* the warehouse? All those thoughts raced through her mind while she transferred her attention to Greene. "You gotta work on your bullet-dodging skills," she said.

"Yep." Otis, resting in the down position at Greene's side, looked up, then licked the man's hand. Greene scratched the dog's ears. "I'm all right, old man." But his clenched jaw and narrow-eyed gaze told her the pain he was in. He met Kenzie's gaze. "Really. I'm good. Like I said, it got my vest. Took my breath away and stings a bit, but I'm not hit otherwise."

Thank God. "Otis?" She ran her hands over the dog's torso that was also covered in a bulletproof vest. "How are you, boy?"

"I checked him. He's good too." Greene's voice was an octave lower and, for a moment, unfiltered gratitude shone at her.

"Okay." She gave the dog an ear scratch and a light pat. He rewarded her with a swipe of his tongue up her cheek. "Then you two hang tight."

"Yep."

With the triage finished and no one in immediate danger of bleeding out, she scurried over to Cole. "Greene will be good. He'll have a bruise where the bullet got him in the vest. Buzz is going to need surgery, but it's nothing life-threatening. Otis is uninjured."

"Good. Stay with them until we find the kid . . . and whoever else might be in here, but keep your eyes peeled and your weapon handy."

"Got it."

He moved toward Butler and Cross. "Come on out, kid. You're not in trouble. We're here to help."

Kenzie strained to see while James used a Maglite to light the way, sweeping the beam left, then right. James' hand rested on Cole's left shoulder and Butler's hand would be on James'. Silent communication. A tap, a squeeze, or pulling a team member out of danger. All possible with that hand.

Movement just beyond a stack of wooden pallets captured her attention. The guys saw it too. "Come on out!" James' order cut through the silence. "Hold your hands up so we can see them!"

A young boy, maybe twelve or thirteen, stepped from behind the crate, hands up. "P-please, don't shoot me. I didn't mean to hurt anyone. I-I'm sorry. He told me to do it. He said it was a training exercise. I didn't think it was real. He paid me and said you knew about it."

The kid babbled while Kenzie listened and exchanged frowns with Greene and Buzz. The kid's words registered. Someone had paid him to toss a hand grenade at the team?

COLE STOOD TO THE SIDE while James patted the kid down. All he found was a hundred-dollar bill, corroborating the payment story. Thankfully, no more grenades. "What's your name, son?" Cole asked, taking the money from James.

"Micah Martin."

"Anyone else in here?"

"N-no, it's just me."

James walked away speaking into his radio, reporting the situation, while Cole nodded to Butler. "Make sure? And find out what's going on with our shooter across the street."

"On it."

"Come on over here. Let's sit for a minute and have a chat."

He led the boy to a pile of stacked crates and motioned for him to sit. Micah did and Cole squatted in front of him, registering the sound of chopper blades beating the air above the building. Kenzie was still off to the side with Buzz and Greene. "Okay, Micah, I need you to be honest with me no matter how scared you are, okay?"

Micah nodded and bit his lip. "I always tell the truth." He rubbed his nose and looked down for a second before he sighed. "Well, maybe not always, but I will with this, I promise."

"Thank you for that. How old are you?"

"Twelve. I'll be thirteen next week."

"Where's your mom?"

"At home, I guess."

So, not being held hostage. "Dad? Brothers and sisters?"

"I have two brothers and two sisters and two cousins who live with us because my aunt and uncle died in a car wreck. I'm in the middle of them all. Don't have a dad. He left when I was nine because he didn't want to be 'saddled'"—Micah wiggled his fingers around the word that he'd probably overheard—"with two more kids."

And he was the middle kid of *seven* children living in the home? "Money tight?"

Micah swallowed and slid his gaze away from Cole's once more but gave a subtle dip of his head.

"Understandable. You can look at me. It's okay. Nothing to be ashamed of." Micah met his eyes. "Tell me who paid you to throw a hand grenade out the window."

Before Micah could answer, James and Butler returned. "It's clear," Butler said. "No one else in here but the rats and roaches."

"Okay. As soon as you get the all clear, get Magic Man in here with the medical supplies. Kenzie can help if he needs it."

"Copy that."

They went to pass on his instructions and he turned back to Micah. "Sorry about that. Go ahead."

"This cop came up to me and asked me if I wanted to earn some money."

"A *cop*?"

"Uh-huh. He was dressed like you."

Cole blinked. "In SWAT gear?"

"Yeah, but . . . different. He had his face covered. I could only see his eyes."

76

Some SWAT officers used gaiter-like face coverings as part of their uniform.

"What color were his eyes?"

"Blue, I think." He frowned. "Maybe."

"How tall?"

Micah studied him. "Can you stand up?"

"Sure." Cole did so. Micah stood next to him and looked up. "Not as tall as you. Maybe like to your nose."

He was six feet two inches, so the guy Micah was describing was less than six feet tall. Five ten or five eleven. "Good, good. That's helpful. Keep going. How did you meet him?" Cole sat down again and motioned for Micah to do the same.

"I live in the trailer park up the road. We have a basketball court. Sort of. Anyway, I was playing with some friends. They left and I stayed behind to shoot some more hoops even though the ball is almost flat. I wanna play on the high school team and I only got two years to practice. Just as I was about to leave, this dude dressed like you walks up to me and says y'all are doing a training thing today and he needs me to throw a fake grenade out the window." He shrugged a bony shoulder. "Then he slipped me a hundred, brought me here, told me to be real careful because it was like a flash bang and could hurt my eyes and ears if I didn't pull and throw. He said there was just smoke in there, I swear."

"That's what he said. 'Pull and throw'?"

"Yeah. He made me repeat it after him like ten times and practice on a pretend one. He said the team would be coming toward the building, and as soon as they got close, I was supposed to throw it. So I did. I pulled and threw just like we practiced." He swallowed. "But the one I threw, that was a real one, wasn't it?"

"It was."

A shudder rippled through his slender frame. "I didn't know. I swear."

"I believe you," Cole said. And he did. There was nothing but truth in the boy's eyes and words. He'd been a pawn in a dangerous man's game.

Micah frowned. "Why would he do that? I'm just a kid. I shouldn't be handling stuff like that."

No kidding. "That guy wasn't a real cop, Micah," Cole said. At least he prayed he wasn't. "No real law enforcement officer would ever ask you to do something like that."

The boy's green eyes with lashes all women would envy widened. "Then who was he?"

"That's what we're going to find out."

"Garrison?" James' voice came through the comms.

"Yeah?"

"Micah's mother is here."

He held a hand out to Micah, who took it and let Cole pull him to his feet. "Your mom's here."

Micah flinched. "She's going to be so mad at me."

"Maybe not. We'll talk to her."

The boy shifted and bit his lip once more.

"What is it?"

"The money. Do I get it back?" Tears formed in his eyes, but he straightened his shoulders and swallowed hard. "Mom needs that money."

Cole sighed. "I have to keep it for right now. It's evidence. But I'll make sure you get it back as soon as the lab is done with it, okay?"

"When will that be?"

"I don't know. Probably a few weeks."

"Oh." His shoulders drooped.

"You have something to spend it on before then?"

"Yeah," he whispered. "They're going to turn the power off tomorrow if Mom doesn't pay the bill. That would have paid the power and bought some groceries too."

Two things no twelve-year-old should be worried about. He patted the kid's shoulder. "We'll see what we can do to make sure the power stays on. Anything else?"

"Um. I don't know if it's important, but something fell out of his pocket when he pulled out the money." He dug into the front pocket of his jeans and pulled out a small label. "I only picked it up because I wanted something to remember the day by. I thought it was going to be a cool one, something to brag about to my friends. Now I don't want it."

Cole's radio went off with the code for the all clear. He took the tiny piece of paper by the edge with forefinger and thumb. No way to get a print off that, but . . . "King, you got an evidence bag?"

"Heard the all clear so I'll get one out of the car."

She left and returned in seconds. He slipped the piece of paper into the bag, sealed it, and labeled it. Then took a good look at it. "It's a label from a piece of fruit."

"Guess that's stupid, huh?" Micah asked.

"No way. This might actually be super helpful. Good job." The boy's eyes lit up and he offered Cole a small smile. "You ready to get out of here?" Cole asked him.

"Yeah."

Cole led the way out with the others following him. As soon as they reached the barrier of the crime scene tape, a woman who looked to be in her midforties gasped. "Micah!"

"Mom!" Micah ran toward his mother. As Cole got closer, he could see Micah was a miniature version of her with his dark hair and green eyes. She wrapped him in a tight hug while tears slipped down her pale cheeks.

She met Cole's gaze. "Will there be charges?" she whispered.

"I can't say for sure, but we'll talk to the DA and explain everything. Micah didn't realize what was going on. There was no malicious action on his end."

She swiped away her tears, sucked in a breath, and nodded her thanks. "Can I take him home?"

"Sure."

Once they were gone in her beat-up minivan, Cole returned to the warehouse to find Magic Man working on Buzz. "He's okay?"

"Will be. Paramedics are headed this way."

No sooner had he spoken the words than the door opened and the medics rushed in pushing a stretcher.

Cole walked to the door, aware of the action going on behind him but his gaze sweeping the area. Someone was out there who'd deliberately planned an ambush and tried to take out his team.

Someone who used a twelve-year-old kid.

Someone who was probably fuming that his plan had failed.

And maybe someone who was already formulating a new one?

SEVEN

LAKE CITY STATE HOSPITAL
AUGUST 1947

Eliza sat in front of Dr. King and sucked in a ragged breath. It was time to come clean and see what would happen. Where the truth led. It was time to see if this man was truly as compassionate and caring as he came across in their sessions or if it was all just an act to get her to cooperate.

He leaned forward. "What is it, Eliza? Have you finally remembered something?"

Did she dare tell him? "I . . . I . . . no."

He frowned and settled back against his chair. "Well, that's disappointing. I thought we might be getting somewhere."

Eliza licked her lips. "I want to see my friend Betsy."

His eyes lit up like she'd announced it was Christmas and he had a free vacation to Hawaii on the horizon. He hesitated, then rubbed his chin and set his clipboard and pen aside. "Tell me about Betsy."

"What do you want to know?"

"Just . . . how did you meet?"

"We go to the same church, but we also went to high school together for a couple of years before the war. She's two years behind me, which makes her twenty years old now. She still lives with her parents. Her two older brothers fought in the war and one died." Sorrow clouded his eyes, but she continued. "So we share that common grief."

All of her father's money couldn't stop her brother from enlisting and coming home in a pine box.

"Betsy worked in a textile plant helping make uniforms. Now that the war is over, we socialize and attend church together. Our families used to be very close, but since my brother died, my father has changed. He and I never really got along before all of that, but now I don't even know who he is anymore."

The doctor's hand covered hers. "I'm so sorry. You've been through so much. And your friend as well." His cheeks pinkened slightly when he referenced Betsy.

Eliza's eyes widened. "You're interested in courting her."

The pink darkened to red and he sat back. "Don't be daft. I'm fifteen years older than she is and I've only met her the one time."

"Why does age matter or how many times you meet someone? When you know, you know. That's how it was with my William too." She'd told him about her fiancé.

A sigh escaped him. "Eliza, why are you here?"

She blinked. "You've never asked me that before."

"I am now. You don't belong here."

"I agree, but my father says I do, and because I've been deemed a danger to myself, he has the authority to keep me here."

He glanced at the healing wounds on her wrists. "Why did you do that?"

"Finally," she whispered.

"What?"

"Finally, after four weeks, you're asking the right questions."

He leaned back and crossed his arms. "Care to explain what you mean?"

"For the past month you've talked and talked, asked me about my childhood, asked me about my family relationships, asked me about my dreams for the future, about my brother's death in the war, but this is the first time you've asked me why I'm here."

He frowned. "Okay, I guess that's true. Do you have an answer for me?"

"I think so. I knew the question was coming, but I wasn't sure I would know how to answer, so I didn't push you to ask it sooner." And she'd felt safe here. Which was insane. She almost laughed at her unintentional pun, then smiled. A mental asylum had been her safe home for the past month while she'd healed.

He clasped his hands and studied her with those exceptionally dark brown eyes. "Why are you here?"

"Apparently, I decided to kill myself and slit my wrists."

"Apparently?"

"That's what I was told." She eyed him. "What you were told as well, I'm sure."

"Yes, but I wanted to know your thoughts." The frown deepened. "You don't remember the night you did that?"

"Not until just recently. And even now, not everything."

"Tell me."

She looked down at her wrists and anguish filled her. "You won't believe me."

"I assure you I will."

Well, it was now or never. "I didn't try to kill myself," she said. "My father tried to buy off my fiancé, saying he wasn't good enough to be a part of our family and he'd give him ten thousand dollars to walk away and never look back." She ignored the doctor's gasp. "I overheard them arguing but stayed out of it. William refused, told my father I was a grown woman and he should trust my judgment. Do you know what my father said?"

"I can't imagine."

"He said if William had two nickels to rub together, he'd trust my judgment more, that William was a gold digger, but he would never get his hands on the family money—or me." She shuddered. "William stood for a moment and told my father he didn't deserve to have a daughter like me. My father threatened to call the authorities, and I made my presence known. My father yelled at me to go to my room. I tried to leave with William and there was a huge uproar. The authorities were called. William finally left with promises to come find me when everyone had a chance to calm down. I . . . didn't try to stop him. I knew this was between me and my father, so I confronted him. He tried to convince me he had my best interests at heart, but he didn't. His only interests, then and now, are his own. And that's me marrying into a family more wealthy than my own. When I told him I'd run away, he hit me. Hard. I fell against the mantel and must have hit my head because when I woke up, I was here." She held up her left hand. "And I had bandages on my wrists."

"Eliza . . ." Dr. King's face had gone pale. "Do you understand what you're saying?"

"Yes." She lifted her chin. "My father tried to kill me. I don't know why he brought me here rather than completing the deed, but I assure you, I don't want to die. But I also don't want to go home. I'm . . . afraid to go home."

"Where is your fiancé? He's not been to visit. Not once."

"I feel sure it's because he doesn't know where I am. If he knew, I'd already be gone."

"What about Betsy? Wouldn't she tell him?"

"She hasn't said anything to you?"

"No. We didn't discuss you. It wouldn't be ethical." He paused. "Does she know what you've told me?"

Eliza shook her head. "I haven't had a chance to tell her. And just so you know, I'm perfectly fine with you two talking about me if it means you can put your heads together and figure out a way to get me out of here."

"I'll bear that in mind. You asked her to find William?"

She nodded. "She said she's looked all over for him and hasn't been able to locate him. She also said that my father has spread the rumor that I'm in Paris living with relatives. I can't help but think

William might have gone there to look for me." But for four whole weeks? She pushed the doubts away.

Dr. King studied her, then picked up his pen and notepad. "Give me his name and address."

Just as she finished providing the information, a knock on the door interrupted them and the doctor's secretary stuck her head in. "Miss Betsy is here for Miss Eliza."

"Please show her in."

Eliza couldn't help but smile at his eagerness. Normally, visitors were escorted to the specified area, but Betsy had special privileges thanks to the doctor.

When Betsy entered, Eliza rushed to hug her. "Thank you for coming," she whispered.

"I'm sorry it's taken me so long to come back, but I've been searching for William."

Eliza pulled back. "And?"

"I finally managed to talk to his sister and she said he's been looking for you. But—" She broke off and bit her lip.

"But?" Eliza gripped her friend's biceps. "What? Tell me."

"He's had the most terrible accident and is recovering in the hospital."

"What!" Eliza stumbled back as though to get away from the news.

"He's okay, Eliza, truly. He's recovering. He was in a coma but woke up briefly to ask about you."

He was okay. He was asking about her. Her pulse settled slightly. "What kind of accident?"

"His car slid on the slick road and he crashed into a tree. Banged himself up really well. But like I said, he's okay. I talked to him myself and he's quite horrified that you're here. Said to tell you he was coming to get you as soon as possible."

"Oh, thank God."

"Um, Miss McCall?"

They both turned at the doctor's voice. "Yes?"

"How did *you* know Eliza was here?"

Betsy shuddered. "I followed them here the night her father brought her."

"What?" Eliza gripped her friend's hands, appalled that she hadn't thought to ask that very question. "What do you mean?"

"I was coming to see you the day you were admitted, remember?"

Eliza forced her mind back to that fuzzy day. "Yes. Yes, I do. You were going to have dinner with William and me."

"Well, I was a little late, and when I arrived, I saw William speed away. He looked so angry. I knew something had happened, so I stood there trying to decide what to do when the door opened and your father came out carrying you. I almost ran to see what was wrong, but I didn't because everything looked . . . off. You had bandages around your wrists and . . ." Tears flooded her eyes. "You were unconscious. I could tell that right off." She glanced at the doctor. "Their drive is lined with trees, so I hid behind one and watched."

"Wouldn't someone have seen your car?" Dr. King asked.

"No. It's a wide U-shaped drive and they left on the opposite side of where I was parked. I always leave room to get out in case I need to leave. I don't want to bother anyone if I have to leave before others are ready. You can't see the front door from there, and I don't think anyone noticed my car there when they left." She waved a hand. "Anyway, I ran to my car and followed them, thinking there'd been a terrible accident and he was taking you to the hospital. When he came here, I was stunned. This wasn't the hospital I had in mind." She swallowed. "And then I figured it was because your father was doing everything in his power to keep you from marrying William."

"Yes," Eliza whispered.

The door opened and a man Eliza had never seen before stepped inside. His eyes landed first on her, then Betsy. They widened and lingered until Dr. King cleared his throat. "Dr. Stephen, I'm in a session."

"I see that." His eyes roamed the trio before him. "Are we now allowing visitors to join in the sessions?"

"If I think it helps the patient, then yes."

The man sighed, but he continued to gaze at Betsy. Finally, he turned his attention back to Dr. King. "You and your modern ideas. I've arranged for Miss Crane's electric shock therapy sessions to begin today. The staff will be expecting her in twenty minutes."

"What?" Eliza nearly screeched the word and Betsy's fingers tightened around hers. "I don't need that." Fear nearly strangled her.

"It was suggested by your father, Miss Crane." To the others, he said, "He's even purchased the latest machine to make sure Eliza gets the best care. It was delivered today. Bring her down when you're finished." He tilted his head toward Betsy. "Miss." Then he was gone.

Eliza turned her gaze to Dr. King, then Betsy. "You can't let them," she whispered. "Please . . . I must go to William. I . . . What do I do?"

Dr. King pulled in a ragged breath and rubbed his chin. "Stay here. I don't know how he can do this. He's overstepping his authority. I'm your doctor, not him."

He swept from the room and Eliza wilted on the chair.

EIGHT

PRESENT DAY

Two hours later, back at headquarters, Kenzie pressed a hand to her head. A tension headache gnawed at her temples, and she tried to remember whether she had any ibuprofen anywhere. The shooter had managed to get away in spite of law enforcement pulling out all the stops.

Buzz and Greene were at the hospital, but both would make full recoveries. She hadn't been worried about that. Much. Not Greene anyway. His vest had done its job. But Buzz had been a concern, and she'd been glad to get the confirmation he'd be fine.

They'd both demanded to FaceTime in on the debrief, but Buzz probably wouldn't be out of surgery in time. He'd be mad, but he'd get over it. Thankfully, Cowboy had been discharged and sent home and would join them from there.

She shut the locker and twisted the combination lock, wishing she could ride the adrenaline crash in front of her television.

After the meeting, she promised herself. If she could stay awake that long.

When she arrived at the conference room, she noted the remaining team members already gathered at the back of the room, heads close together. All at once, they nodded in unison at something

Cole said. Once again, the feeling of being left out stung. "What's going on?"

The men separated, turned to face her, and began clapping one by one. James, Cole, Commander Judson Hill, and Magic Man. Butler simply stood there, eyes narrowed.

Kenzie blinked and met Cole's gaze, then the others'. "Uh, what?"

James laughed. "You're a hero, Kenzie. You waltzed right into the line of fire like the dude was shooting potatoes, not bullets, grabbed Buzz like he was a toddler, and got him to safety."

Cole didn't look nearly as thrilled with that, but he did have a small smile on his face.

"Oh," she said. "Well. I mean, I couldn't just stand there while he was lying there wounded with a chance of a more deadly bullet headed his way."

"Exactly," Cole said. "Brave and heroic. Well done."

Kenzie didn't think her face could get any redder or hotter, but at Cole's praise, she was proven wrong. "Uh, thanks." She cleared her throat, desperate to stop stammering and turn the attention elsewhere.

The commander shook her hand. "I know there's been some question about your presence on this team. I hope this proves the decision to put you here was the right one. I know I have no doubts whatsoever."

"Thank you, sir, I really appreciate that." Kenzie's throat tightened briefly and she drew in a deep breath. This was not the time for emotions. "So, what else did I miss?"

Thankfully, Cole let her redirect. "I was just asking the guys what they thought about taking up a collection for Micah's family."

In the almost six months she'd been on the team, they'd done this a few times. It was always the kids who triggered it. Kids trapped in situations they had no say about. "I'm in." She had about fifty bucks in her wallet. She pulled it out and passed it to Cole, then leaned back, willing herself not to yawn.

Cole tucked the money into his wallet. "I'll go by there when we get done here. Want to go with me, King?" Butler snorted and Cole raised a brow at the man. "You want to go too?"

"Naw, just wondering why she gets the invite."

"You're all invited. I just thought it might be good for Micah's mother to have a woman present."

James rolled his eyes at Butler and shook his head. "You're an idiot, man. Zip it." The words directed at his team member were soft. The warning look was not.

Butler huffed but fell silent, leaned back, and crossed his arms.

Kenzie ignored them all. "Sure, I'd love to go."

They settled around the table, and Butler rose to set up the technology to bring Greene and Cowboy in via video. Greene's face appeared on the screen and he scowled. "I could be there, you know," he said by way of greeting.

James leaned back in his chair. "Dude, take it from someone who's been there. Go easy on yourself. You're going to be hurting for a few days." James had taken a bullet to the vest in his back just a few months ago while rescuing a young child from the father who'd taken her and her family hostage.

"Yeah, yeah," Greene said. "You get the joker behind all this?"

"No," Hill said, "not yet. The manhunt is still ongoing, but it looks like he's managed to evade everyone. The dogs picked up his scent and trailed it for a while, but he must have had a vehicle stashed somewhere not too far from the scene. We left when there was nothing else for us to do but wait. Any word on Buzz?"

"I've got a nurse keeping me informed," Greene said. "If I didn't want the every-fifteen-minute play-by-play update, I'd get out of here. At least I'll be here for Buzz when he gets out of surgery." He glanced away from the camera for a moment. "Which, according to Nurse Byron, should be soon."

"His parents there yet?" Cole asked.

"Yep. They've already checked in on me."

"Perfect. Keep us in the loop. We'll stop by to see you two in the morning."

Greene snorted. "I won't be here. Just waiting on my discharge papers."

"Glad to hear it. You need a ride home?"

"I'll give him one," Cowboy said, chiming in for the first time.

Greene rolled his eyes. "Right. No thanks. I don't like your driving on a good day." He turned serious. "My sister is on the way. Now, let's get down to business. First things first, if I may?"

Cole nodded his permission for the man to continue.

"King, that was some kind of move you pulled getting Buzz to safety." His throat worked and he cleared it. "I don't even know how he or the team will ever be able to thank you for that."

Again with the blushing. She sighed. Just when her cheeks had finally cooled off. "I'm glad everyone is going to be okay."

"All right, then, I'm done now. Just had to thank King. What's next, Garrison?"

"I've been thinking about that." Cole rubbed his chin and shook his head. "So, we've got one incident that could have been aimed at Kenzie. Then the one where the guy definitely broke into her house. I don't think those were random. Now this ambush at the warehouse? It doesn't take a genius to figure out someone is targeting one or all of us."

"Well, what are we going to do?" Butler asked. "Go into hiding?"

"No way." Commander Hill shook his head. "We couldn't even if we wanted to. We—you—have this job for a reason. And that means you keep doing it, you just do it with your guard up and have each other's backs. Stay alert and don't go anywhere alone—or to a location that seems like it could be a setup for an attack."

Kenzie rubbed her eyes. Great. They needed a plan to get this person as fast as possible. Lives were at stake whenever they had a call to a scene. If they had to look over their shoulders—more so than usual—while trying to deal with everything that went on at a call, then . . . people would die.

And that was unacceptable.

They *had* to get this guy. ASAP.

"One other thing," Cole said. "Does anyone recognize this label? It has a small logo on it. The kid, Micah, said the guy who paid him dropped it when he pulled the money out of his pocket." He passed his phone so everyone could take a look.

When it got to Butler, he raised a brow. "Yeah, that's the farmers' market off the parkway. Not the big Lake City one, but a privately owned spread. Coleman's. Out behind Coleman Stables."

"No kidding." Cole squinted at the picture once more. "I guess I need to get out more. I didn't recognize it."

Butler shrugged. "I go there a few times a month. They have some really great produce. They also have a small grocery store at the back past some of the local booths where you can get cold stuff. One-stop shopping."

"All right, everyone," Commander Hill said. "If no one has anything else, that's it for now. Stay safe out there."

He left and the others filed out, leaving Kenzie and Cole behind. Cole looked at her. "Ready?"

"Ready."

THANKFULLY, the trip to the Martins' home was uneventful, and Cole pulled to the curb. Micah's trailer was almost all the way in the back of the mobile home park, and while the structure itself looked sad and run-down, the little yard to its right bloomed with flowers he had no name for.

They'd made a stop at the local sporting goods store to purchase a new basketball, then a trip to the grocery store for a few staples. Cole pointed to a small fenced area. "Guess that's the basketball court."

"Yikes. That looks dangerous." Trash, broken cement, glass, and drug paraphernalia littered the area that was supposed to be a fun space for kids. The bare hoop needed a new net.

Cole shook his head. "How hard is it to keep something like that clean and safe for the children who want to play on it?"

"You have to care," Kenzie said, her voice low.

"Yeah. Yeah, I guess you do."

Still dressed in full gear, he led the way up the rickety wooden steps to the small porch. Kenzie waited at the bottom. He raised a brow at her and she shook her head. "I'm not sure that wood will hold both of us."

He shifted and the porch groaned. She could be right.

"How much did you collect?" she asked him.

"Three hundred bucks." He knocked, then turned to look at her. "Everyone always puts something in." He smiled. "Even Butler."

She nodded. "I know it's not really that much, but for this family, it'll help."

"Yeah." He knocked again, even while he noted Kenzie's gaze roaming the area. She was definitely on high alert.

Good. They needed to be.

The deadbolt clicked and the door creaked open. A little girl about four years old with stringy blond hair and big blue eyes looked up at him. "Hi."

Cole set the groceries on the deck, then squatted, one knee popping and his gear creaking. "Hi. I'm Cole."

"I'm Randa." She brushed the hair out of her eyes with a gesture that looked automatic. "What you want?"

"Is Micah home?"

"Uh-huh."

"Good. What about your mama?"

"Yep." She continued to study him.

"You want to tell her we're here? We have something we want to give her."

"Okay. Be right back." She shut the door and he could hear her little footsteps on the linoleum floor.

He turned to Kenzie once more. "That's a little unnerving. Not sure it's a good idea for that baby to be opening the door around here."

"Agreed."

"She did have it locked, though."

"And we have our uniforms on, so maybe she's not been taught to be leery of the police yet."

"Good point."

Hurried steps of an adult came toward the door, and through the thin wood came a woman's voice. "Randa, how many times have I told you not to open the door? You come get me."

"Sorry, Mama."

The curtain on the dusty window to the left moved, and eyes that matched Randa's appeared for a moment, widened, then disappeared. The door opened a crack and Mrs. Martin looked out at them. "Yes?"

"Hi, Mrs. Martin," Cole said. "I'm Cole Garrison, the officer from this afternoon that talked to Micah about the situation at the warehouse. This is Kenzie King. Do you have a minute?"

"Sure. And call me Melissa, please." She bit her lip, then shrugged. "Come on in. It isn't much, sorry."

"It's a home," Kenzie said. "As long as there's love, the packaging doesn't matter much."

The woman's eyes teared and she swallowed hard, then gave them a shaky smile. "Well, there's love for sure." She waved them in, and Cole grabbed the three bags of groceries. As soon as he entered, he noted right away the place was clean. Worn and old, probably hand-me-downs and thrift store items, but clean. A hint of pine filled his nose, reminding him of his grandmother's house. A couch was against the far wall. An old recliner with a torn arm was beside it. He noted there was no furniture in front of the window. Smart woman. Everyone who lived in this area worried about stray bullets.

Micah stepped into the room from the hallway and stopped when he saw them. "Randa said two cops were here. I didn't expect it to be you guys." Fear flashed. "You coming to take me to prison?"

"No, no, not at all," Cole said. He turned back to Melissa. "Micah said you were taking care of him, his siblings, and two cousins."

"That's right. The others are at the church for a weekend activity.

Randa and Micah didn't want to go so I let them stay home." She rubbed her palms down the sides of her jeans and eyed the bags he and Kenzie held. "Why?"

"Well, Micah was trying to help you out today, not realizing he was being tricked by a criminal. He said you needed money to keep the power on and for groceries."

She sighed and a single tear leaked down her cheek before she swiped it away and drew her shoulders back. "That's true, but I've always found a way before. I'll find one this time." She shrugged. "God provides. Sometimes when it's last minute and it looks like he's forgotten me."

"Well," Cole said, "then I guess God decided to use us this time." He hefted the bags of groceries. "We weren't sure what you needed, but figured we couldn't go wrong with the usual. Milk, butter, sugar, salt and pepper, bread, some pasta and sauce. Got you a few bags of chips, ten pounds of hamburger meat and chicken. And some treats for the kids. There's a basketball in there somewhere for Micah. He mentioned his was going flat."

"What?" she whispered. Her wide green eyes bounced between him and Kenzie.

"I hope you don't mind," he said. "I promise this isn't pity. We all need help every so often." Which was completely true, but some people got touchy about receiving help from others. Sometimes all a person had was their pride, and that could be good or bad, depending. Not taking the groceries she obviously needed would be bad.

"Mind?" She blinked and let out a shuddering sob before biting her lip. Her eyes shimmered with new tears. "Are you kidding? I have pride, but I also know an answer to prayer when God lands one on my doorstep." She motioned to the kitchen. "You can put them on the table if you don't mind."

"Don't mind at all."

Cole carried the bags to the nice-size kitchen and set them where she indicated. Micah and Randa hurried over to help unload their bounty, giving exclaims of delight, first at the basketball that Micah held like it was made of pure gold, then at the huge bag of M&M's Kenzie had insisted on.

"Mama," Randa squealed, "can we have some?"

"A handful each."

Randa frowned. Looked at Micah's hand, then her own. "How about we count out the same amount?"

Cole smothered a smile, heard Kenzie cover a chuckle, and even Melissa pressed her lips together while her eyes sparkled with a brief flash of humor. "Sure. That's a great idea. Twenty each."

"Twenty-five?" Randa asked.

"Nineteen."

The girl gasped her horror. "Twenty is fair."

Melissa nodded. "I thought so."

Micah ripped open the bag, and Cole and Kenzie passed his mother the rest of the groceries until they were put away. Melissa sniffed, swiped her face, and led them out of the kitchen and back into the den. She motioned to the couch. "I honestly don't even know how to thank you."

Before Cole sat, he pulled the envelope with the money from his pocket. "Our team collected this and wanted you to have it. I called the power company, and if you pay it tomorrow before they close, they won't shut it off."

She gasped and took the envelope with a shaky hand. "I . . . I don't know what to say. This on top of everything else?" Tears now slipped unchecked down her cheeks. She ignored them and looked up to meet Cole's gaze, then Kenzie's and back to Cole.

He smiled. "No need to say anything. Just please call us if you need anything." He handed her a card with his contact information and Kenzie did the same. "We really do want people—especially kids—to see there are good officers in law enforcement."

Melissa clutched the envelope to her chest. "As far as I'm concerned, you're the best."

NINE

The next morning, Kenzie rolled over in bed to stare at the ceiling, her mind replaying the events of yesterday, but mostly she couldn't get the look in Micah's mother's eyes out of her head.

Gratitude. Surprise. Relief. Resignation. Grief. Guilt. Weariness. A bone-deep tired that all the sleep in the world wouldn't be able to dispel. The one thing Kenzie didn't remember seeing was hope.

And that bothered her.

Everyone needed hope.

It took her thirty minutes to dress for her day of . . . what? Some days she hated not being on the schedule. Technically, she was on call 24/7, but when it was her day off and no calls came in . . .

Okay, no calls was a good thing. She climbed out of bed and walked to the window to peer through the blinds. Yep, her "bodyguards" were still there. She itched to take a run or hop on her bike and get in a few miles on her favorite trails around Lake City, but the fact that Cole thought she needed security held her back. He had called in a few favors, and officers and the other off-duty unit members had stayed on her home.

The clock said she'd actually slept for seven solid hours, and that spoke volumes as to how tired she'd been.

Cole had offered to stay on her couch once more last night and she'd refused. She had protection on her home, her gun on her end table, and her alarm armed. Having Cole in her home would rattle her too much to relax. That very fact bothered her on so many levels. Why was she attracted to him all of a sudden?

She snorted. If she were honest, it wasn't all of a sudden. She'd always thought Cole was good-looking but had considered him so far out of her league she hadn't allowed herself to crush on him. So why did her attraction meter go off every time he walked in the room?

It was ridiculous and she needed to get over it.

Her phone buzzed on the pillow, and she unplugged it from the charger to see a text from Cole.

I know today is your day off, but you up to trying to track down the guy who set us up yesterday?

More than up to it.

I figured. I thought we'd head to the farmers' market and see what kind of fruit that label belongs to.

Pick you up in 30?

You really think that label is going to tell us anything?

No idea, but figured it wouldn't hurt to try. You game?

I'll be ready.

Kenzie set her phone aside and frowned. Why was he being so chummy with her lately? Was it really because he was trying to get the other guys to warm up to her? Maybe. Or maybe he had another motive.

Like what?

No idea.

Not that she wasn't grateful for the change, but it was . . . un-nerving. Weird. Just like her stupid attraction to him. He was still out of her league, and the quicker she got that through her head, the better off she'd be.

Her phone buzzed again. This time with a call from her father. Great. Ignore or answer? She swiped the screen. "Hey, Dad."

"I need you to take me to the cemetery today."

Kenzie froze. "Why?" The word slipped out even though she already knew the answer.

"Why?" He snorted. "To visit your mom, of course."

"I didn't know we were doing that today. No one told me." He went a couple of times a week, but it was usually one of her brothers who took him.

He swore and she grimaced. Her mother's death, his injuries from the wreck, the rumors swirling about him being a dirty cop, and his subsequent "forced" retirement from the force had turned him into a very bitter man. Being around his abrasive bad attitude was like fingernails on a chalkboard to her nerves. And it hurt, as it seemed to be reserved mostly for her. She loved him but spent as little time as possible with him for her own mental health.

"I can't go to the cemetery today, Dad, I'm sorry. I already have plans."

"More important than visiting your mother?"

"Dad . . ." She sighed. "I get that you want to visit her grave, but Mom's not there. She's in heaven living the good life, and she would want you to do the same—as much as possible during our limited time here on earth."

Click.

Another sigh mixed with a groan slipped from her, and she shook her head, trying to ignore the sudden surge of guilt. Why did she bother? She should just keep her mouth shut.

He hated being in a wheelchair and she didn't blame him for that. Of course not. But he refused to even try to make peace with it. And after all these years, she'd almost lost hope that he ever would.

She called him back. He answered on the first ring. "What time are you wanting to go?" she asked.

"This afternoon around three o'clock."

She bit back another sigh. "I'll see what I can do. Can I text you?" He fell silent. "Dad?"

"Really?"

She blinked at the hint of vulnerability in his tone. "Yes. Really."

"Good. I'll be ready. You can drive the van." He hung up again. Whatever she'd heard in his voice was gone, and now she wondered if she'd imagined it. And she hated driving his van. It was big and bulky and needed a new muffler.

But she'd do it just like she always did.

It didn't take her long to shower and get ready for the day. When she walked into her kitchen, she could almost believe the previous couple of days were just a bad dream.

Except now a tension headache was starting behind her eyes. She loved her dad, she did. She just didn't *like* him very much.

Neither did most of the people who knew him.

"Well, it's your own fault for calling him back," she muttered. "Should have just let it go." But she couldn't, and that bothered her more than she liked.

While she waited for Cole to arrive, she did some housecleaning, her mind spinning back to childhood memories. Back to when her mother was alive. Back when they would come to this very house to visit her father's mother. Grandma Betsy was a wonderful woman who loved Jesus with every fiber of her being.

Those had been good days, even though Kenzie knew her parents were having marital difficulties. Never had there been arguing or blowups or anything obvious. Just the silences. Her parents had gotten to the point where they would go days without speaking. Her mother's smile had been fake for weeks before her death, and no amount of asking what was wrong had been able to pull the truth from the woman.

One of Kenzie's last moments with her had been finding her crying in the kitchen. Anger surged, but she bit it back. "Mom, something's wrong with you and Dad. Why won't you tell me?"

A sigh slipped from her and she smiled through her tears. "Sometimes you've just got to have a good cry."

"And you're crying because of Dad. What's he done?"

Her mom cupped her face and kissed her forehead. "Partly because of him, yes. I won't insult your intelligence by denying it. We're just having some tough times right now, Kenz, but I love him and he loves me and I know we'll work it out in the end. We just have to walk through the fire to get there."

"I'm never getting married."

"Aw, honey, don't say that. The good times far outweigh the bad. And besides, I wouldn't have you or your brothers if I hadn't married your dad, and I'd never change that."

Kenzie grunted. "I'm not sure pointing that out is a good marketing strategy for the benefits of marriage. Four kids? Three of them boys, Mom? Really? Then again, I get why you had to keep trying. You had to get to me."

"What do you mean?"

"So you could finally hit perfection," Kenzie deadpanned.

Her mom had laughed. Loud and long and then had hugged her tight. "I love your humor, sweet girl, and your ability to make the sun come out amidst the clouds. Don't ever lose that."

"Sorry, Mom," she whispered to the silence of the house, "I think I lost it and don't know how to get it back." She walked to the mantel and picked up her favorite photo. Just her and her mother. Grandma Betsy had taken it during a vacation week at the beach. Kenzie was twelve and just starting seventh grade, with no clue of the tragedy that was coming. "I miss you, Mom."

When the doorbell rang, Kenzie turned from the photo and pasted a smile on her lips.

COLE DIDN'T KNOW WHY he had a hard time pulling in a breath when Kenzie opened the door, but this reaction when he was around her was getting ridiculous. She wore a light blue oversize sweatshirt and faded jeans with fashionable holes in the knees. He could tell she had her vest on under the sweatshirt. With her dark hair pulled into a ponytail and a few wispy bangs playing tag with her eyebrows, she looked about eighteen. Her eyes were decades older, though.

"Hey," she said, "come on in for a sec. I just need to grab my piece."

He stepped inside and shut the door behind him. A hint of lemon and pine tickled his nose. She'd been cleaning.

When she returned from the kitchen, her eyes met his. "Ready?"

"Ready."

It didn't take long to get to the farmers' market. Kenzie lived about three miles from the place, and he knew she was a frequent visitor, thanks to the baked goodies she often brought to headquarters.

"What good do you think this is going to do? I mean, anyone could have bought that. It could have been in a gift basket. It could have been—"

"I know, Kenzie. I honestly don't expect to figure out who bought it, but if he's been here once, maybe he's a regular."

"True. And if we know the booth he bought from, we can watch it."

"Exactly."

He backed into a spot near the entrance and displayed his law enforcement status on the dash. The open-air market was already bustling with visitors, and the breeze carried the stomach-rumbling scent of croissants and cinnamon rolls. He was going to have a cinnamon roll before they left.

But first, business. He examined the setup of the place. At the entrance, there were stalls, one after the other, with everything from children's toys to clothing for sale. This part of the market opened to the parking lot. From a previous visit, Cole could envision the rest of the layout. Long rows of indoor vendors with an exit on the far end and multiple exits along the walking paths.

"Produce is all the way to the back and to the left," Kenzie said, pointing down the main aisle. "In front of that temperature-controlled building."

"It's like a grocery store, right?" He'd been in it once? Maybe?

"Yeah, but with vendor booths inside, so you pay at each booth, just like out here."

"Right."

They found the produce aisle easily. The place had been built back at the start of the city's founding and had been the place to trade and sell goods since day one, according to history. Improvements had kept the market up to code, and business still boomed.

With a picture of the label on his phone, he walked to the first interior booth and showed the teen worker the screen. "Hi, could you tell me what fruit this was on?"

She frowned. "Dunno. Lemme ask my mom. Mom!"

Cole smothered a laugh under the guise of a cough while Kenzie pressed her fingers to her lips to cover her smile.

A woman at the back of the booth spun and shot a ferocious frown at her offspring, then hurried to stand in front of them. "Yes?"

"These people want to know what fruit a label came off of." She rolled her eyes. "Like I can tell them that."

"Go see if Mr. Boyle has anything you can help him with. Something that doesn't involve customer interaction." With another exaggerated roll of her eyes, the girl stomped off, and her mother turned a weary smile on them. "She's such a delight these days, as you can see. She doesn't want to be here, but she's grounded, so . . . I apologize. Now, what label do you have?"

Cole showed her.

"I don't recognize that one. Miranda Tollison might know. She's been here longer than some of us."

"I know Miranda," Kenzie said. "Thank you."

Cole followed Kenzie to the booth at the end of the row, and Kenzie introduced them. Miranda looked at the picture. "I've seen it, but it's not one of mine. Why don't you try Jonathan?"

They said their goodbyes and found Jonathan. The redheaded man with a sunburned nose nodded. "Yeah, that's my label. According to the number, that's for the pears." Jonathan reached over and held one up with a matching label. Finally.

"Well, that explains why I didn't recognize it," Kenzie said. "I hate pears." Cole shot her a look of amusement, and she shrugged, then turned back to Jonathan. "Do you have a lot of law enforcement customers?" Kenzie asked.

The man shrugged. "Sure. All the time."

Cole planted his hands on his hips. "Anyone in particular who likes pears?"

Jonathan laughed. "You're kidding, right?"

He wished. "I know. It's a crazy question, but I have a reason for asking."

"Naw, man. I don't have a clue who bought the piece of fruit that was attached to that label."

"I know. We didn't really expect you would. We're just asking a few questions." Cole shot him a tight smile. "Thanks."

"Sure. That it?"

Kenzie hesitated. "Actually, no. One more thing. The next time a guy comes in dressed in SWAT gear or police gear and buys a pear, will you see if you can engage him in some conversation? Maybe introduce yourself and get a name?"

Jonathan's eyes narrowed. "What's this all about anyway?"

"Just running down a lead," Cole said. Which was probably going nowhere, but shots in the dark had panned out before. Might as well give this one a try.

Kenzie shifted and Cole noted her gaze had snagged on something in the far-right corner. "Kenz?"

TEN

Kenzie glanced behind her, the feeling that someone was watching her creeping up the back of her neck and settling at the base of her skull.

"Hey." Cole placed a hand on her shoulder and narrowed his eyes at her. "What is it?"

"Just a feeling. I may be a little sensitive after what's happened."

He nodded. "It would be weird if you weren't."

The market was busy but not overly crowded. People pressed past and went about their business while she and Cole examined the area around them.

Kenzie spotted a man wearing a hoodie, his hands shoved into the pockets. He wore tattered jeans and hiking boots that had seen better days. She couldn't get a good look at his face. She nudged Cole and nodded toward the guy. "I don't want to profile, but—"

The figure had his back to them but seemed to be trying to look over his shoulder unobtrusively—and honestly, Kenzie probably wouldn't have noticed him if she hadn't been looking at every single person in the market.

"Should we see what he's up to?" Cole murmured.

The man turned once more and met her gaze. It was then she noticed the rag tied across the bottom of his face. He hunched his shoulders and looked away. Well, that wasn't suspicious at all. She had a hard time seeing him dressed up in a SWAT outfit, paying a twelve-year-old to throw a hand grenade at the team. Then again, criminals came in all shapes, sizes, abilities, and surprises. Who knew what he was capable of? And Micah had mentioned he'd kept his face covered.

She and Cole started walking toward him. He moved away and seemed to exhibit an interest in the display in front of him. A case of knives. He picked one up, and Kenzie tensed, her hand going to her weapon that her sweatshirt covered. Cole did the same.

Their suspect looked at the knife, then set it back down to move a few more steps to his left. Kenzie picked up the pace a bit and Cole stayed with her.

Her target turned, met her gaze once more, then hurried toward one of the side exits, which would lead him to the sidewalk and then down to the riverfront. Kenzie bolted after him and Cole was right beside her.

"Fire!" The shout echoed from the fleeing man. "Fire! Run!"

Panic stirred. People who had only moments before been a relaxed group of shoppers were now a desperate, writhing mass, pushing and shoving in their desire to escape the building.

"Fire!"

Smoke billowed from the store and into the rest of the market. Screams mingled with shouts.

"Kenzie!"

She whirled to see Cole hunched over a woman who had fallen, protecting her from the stampede of feet. A lightning bolt of pain stabbed her side just under the edge of her vest. Before she could spin back around, a hard shoulder shoved her. She bounced off an older man, who fell against a younger woman who let out a harsh cry and tried to keep the old man from tumbling to the ground.

The screams continued to echo around her while smoke stung her nose. Another hard push sent her and the other woman, still gripping the man, to the cement floor. Kenzie ignored the pain sweeping through her and searched for the one who'd started this amid the panicked people trying to get out.

She caught a glimpse of him, aiming his way to one of the side exits, shoving people out of his way to create a path.

Once he reached it, he would be in the parking lot and could easily disappear. Kenzie pushed herself to her feet, slightly lightheaded but wanting to go after the guy. She started forward and stopped when pitiful cries reached her. A young girl no more than four years old stood in the middle of the chaos, weeping.

Kenzie snatched her up, wincing at the pain the action caused. "It's okay, baby. We'll find your mama."

She shook her head. "Granny."

"Okay. Granny."

"Mia! Mia!"

The little girl's eyes went wide and her head whipped toward the voice.

"Mia! Where are you?"

The panic in the woman's voice was clear.

"I have Mia," Kenzie called out. "Keep saying her name!"

"Mia!"

"Granny!"

In less than five seconds, an older woman took the little girl from Kenzie's grasp and held her, tears dripping off her cheeks. "Thank you," she said. "Thank you."

"Yes ma'am. You're welcome. Now, y'all head for that exit right there." She pointed to the open door behind one of the vendor stalls. "You got it?"

The granny nodded and fell in with the crowd, clutching her granddaughter tight. Kenzie stood still while the last of the crowd slipped out the door. The smoke hovered in the air, but it wasn't too bad. Not like a fire raging out of control.

She spotted Cole helping another frightened older woman to her feet. "Cole!"

She hurried to him, and he shot her a relieved look. "You okay?"

"Yeah, I'm fine. Get her out. I'm going to see where the smoke is coming from and make sure no one else is in here."

"Got it. I'll be back to help you clear it."

Black dots swirled in Kenzie's vision for a moment, and she stayed still, waiting for it to pass.

"Kenzie?"

"Yeah. I'm good. I'll be right back." Her side throbbed just under her rib cage and she pressed a hand to it, the intensity of the pain taking her by surprise. A sticky wetness slid between her fingers, and she hissed a breath through her teeth while she hurried to the back of the store, looking for the source of the smoke. She wanted to stop and check out whatever wound she'd managed to acquire, but needed to make sure the store wasn't going to burn down around them or anyone else in the place.

Sirens screamed into the parking lot while Kenzie cleared the bathrooms. Empty.

Squinting through the thin layer of smoke, she hurried toward the row of freezers against the back wall. Smoke rolled from underneath them. A short in the wiring?

Maybe. But no flames in sight.

Her lungs protested the harsh treatment, and she pulled her sweatshirt up around her nose and mouth while she squinted, searching for the source of the smoke.

It dawned on her that there was no heat, and the thickness of the smoke was concentrated in one area now. Under the last freezer. Kenzie hurried to it, wondering why her side hurt so bad, but had no time to stop and check it. She dropped to her knees and, using her phone's flashlight, looked underneath the freezer.

"A smoke bomb," she muttered. "Of course." Thankful that the place wasn't in danger of burning down, she turned and gasped at the sudden appearance of the firefighter next to her. Then choked on a lungful of smoke.

She pressed a hand against her chest, her heart pounding a triple-time rhythm against her palm.

"Ma'am? You okay?"

"Yes, it's a smoke bomb. I have to call it in." She fumbled for the radio that wasn't there. Right. All she had was her phone. In her hand. When had she grabbed it? Whatever. Grateful for instincts, she lifted it, then stopped when she noticed the coating of red over her palm. She'd known she was bleeding, but that much?

The firefighter grabbed her while her head swam. She blinked, feeling the hard grip on her bicep even as she studied the blood covering her fingers.

"Where are you hurt?" he asked.

"I don't know." Her side? Had to be.

"Come on," the man was saying, "we need to get you out of here."

"Kenzie!"

Cole's voice came through the fog that had invaded her mind.

Weakness hit her. Why was there blood on her hand?

She allowed the firefighter to help her to her feet and guide her toward the exit. And truthfully, without his support, she didn't think her legs would have held her up much longer.

At what she guessed to be the halfway point, the smoke had thinned to a faint mist.

Cole appeared, rag over his face, eyes squinting. When he spotted her, relief flashed across his features. "You okay?"

That was going to be the question of the week. She could hear it now. "I'm good! Fine!" Okay, that was stretching it, but she pulled away from the firefighter's grasp, not wanting Cole to see her leaning on the man. Her lungs burned, her eyes leaked tears . . .

. . . and her knees buckled.

Cole swept in and grabbed her up into his arms before the firefighter had a chance to act. And while she hated the outward appearance of weakness, it was better than falling on her face. She closed her eyes, coughed, and allowed Cole to hurry her out of the building.

Once outside, she noted the abundance of law enforcement, firefighters, and medical personnel. Cole headed toward the waiting ambulance.

"Hey, put me down. I'm fine."

"You're bleeding."

"I know. I figured that out, but it's probably nothing. I must have caught my side on a metal shelf or something."

"There's more blood than that would cause. You're not fine and you're going to get checked out."

The order rankled, but the tight-lipped concern registered. As well as his narrowed eyes and flared nostrils. The bystanders parted like he was Moses at the edge of the Red Sea.

He set her on the stretcher, his actions careful and gentle, yet she couldn't suppress the low groan at the arc of pain that swept through her.

"What happened?" She ended the question with a hacking cough. One of the paramedics slapped an oxygen mask over her mouth, and she noted Cole trying to stay out of the way yet not going far.

When the paramedic peeled her shirt up from the bottom hem, Cole gasped.

Kenzie's gaze flew to his and she pulled the mask off. "What?"

"Uh, I think you got sliced." He looked at the wound, then back to her, his face pale. "Kenz, I think a knife got you."

SHE BLINKED, shock written on her face. "Stabbed? What? By who?"

Cole ground his teeth for a brief second to ward off the alarm racing through him. "Think back to when you first felt pain."

"Um . . . it was when we were heading to exit the store. I looked back and you were helping an elderly woman who'd fallen. So . . . couldn't have been a metal shelf. I was in the middle of the aisle when I felt this pain in my side."

"All right"—the paramedic shooed Cole back—"sorry, but we're going to get her to the hospital. You can meet us there."

"No, wait." Kenzie tried to sit when another wave of coughing left her gasping, and the paramedic attempted to put the mask back on. Kenzie shoved the woman's hand away with a glare. "I can't go to the hospital. I'm supposed to take my dad—" More coughing cut her off, and when she caught her breath, her gaze bounced between Cole and the frowning paramedic. "Fine," Kenzie muttered. She took the mask back and covered her face before the woman could do it for her. Then she took a deep breath.

Cole nodded. "I'll call your dad for you and let him know what's going on." She frowned but didn't protest. "I'll be right behind you."

The ride to the hospital was smooth and quick, and Cole soon found himself pacing in the waiting room while the rest of the team arrived one by one.

He'd honestly wondered if they'd show up and squelched the shame at his doubt. Greene walked in—moving carefully, but moving—with Otis at his side, followed by James.

Even Cowboy had made it. He was dressed in his trademark blue jeans, boots, and Stetson since he wasn't on the job at the moment.

The only one not there was Butler, who'd driven Dolly and said he'd wait in the vehicle. Cole found himself pushing aside his anger with the man. Commander Hill had called, and once he was assured Kenzie was going to be fine, he apologized for not coming due to a previous engagement with the mayor. "She'll understand, sir," Cole had told him.

"Yeah, she will. Thanks."

As soon as he hung up with the commander, he tapped a message to Esther Hemingway, their analyst who could find information at the drop of a hat. A former independent hacker, she now used her skills to catch the bad guys.

I need security footage from the Coleman's
Farmers' Market today.

He gave her the approximate time range and tapped send.

Urgent tasks done, Cole now waited with the others. And waited. And paced a little.

Finally, James caught his eye and nodded for Cole to look behind him.

He spun to see Lainie headed toward him. She had her stethoscope wrapped around her neck and her scrubs had seen better days. She'd had a busy time in the ED over the last few hours, but she was the best physician assistant he knew. Better than some doctors. Having her taking care of Kenzie lowered his blood pressure considerably. "I know she's okay, technically, but how is she? For real?"

"Ornery. Ready to get out of here."

He let out a slow breath. "Good. Then . . . normal."

Lainie smirked. "Yes. The wound isn't deep, more like a bad graze instead of a stab. I stitched it in a couple of places—refusing to let her do it herself—but it shouldn't hold her down for long, so that's good."

"Yeah, very good." Of course she'd offer to do it herself. He shook his head.

"You can go on back and see her if you want."

"I want."

"Room 3. You know the way. But tell her that I'm going to keep a room reserved for her if she keeps showing up like this." She let her gaze roam the rest of the guys in the unit. "In fact, I may need to rope off a wing."

"That's the one thing I'll be sure *not* to tell her."

Lainie laughed. "I'm going to hang here for a minute." She had her eyes fixed on her fiancé. And since James could put aside his concerns about Kenzie, Lainie now had his full attention.

Cole refrained from rolling his eyes. He couldn't picture himself that gaga about someone. Not after the number Tracy Rochester did on him. Trusting someone with his heart again would take too much work. Too much effort.

Nope, he was done with romance. For now anyway. But if the right one came along, he might not argue the idea.

"Hey, tell Kenzie we're thinking about her and glad she's okay," Cowboy said.

The others echoed the sentiment, and Cole aimed his footsteps toward Kenzie's room.

"Come in." A cough followed the words and he pushed into the room.

"Hey."

She raked a hand over her dark hair and shook her head so the mass tumbled around her left shoulder. He'd rarely seen her with it down, and he realized how stunning she was. Maybe not fake beautiful in a photoshopped-magazine-cover kind of way, but her intellect, professional skills, and personality were so big that he found himself fighting the attraction.

And just like that, his whole "I'm not trusting my heart to anyone ever again" vow scattered like ashes.

Because he was falling for her. And had been for a while now.

Put the brakes on, man, that's not happening.

She snapped her fingers at him. "Hello? Cole? You in there?"

He blinked and cleared his throat, thankful she couldn't read his thoughts. "Yes, I'm here. I was just thinking."

"Obviously."

"I asked Esther to see if she could round up some security footage from the market. Maybe we can piece together the events, see who set off the smoke bomb—and who stabbed you."

She pressed a hand to her side and winced. "I'd like to know that too."

"I'll let you know when she gets back to me. How many stitches?"

"Just a couple and some glue. The wound isn't that deep."

"I'm glad. Could have been a lot worse."

"Yeah." She chewed her lip for a second, then waved him to the chair. He pulled it up to the bed, then settled on the edge of the cushion while she narrowed her gaze at him. "What's going on, Cole? Are we all being targeted, or is it just me, and the others are collateral damage?"

"Good question, one that—"

A knock on the door interrupted him. She frowned, but called, "Come in."

The door opened and her father rolled in. Cole stiffened, knowing the relationship between the man and Kenzie wasn't the best, but pasted a benign expression on his face and nodded. "Hello, sir."

"Dad?" Cole didn't miss the shock in her voice. A younger man followed. "Paul?" The door swung open again and a third man about Cole's size stepped in. "Kash? What in the world are you three doing here?"

Kash raised a brow at her. "Really? We get word that you've been injured and are in the hospital, and you think we're not going to show up?" His eyes flicked with hurt that Cole wasn't sure Kenzie caught.

"Well, I—" She snapped her lips together and cleared her throat. "Well, thanks, but it wasn't necessary. I'm fine."

"Sure you are." Paul stepped closer and took her hand. "What can we do for you?"

Kenzie gaped and shot a look at Cole that he could only describe as a plea for help. Unfortunately, he was blanking at what to do. "Thank you, Paul, for offering," she finally said, "but I should be out of here before long. I really don't need anything."

"Of course not," he murmured. "You never do."

She blinked at her brother. "What?"

"Nothing." He turned to the others. "She's fine. I'll let Logan know he doesn't need to bother coming, then I'm going back to work." He ruffled Kenzie's hair. "Glad you're okay, kid." And then slipped out the door.

Kenzie sucked in a breath like she'd been sucker punched and looked at Kash, then her father. "What was that all about?"

Kash shrugged and caught Cole's eye. "Guess we'll get out of your hair." He gripped the handles of their father's wheelchair and had the man out of the room before Cole could do more than offer a small protest.

Once the door shut behind them, he turned to find Kenzie sitting up, hand pressed to her wound, eyes wide with massive amounts of confusion. She looked at him, her deep frown creasing her forehead. "What just happened?"

ELEVEN

Cole's mouth opened, then snapped shut.

"No," she said. "Tell me. What did I do?"

He shrugged. "You shut them out. Said you didn't need them. I think it hurt their feelings."

Her jaw dropped. "You've got to be kidding me. I didn't say that."

"Not completely with words, but you definitely did. I suppose I could be wrong."

Unfortunately, she didn't think he was, guy or not. And if the look on his face was any indication, neither did he.

She dropped her face into her palms and tried to gain control of the emotions swamping her. Cole's hand on her shoulder pulled her attention up to him. "I didn't mean to do that," she whispered.

"Yeah, I can tell."

"Well, great. Now what?"

"Apologize?"

She scowled. "Apologize. To them. For . . ." She'd learned long ago to never apologize because they would take it as a sign of weakness.

Cole shot her a confused smile. "Well, yeah. They're the ones you wronged."

"But did I? Wrong them? I just told them I'm fine. Which I am"— she coughed—"other than a small cough. Now that I think about it,

I just spoke the truth. So, how exactly did I wrong them? Maybe it's their interpretation of what I said that was wrong."

Cole simply watched her with a knowing expression on his face, and she flopped back onto the pillow with a huff. And a grimace. "Ugh. I don't do apologies well," she muttered. "At least not with my family. They're very hard to apologize to because they usually throw it back in my face."

"It's totally your decision, but you asked me what happened and that's my take."

"Fine. I'll apologize." She would do so if it was anyone else in her life. The fact that it was her family she needed to apologize to shouldn't cause her stomach to knot. They'd see her as weak. And while that had mattered when she was a teen on into her early twenties, did it matter now? As long as she knew the truth?

It shouldn't.

"Good." He patted her hand and started for the door.

"Cole . . . do you think it was a mistake? My joining SWAT?"

He paused, his back to her, then his head dropped and he sighed. Then turned. "Kenzie, we've known each other a long time. Not like best friends or anything, but our families have. Kash and Paul and I weren't really friends, per se, since they're so much older than I am, but Logan and I were tight. Still are."

"I know. I used to be jealous of y'all going down to the lake to go fishing. I wanted to go, but Grandma Betsy wouldn't let me. Said you two needed 'guy time.'"

He laughed. "We did."

"Well, I'm going on record as officially feeling left out."

"If I could turn back time—"

"You two would still leave me behind."

"Yeah, we probably would."

She sighed. "We had a pretty good childhood before my mom died. After that, everything seemed to fall apart." She picked at the fuzz on the blanket covering her from the waist down. "Except for summers with Grandma Betsy." Tears filled her eyes and she blinked at the wetness. When was the last time she'd cried? And why now? "I need to go visit her. It's been way too long. I'm ashamed."

"I'm sure she understands."

"She does, but still . . . she gave me a house. The least I can do is see her on a regular basis." And ugh. More tears. *Stop it.*

She brushed away the sign of weakness only to look up and see Cole watching her with such compassion that more tears pushed their way to the surface. She sniffed and shook her head, willing her throat to relax.

He nudged her. "Move over. Gently. Be sure not to hurt yourself."

"What?"

"Move over. I need room."

What in the world? She scooted—carefully as instructed, hand pressed to her wound—and Cole settled onto the mattress next to her, sliding an arm around her shoulders and pulling her against him. Confused, but not in the least little bit of a hurry to get away, she settled her head against his chest, mind spinning. "Is this how you comfort the other guys on the team?" she murmured.

A chuckle rumbled under her ear, tickling her eardrum. "That would be a negative. I have to say, this is a first." His laughter faded and he pulled back a fraction to look down at her. She lifted her chin to meet his gaze and the action brought their lips in close proximity. *Very.* Close. Proximity.

She froze and so did Cole.

He cleared his throat and she tilted her head down, hoping against hope he couldn't feel her runaway pulse pounding like . . . like . . . well, like it never pounded. Ever.

"Your side okay?" he asked, his voice a little more husky than normal.

What side? Oh. Ahem. "Yes, it's fine." Well, it hurt, but she didn't want to move, so . . .

She *should* move. She really should. "Cole?"

"Yeah?"

"I'm confused."

"I know. I am too."

"Well, as long as it's both of us . . ."

"We'll figure it out, Kenzie. For now, let me try to answer your question."

She had a question? Well, yes, she had a lot of questions, but this . . . whatever *this* was . . . was the biggest question she'd ever faced.

"So," he said, "when all the applicants for your position with SWAT were reviewed, it was easy to discard a lot of them. Most of them. But there were some really, really good applicants."

"I'm sure."

"We narrowed it down to five. Then three. Then two."

"Me and . . ."

"Yes."

"You're not going to tell me who the other one was."

"No. If he wants you to know, he'll tell you."

She reared back and gasped at the shaft of pain that shot through her wound. Then ignored it. "It wasn't Butler, was it?"

"No, he didn't apply."

Kenzie knew her jaw was swinging, but couldn't seem to do anything about it. He tapped it shut, but she didn't return to his comfortable, very nice, rock-solid, Shemar Moore chest. No, no. Not yet anyway. "B-but, I thought that was why he was being so . . . antagonistic about me being on the team."

"No, Butler's just a jerk."

"So, it really is a gender thing." She didn't know why she was so shocked about that.

"Yeah, I think so. I can't think of any other reason. Now, can I finish?"

"Oh, right. You were answering my question. Go on."

"Anyway, most everyone knows I'm friends with Logan, and I didn't want that to influence the decision, so I stayed out of it."

"And the guys know that."

"They know. And I think they're not happy with me for that decision. So, I've tried to stay neutral. Keep you at arm's length, as you put it, and not show any favoritism."

"Which I do appreciate."

"But do I think it was a mistake hiring you? No. Now more than ever."

She sighed. "I know that men and women are made differently—"

He muttered something.

"What?"

"Nothing, go on."

Kenzie frowned. She could have sworn he'd said something that sounded suspiciously like "Thank God for that."

"Anyway," she said, "I know that in this kind of job, sometimes brawn wins. I get it. Hands down, every guy on the team would win a strength contest with me."

He narrowed his gaze at her. "You overheard us talking about this, didn't you?"

"What? Who? When?"

"Uh, never mind. Continue please."

He'd been talking? About how she was weak? Or the guys were stronger? She'd address that later. "But I'm smart. And I have other abilities. And truly, thankfully, in my position, I don't have to rely on strength much. I can leave that to you guys."

"But . . ."

"I don't know, I guess I'm naive. I suppose I thought that even if the guys—you—had reservations at first, that I'd be able to prove I deserved the spot I was given."

"You have, Kenzie," he said, his voice low. "You've proven it."

She tilted her head at him. "So, is that why you feel like this is okay now?"

COLE FROZE ONCE MORE. Was it?

"No." He sighed and slid off the bed, careful not to jar her side.

119

She shot him a skeptical look, and he couldn't blame her. "No," he said again with more conviction. "I . . ." He waved a hand. "I don't know what this was. I'm sorry." And he was. He had no business treating Kenzie different from any other team member. He was an idiot. "I just felt so bad for you that I—"

She flushed. Then her eyes did that glitter thing that told him he'd just messed up big-time. "That you thought I needed a pity cuddle?" she asked.

He blinked. "A . . . a what?"

"You felt sorry for me, so you decided to give me a pity cuddle. Well, I don't need your pity or your . . . your . . . stupid cuddles, so just treat me like one of the guys and we'll forget this ever happened."

Cole gaped. "Have you lost your mind?"

"Probably," she muttered. "If not, I'm getting close." She sighed before he could respond. "Just go away, Cole."

He was not going away. "Sorry, you don't get to do that." He planted his hands on his hips. "I have no idea what a pity cuddle is, but that was not one. I saw a fellow human and friend in pain and wanted to help. That was the only way I knew how to do that, and I'm not going to feel guilty for it. As for treating you like one of the guys, I've done that." And he was over it. She wasn't one of the guys—well, she was and she wasn't. Professionally, yeah, okay. But personally. Nope. And now he was going to have to figure out how to deal with that. Or run. Running was sounding better and better by the moment. But he wasn't a runner.

He sighed. "I guess I should take my own advice then, huh?"

She frowned. "What?"

"About apologizing. I'm sorry, Kenzie, it was my intention to comfort, not come across as offering pity. I offended you and I'm sorry."

It was her turn to blink. And swallow. Then meet his gaze.

She deflated with a heavy sigh. "It's okay, Cole. I appreciate the comfort." She offered him a small smile. "It helped. It's me, not you."

He barked a laugh. "I've heard that one before." Boy, had he.

Curiosity flickered in her eyes, then knowledge. "Oh. Tracy."

"Yeah. When she dumped me, she said it was her, not me."

"And it probably was."

For the first time since the breakup, he thought that actually might be the case. His phone buzzed and he frowned. "It's Micah."

She raised a brow. "What's going on?"

"He sent a picture with a text. Said the guy was back hanging around the court and he's scared he's going to dupe someone else into helping him hurt someone."

She straightened. "What if he's looking for Micah?"

"Yeah." He tapped a message back.

> Stay away from him. Don't let him see you.

> Too late. He's already seen me. And I think he's watching me.

> Then stay with your friends. Don't let him get you alone.

Cole dialed 911, made the report, and asked officers to detain the man, saying that he was wanted for questioning. Dispatch assured him officers were on the way.

Kenzie slid her legs to the side of the bed.

"What are you doing?" he asked.

"Getting out of here. I want to know who this guy is and what his beef is with me and the team."

"Uh, you need to stay put."

"I'm good to go."

"Says who?"

"Lainie. She said when I felt good enough to leave, I could. I already signed the discharge papers. Now, can you help me with my shoes?" She pointed to them on the bench by the window.

He grabbed them but frowned. "She didn't tell me that. Just said you were ornery and wanting to get out of here."

"Ornery, huh?"

"Uh, don't tell her I told you that."

She wiggled a foot at him. "Please?"

He didn't bother to protest any more. If Lainie said she could go, he couldn't make her stay. And Kenzie was a doctor, so . . .

Five minutes later, they were out the door and heading to the waiting area. He texted Micah.

> Officers are on the way. Is he still there?

The reply came instantly.

> Yep. Sitting on the bench on the other side of the court thinking no one is noticing him.

> Is he in cop gear?

> Nope. But he's got that same rag thing over his face. Not sketchy at all.

The kid's sarcasm made Cole smile.

> Text me when the cops are there and have him in custody. They'll get there before I can.

> 10-4.

He and Kenzie walked into the waiting room. The team was there. All except Butler and Buzz. At least Buzz had an excuse.

Greene nodded. "Looking good there, King."

"Thank you." She scratched Otis's ears and the dog leaned against her leg. She glanced at Cole. "At least someone doesn't mind my gender."

Her words were low, for his ears only. He felt quite sure he shouldn't reassure her that he was more than happy with her gender and pressed his lips together to keep the words from slipping out.

Cowboy stood and sauntered over to stand in front of her. "You stitch yourself up?"

She laughed. "No, not this time."

"This time?" Cowboy looked intrigued, and Cole couldn't say he blamed him.

"Hey, Kenzie," Lainie called from the desk. "I have one more paper that needs your signature."

"Be right back," Kenzie said and walked over to Lainie.

Butler chose that moment to step through the sliding glass doors.

"Took you long enough," Cole said.

"What happened?"

"Someone tried to kill King." Just saying the words burned a path along his tongue.

"No kidding. She okay?"

"She is."

A smirk pulled at Butler's lips. "Huh. How about that? I just wanted her off the team. Sounds like someone else wants her off the planet."

Cole scowled. "Not appropriate, man."

The others also turned looks of disapproval on their fellow teammate. Behind him, he heard a soft sigh. Kenzie. He turned just as she hid the flash of hurt, but the hard set of her jaw said she was angry too. "Sorry, Kenzie, he didn't mean that."

Her anger focused on him. "Don't apologize for him. That's not your job." To the others, she said, "Thanks for coming, guys, but I'm fine."

Butler looked like he wanted to say something, then snapped his lips shut and cleared his throat. "Um, I gotta go. Rest up, King," he muttered.

Cole took a deep breath to get himself under control. He couldn't go after the man and punch him no matter how much he might want to. That wasn't the way to handle this.

Butler left and the others shuffled out behind him. Cole turned to look at Kenzie, and the haunted look that flashed for a brief second in her eyes made him want to wrap her in his arms. Again.

Figuring that wouldn't go over well and would be interpreted as another pity cuddle, he curled his fingers into tight fists and released the breath he'd been holding. "Kenzie—" His phone buzzed and he pulled it out of his pocket to glance at it. "It's Micah again," he said. "The guy left before the cops could get him."

"Scared him off."

"Yeah. I'm going to tell him to keep watching the area and let me know if he comes back, but to be careful and definitely don't approach him or be caught alone with him." He finished the text and received Micah's agreement.

Kenzie rubbed a hand over her lips and sighed. "You think he's behind it?" she asked. "Butler? Could he want me off the team so bad that he'd hire someone to actually put us all in danger to get rid of me? Or am I giving myself too much credit?"

TWELVE

The fact that Cole didn't immediately come to Butler's defense spoke volumes to Kenzie. She studied him, the conflict in his eyes stirring her guilt. If she hadn't applied to—and been chosen for—the team, he wouldn't be dealing with all the turmoil her presence caused. "Cole . . ."

"Stop it," he said.

"What?"

"Whatever it is that put that guilty look on your face."

"This is the first time you've noticed it?"

"What?"

"Some days . . . no, make that *every* day . . . I have some kind of guilt related to this position."

He frowned. "That's crazy talk." A pause. "Why?"

She scoffed, a quick puff of air that she made no attempt to suppress. "Seriously?"

"Well—"

"I beat out my own brother for it, for one thing."

"I'm aware."

"I know you're aware. I'm the one who wasn't aware. I had no idea he'd applied until my dad mentioned it. With a snarl to go with the words. He really wanted Logan to get it apparently." She shook her head. "I'll never do anything right in his eyes." She clamped her lips together, kicking herself for revealing more than she'd intended. She'd thought her father would be proud. That finally she'd done something worth his praise. She was an idiot.

"Would it have stopped you from applying, had you known Logan had done so?"

She went still, then swept stray hairs behind her ears, thankful he'd let the comment about her father go unaddressed. "I don't know." She scowled, her spirit troubled. "I've asked myself that question quite a bit. And I just . . . I don't know." She pressed forefinger and thumb to the bridge of her nose and shook her head. "Probably not."

"He was a good candidate, Kenzie, but you were better."

She glanced at him sideways. "I know."

"You're a doctor. He was an advanced paramedic before he became a cop. And while you both have police training, it all came down to who was the better qualified applicant. You were."

"I . . . I know. Thank you for that. But I also know Logan was terribly disappointed that he wasn't chosen." Just one more thing to add to her guilt load.

"Kenzie, remember I said it came down to two people in the end?"

"Yes."

"The other person wasn't him."

She blew out a slow breath. "Thank you for telling me. That helps. A lot."

"Good."

"Okay, now on to other things. I need to go by my dad's house."

"Today?"

"You said I should apologize. I agreed. It's going to be unpleasant and I need to get it over with. Otherwise it will just nag at me until I do it."

"You're a 'take the bull by the horns' kind of person, aren't you? Rip the Band-Aid off and be done with it, huh?"

She raised a brow at him. "You really have to ask that?"

"No. It was a rhetorical question." He nodded and tucked a hand under her elbow to lead her to the exit. "We'll swing by your father's place as long as you don't mind me being there?"

Mind? She'd prefer it. She often found herself holding back tears whenever she was around her father—probably one of the main reasons why she avoided him—but if Cole was there, she'd be stronger.

And she wasn't going to investigate why she felt that way.

When Cole pulled into her father's driveway, Logan's vehicle was already there. He lived there so his car in the drive wasn't unusual, but she'd thought he'd be at work.

Kenzie shoved aside the feelings that always rushed back at her when she came to her childhood home. Trapped, stuck, no way out. They were all synonyms that she'd shed the last time she walked out the door, her final load grasped in her arms. When she'd pulled out of the neighborhood and onto the main road, freedom, the ability to breathe, and the excitement that came with stepping into life with a new start had filled her.

"Kenzie? You awake?"

She jerked. "Yes. Sorry. Just thinking about when I moved out."

"A good day, right?"

She shot him a grin. "The best."

He laughed. "I remember Logan's shock that you actually did it. He honestly didn't think you would."

Her brief flash of joy faded. "I know. None of them did. They think I'm a coward because I waited until they were all out of the house to make my move, but I had no intention of listening to the four of them list all of the reasons I should stay and how selfish I was for leaving them. Especially Dad. And besides, it wasn't long after Paul and Kash moved out. It's the cycle of life, right?"

He frowned. "Selfish? You moved out two years ago at the age of thirty-two—and only after you arranged for your dad to have care around the clock should he need it. I think you're anything but selfish."

She pursed her lips and nodded. "Hm. Well, I appreciate that, but I assure you they'd disagree with you. On the flip side, living at home as long as I did allowed me to pay for my school expenses and finish debt free. So there's that." She needed to stop jabbering, get out of the vehicle, and go inside.

She pushed the door open and winced. The movement had pulled the wound, but she ignored it and climbed out.

Logan opened the front door. "What are you doing here?"

"Hello to you too."

"Aw, you know you're always welcome, but Paul said you'd been hurt and didn't want any company or help."

She winced again—this time from the pain in her heart, not her side. "Apparently that's the way I came across, but I didn't mean to."

Logan simply raised a brow. "All right."

"Thought you'd be working today."

"I asked for the day off. Tomorrow too."

"Okay." She wasn't going to ask why. She didn't need to know.

Kenzie sighed and aimed herself for the open front door. "I'll go apologize." She paused. "Is the nurse here?"

"No, he sent her home when I got here."

"Did he ask you to take him to Mom's grave?"

"No."

She stopped and turned to meet her brother's gaze. "Then why did he ask me?"

Logan shrugged. "No idea." She glanced at Cole, who stood a discreet distance away, giving them the illusion of privacy. "Go on in," Logan said. "He's in the recliner. I'll let you have him to yourself for a while."

Great. She walked in to find him exactly where Logan said he was, head back, eyes closed, his mostly useless legs on the raised footrest and covered with a blanket she'd given him for Christmas last year. For the first time, he looked old to her. She flinched, then schooled her features. "Hi, Dad."

His eyes opened. "Hi. What are you doing here?"

Why did everyone keep asking her that? "You wanted me to take you to Mom's grave."

He frowned. "You get out of the hospital and you come straight here? Are you crazy?"

She bit her tongue for a full five seconds. "Not crazy, just not hurt that bad. Like I told you in the hospital, I'm fine. The wound required two stitches and some glue."

He grunted. "That doesn't sound serious."

She was going to stomp her feet and yell any second now. Instead, she pulled in a slow, deep breath and then let it out while she squelched the desire to have a good old-fashioned temper tantrum. "Like I *said*, it's not."

He studied her for a brief moment, and a hint of a smile curved his lips before it disappeared. What was that all about? "You don't have to take me to the grave today," he said. "We'll go another time."

She sat. Stood, then sat again. He raised a brow. "Something on your mind or you got ants in your pants?"

"I need to apologize. Cole said I blew you guys off at the hospital. That's not . . . I didn't mean to do that."

His still laser-sharp gaze cut into her. "We wanted to be there for you."

Kenzie swallowed the "why?" that almost tripped off her tongue. "I know and I appreciate that. It's just . . . I didn't . . ."

"Say what you want to say, girl."

She sighed. "Okay, fine. I don't mean this as a criticism against you, so please don't take it that way. It just is what it is. I guess what I'm trying to say is that you raised me to show no weakness, and admitting that I might need help is showing weakness. And as much as I try to overcome that—because I don't believe it's true—it's so ingrained in me that I find myself falling into that mindset when it comes to you and my brothers. So, I'm sorry. Thank you for coming by the hospital. It means a lot." She found herself surprised she meant it. This time when she stood, she planned on walking out the door.

"Hold up, Kenzie."

She turned back.

"Where's Logan?" he asked.

"Outside talking to Cole."

He nodded. "Can you help me into my chair?" He could stand as long as he had something to hold on to, so getting him in the chair wasn't as difficult as it would be if he had no use of his legs at all.

"Sure, but I don't mind getting you whatever you need so you don't have to get up." She rolled the chair over next to him while speaking.

"You can't give me what I need." He hesitated. "At least not a new pair of legs, but you might be able to help with something else. Something that I need to show you and a story I need to tell you. I was going to tell you the story on the way to the grave, then show you the room when we got back, but this will do." He shot her a wry smile. "See? Asking for help isn't so hard."

"Are you feeling okay?" She wasn't even kidding.

He laughed and she blinked. Okay, that was a weird interaction, but she was also curious. And a little freaked out.

Once she had him in the electric wheelchair, he motored himself down the reconstructed hallway to the room across from his. The room he made her promise to leave alone. The room that her mother had been sleeping in toward the end. After her mother had died, he allowed Kenzie to take whatever she wanted from it, then shut the door and told her to stay out of it. She'd complied, having no interest in visiting the room that symbolized her parents' marriage. Separation. Isolation. Arguments. Stoic silence. Bitterness. Anger . . .

She could go on, but he pushed the door open and rolled inside.

She swallowed hard, stepped over the threshold, and her jaw dropped. A crime scene board covered one wall. Well, the lower part of it. A large blown-up picture of the intersection where the accident had happened was on the adjacent wall. But it was the list of suspects and their pictures on the crime scene board that captured her attention. She walked over to it. "Dad?"

He closed his eyes for a moment. When he opened them, there was more emotion there than she'd ever seen. Ever. And then it was gone in a blink. "After you left," he said, "I needed something to distract me. So I went back to something that I suspected but could never prove."

She ran her fingers over her mother's face smiling out at her from the wedding picture her father had tacked to the wall under the label "Victim."

The breath caught in her lungs and she turned. "You don't think . . . no . . . I mean, it was an accident."

His eyes locked on hers. "I think it was murder."

COLE STOOD IN THE DOORWAY just behind Logan, who strangled on a gasp. "What? *This* is why you refused to let me come in this room?"

Mr. King spun in his chair, an expert maneuver that would have been impressive if everyone's attention hadn't been on the scene before them, ears ringing with his pronouncement.

"What are you doing sneaking around?" Mr. King snapped, eyes blazing his irritation. "I told you to give me some time alone with her."

"So you can tell her you think Mom was murdered?" Logan scoffed and Cole wished he could disappear—or at least walk away. Kenzie looked like she felt the same. But she wouldn't. She'd be going after every single detail from this point on.

She cleared her throat. "Dad, it's too late to keep this just between us now. Can you please explain without the attitude and snark?"

For a moment the man looked offended, then he sighed and swiped a hand down his face. "Fine." He eyed his son. "But don't you go blabbing this to your brothers."

A muscle pulsed in Logan's jaw. "I won't. Now please explain yourself." He swept a hand toward the walls. "And this."

Mr. King stayed silent, as though trying to organize his thoughts, then he shoved his jaw out and clasped his hands. "I've tried for years to figure this out on my own, but I'm limited. Not just my mobility, but with contacts. Almost no one in the department will talk to me even after all these years. Some have retired and moved on. Even more don't know who I am." He barked a hard laugh. "Or they've heard the rumors and don't know what to do when they find themselves on the other end of the line."

"Dad . . . ," Kenzie whispered.

"Just be quiet and let me tell it. No questions until I'm done."

"Can we at least go into the den?" Logan asked.

"No. I need the board, the timeline." He waved a hand.

"Should I leave you guys alone, Mr. King?" Cole asked.

Mr. King eyed him. "No. And call me Ben. You and Logan are tight. He'd just tell you anyway. Might as well save you both some time. As I was saying, I'd almost decided to give up on trying to figure it out—if there was anything to figure out—but I . . ."

"But what?" Logan asked.

He shook his head. "But it keeps nagging at me." He huffed a humorless laugh. "Actually *haunting* might be a better word. There is something I'm missing. Something besides . . ." He trailed off. "I'm not going to say I wasn't drinking that night. I had one glass of wine with dinner. But they said my blood alcohol level tested at .10."

From the siblings' expressions, they hadn't known this. The legal limit was .08 and grounds for arrest.

"You were drunk?" Logan ground out, his hands curled into fists. "Mom died because you drove drunk?"

"No!" Ben slammed a hand on the arm of his chair and took a moment to pull himself together. "No," he said in a more civil tone. "But no one was going to believe that. Then or now. I swear I only had one glass of wine. I had just been promoted to chief of police six months earlier. I wasn't about to do anything stupid like drink and drive."

"How did the media not leak that information out?" Logan asked.

"I had a buddy in the force who managed to keep it quiet."

"Which buddy?" Kenzie asked.

"It doesn't matter. He's not there anymore." His jaw worked. "I

132

agreed to take an early retirement and keep my pension, and he buried the information. It was ruled an accident, and I was allowed to bury my wife and try to keep my family from falling apart."

"Keep your family fr—" Kenzie snapped her lips shut at Logan's glare.

"At first I refused," her father said. "I knew I hadn't been drinking enough to warrant that blood alcohol number. It had to be some kind of malfunction of the test or whatever." He rubbed his chin. "Unfortunately, I had no way to prove it, and I wasn't about to take my chances in court to try and do so."

Kenzie walked to the desk chair and sank into it, her face two shades lighter and her eyes locked on her father. "I don't know what to say. Or think."

"Think about this," Logan snapped. "If it was murder, who's responsible?"

That had been Cole's first question. He was glad Logan had finally gotten around to asking it.

"I don't know," Ben said with a slight shrug.

Kenzie was still staring at the man, her eyes narrowed now. "That was twenty years ago, Dad," Kenzie said. "Why are you bringing this up now?"

He sighed. "Because it's time."

"No," she said. "There's something else. What is it?"

Ben tilted his head. "What do you mean?"

"There's got to be more than this for you to say Mom was murdered."

He nodded, a slow, grudging nod. "She wasn't even supposed to be in the car that night."

Kenzie gasped. "What?"

"We fought. I was going to the dinner and told her to stay home, that I didn't have the energy to pretend all was well in front of everyone." He cleared his throat. "At the last minute, she got ready, said she wasn't going to let me avoid talking anymore, and if I didn't let her ride with me, she'd just take her own car and meet me there. I let her ride," he finished on a whisper. After a few seconds of silence, he shook his head. "I'd already told Harold I'd be coming alone and he and I could talk business. He wasn't too happy when I showed up with Hannah." Hannah, Kenzie's mother.

"Wait a minute. Harold Woodruff?"

Cole blinked. Harold Woodruff, the man Ben had beat out for the position of chief of police way back when.

"Yes."

"I didn't think you guys were speaking to each other."

"We're not now. Back then we worked together and had no choice. And we both decided the family feud started by our fathers was stupid. We decided to end it long before that night."

Kenzie and Logan exchanged glances. "Family feud?" Logan asked. "What feud?"

Ben waved a hand as though that wasn't important. "It's a long story." He glanced at Cole. "You probably know more about it than I do."

Cole raised a brow and shoved his hands in his front pockets. "Why would I know anything about your family feud?"

"Because your grandparents, Eliza and William Garrison, were at the middle of it. Somehow. I've never gotten all the details straight and my mother isn't much for revisiting the past. Figured you'd have heard some of the stories."

He had, but he hadn't paid much attention. "I just know that my grandmother, Eliza Crane at the time, was admitted to Lake City State Hospital for trying to kill herself after an argument with her father. She was best friends with your mother, Betsy, right?"

"Yes."

"And somehow Betsy and Dr. King worked to get my grandmother out of the institution, but it caused a big ruckus with a lot of people. That's about all I know. Why don't you fill me in?"

"Eh, ask your father. That's all history. I need to focus on this for now and reiterate that I didn't run that stop sign because I'd had too much to drink, regardless of what the test said. I ran it because my brakes failed."

"But the report doesn't mention failed brakes," Kenzie said, while Cole wanted to return to the conversation about his grandparents and how they were involved in Kenzie's family's feud. But he set that aside, not wanting to interrupt her.

"It says that you ran the stop sign and hit the other driver, who was in a stolen car. The other guy left the scene and you were ruled at fault."

Her father's gaze sharpened and Cole raised a brow. "You read the report?" Ben asked.

Kenzie scoffed. "Of course I did. To the point that I have it memorized."

Ben scowled and stared at the crime scene wall he'd created. "It's like it happened yesterday, but the details are fuzzy at the same time. But I distinctly remember the brakes failing. I also remember seeing the other driver running from the scene and never being found. And the pain of realizing your mother was dead." His fingers worked themselves into a fist over and over. Open, close. Open, close. "I worked so hard to recover from that accident. I'd lost my wife . . ." His voice cracked and he stopped to draw in a ragged breath. "And I wasn't losing my job. The day I was ready to return to work, the mayor and two officers came to my house telling me I was going to be arrested for stealing evidence if I attempted to return, but if I took an early retirement, out of respect for me and my years of service—and recent trauma—they'd bury it."

Kenzie gasped. "Bury it?"

Logan stepped forward. "What was the evidence, Dad? I can't see you folding like that."

Kenzie ran a hand down her cheek and pressed her palms to her eyes before dropping her hands to her lap. "They had pictures of him meeting with Shady Talbot."

Ben's face paled. "How'd you know?"

"I came across the pictures in the evidence room. They were in Mom's case box."

He blinked up at her. "They're still there?"

"Yes, of course."

"You didn't think to destroy them?"

Cole flinched and she stared at her father. Then let out a low breath. "I won't lie and say it didn't occur to me, but I couldn't do that." Her eyes narrowed. "Any more than you could. Why were you seen with him? Much less put yourself in a spot to be photographed with him?"

"He was my CI! He picked the place. He always picked the place because he wanted a different spot each time. Said he was safer that way and I agreed. Obviously, he was followed that day—or I was—and I don't know who took the pictures, but they set me up. And then Shady was arrested and his evidence disappeared, which allowed him to be released and free to kill the man he attempted to rob the very next day!"

Cole wanted to intervene, but Logan waved him down and held a finger to his lips. His friend obviously wanted him to let this play out.

"And they think I stole the evidence because Shady blackmailed me, but he didn't!" A vein throbbed in Ben's forehead and his shout bounced off the walls. Kenzie's chest heaved with harsh breaths. For a moment father and daughter glared at one another.

"Your signature was on the evidence logbook the day the evidence went missing," she said, her voice lower, under control. "How do you explain that?"

"I can't," the man said, his words raw and ragged. "Why do you think I took their offer to resign with my pension intact? Do you really think I'd be so stupid to sign in and steal evidence? I'm smarter than that, argued that very thing when I was accused. Harold agreed it was all circumstantial and he worked to prove it, but eventually said he couldn't and"—a deep sigh escaped him—"I couldn't either. If I'd fought, wound up on trial, I could have lost and I wouldn't just have lost my job, I might have lost you kids too. I couldn't risk it."

136

They fell silent, Kenzie's eyes on her father, Logan's face pale and his throat working. He hadn't known everything Kenzie had. He'd told Cole he'd never looked at the case because it just brought up bad memories better left in the past. Cole had never understood that kind of thinking. If it had been him, he would have done exactly what Kenzie had. Memorized every detail.

"Sir," Cole said, "why now? You've kept all of this under wraps for twenty years. What's happened to spur you to talk to Kenzie—or anyone—about this now?"

"After the wreck and my recovery and everything, I tried to find Shady Talbot only to learn he'd died of a drug overdose. I wasn't too surprised by that, but I also learned something else. His DNA was found in the stolen car."

"What?" Kenzie breathed the word. "How did you find that out?"

Ben pointed to a file on the desk under the crime scene board. "That was in my mailbox last week, and yes, it has my prints all over it now because I didn't know what it was when I opened it. I've used gloves to handle it since." He nodded to the tray on the table.

Kenzie rose, strode to the box, and snagged a pair of gloves. Once her hands were encased, she opened the manila folder. Cole watched her, itching to see what it was. Logan shifted and took one step forward before he stopped and crossed his arms.

When Kenzie looked up, she drew in a shuddering breath. "Who sent this?"

"I have no idea."

"Come on, Kenz," Logan said, "what is it?"

"A lab report identifying DNA found in the car, and a second report with proof that someone lied about the brakes," she said. "There are two reports in here dated the same day, signed by the same person, with all of the same information except for one thing. The original report said the brakes were cut." She pulled one sheet from the file and held it up. "This one says there was nothing wrong with the brakes. The forensic mechanic lied."

THIRTEEN

"Yeah," her father said with a grimace. "And since I have no pull or friends in that department anymore—and no idea if the person who set me up is still there—I'm asking for help." The last four words came out through gritted teeth, and Kenzie figured his blood pressure shot into the dangerous range.

So, it wasn't easy for him to ask for help. Surprise, surprise.

"Who's the mechanic on the forms?" Cole asked.

"His name is Cliff Hamilton. Do you know him?"

Cole shook his head. "The one I know is Tabitha Lewis."

Logan clasped his hands behind his back and rocked back on his heels. "Dad, I'm a detective, you know that, right?"

"I know."

"So why were you trying to keep this from me? You know I'd help you."

Her brother looked deeply hurt, and Kenzie couldn't help feeling sorry for him. And curious to know the answer.

Her father sighed. "Because I know the cases you have on your desk and you don't have the time to devote to this. She does."

Kenzie scoffed. "What?"

He shrugged. "You're a SWAT medic. You have more time than most and you have access to resources to find out what's going on."

"Yes, I'm a medic, and yes, I'm on the sidelines some, but I also work at the hospital now two days a week, remember? Not to mention I have a house to renovate."

"Well, you're wounded now. I doubt you're going to be doing much renovating, and surely they gave you a few days of sick leave from both jobs."

She simply stared at him, then laughed and shook her head. "You're unbelievable." She should walk out now. Let him wallow in his bitterness and self-pity, but her gaze slid back to the wall. He thought her mother was murdered, and he had some weird potential evidence that somewhat backed up that belief. She wasn't going anywhere. "Fine. I'll do what I can." With her phone, she snapped pictures of the wall and the mechanic's reports and tucked the file folder into an evidence bag. "If we want to open a case, I'll have to take this to Commander Hill and—"

"No," her father blurted. "You can't make this an official case. If you do that, you can't look into it. I don't even know where that file folder came from or if it's legit. And I certainly don't know who to trust in the department. Someone went to a lot of trouble to knock me down. If they're still there, they're not going to want you, or anyone else, investigating."

"But—"

"No. Just look into it, see if there's anything to it. If there is, then . . . I'll decide where to go from there."

"Sir," Cole said, "I noticed you have a camera on your front door. I know you checked. Is there security footage of someone placing that in your mailbox?"

"There is. You're right, I looked. But it's not helpful. Whoever it was rode on a bike and slid it in the box, then pedaled off. Shockingly," he said with an eye roll, "he had on a hoodie, jeans, sneakers. I studied that footage like I'd win a million dollars if I could find an angle with a shot of his face. Nothing. He knew the camera was there and kept his face covered at all times. His clothes were baggy too. I can't even give you a weight range. Height is probably somewhere between five nine and six feet. Could be a couple inches taller than that." He shrugged. "Useless information."

"Send me the footage," Cole said. "We'll look at it anyway."

"Yeah," Logan said, and Kenzie flinched. She'd almost forgotten he was in the room. "I want to see it too."

Her father rolled to the desk and opened the laptop, clicked a series of keys, and her and Logan's phones pinged. "Don't have Cole's number." One thing she could say for her dad, he'd learned how to be tech savvy.

She glanced at Cole. "I'll send it to him." With a few taps of the screen, she did so, and he nodded he'd gotten it.

Kenzie tucked her phone away. "We'll see what we can find out. Unofficially." She paused. "Dumb question alert. Where's the vehicle now?"

"Scrapped, of course."

"Yeah."

"Now don't ask any more dumb questions. Try smart ones."

"Sir—" Cole shut up when Kenzie lasered him with the fiercest look she could muster. She didn't need him to run interference with the unit, and she didn't need him to do so with her father. He held up a hand in surrender.

Her father's gaze flicked between her and Logan and a look she remembered from her late teen years crept into his eyes. "Why don't you two battle it out? See who can figure this out first? Be like old times, right?"

"Or Logan and I can work together." She kept her eyes on her brother, refusing to let herself get pulled back into the desperate desire to prove herself worthy of her father's love. She bit her tongue on what she wanted to say while Logan shot her a small smile and gave a half nod. His response lowered her temperature, and she was able to keep her cool. "If this report is legit, there should be pictures somewhere," she murmured.

"Should be," her father said, looking disappointed she hadn't taken his bait. "But if so, they weren't included."

She nodded. "All right, then I guess we start with Tabitha Lewis and go from there. She'll have access to all the reports from twenty years ago."

"And I'll see if I can track down Cliff Hamilton," Cole said. He glanced at her. "Come on, I'll take you home. You can work from there, right?"

"Sure." They said their goodbyes and she followed him out of the room, leaving Logan and her father in quiet conversation. That was good. At least they weren't yelling.

"What time do we need to leave to head to the lake?"

He raised a brow at her. "You think you'll feel up to that?"

"Um, yes. I need s'mores."

He chuckled. "I don't guess it would hurt and there's definitely safety in numbers."

"There you go."

"No swimming, though. No telling what kind of bacteria you could get in that wound."

"Thank you, Dr. Garrison, I never would have thought of that."

Ten minutes later, she walked into her home and finally decided she should probably check her phone. Sure enough, she had sixteen messages on the friend group thread asking her to let them know she was good and if she needed anything. How had they known? She looked up to find Cole watching her.

"So you do know how to do that," he said.

"What?"

"Check your messages."

"Ha ha. Cute. Apparently, James sent a prayer request for me."

"He only meant to do a good thing, Kenzie, don't be offended."

"Offended? Not in the least. I'm . . . touched."

He smiled. "Good."

"There are texts from Kristine, Jesslyn, James, and Stephanie, all discussing my well-being . . . and praying for me." She swallowed hard. "I've never had anything like this before," she whispered.

"I pray for you too."

Her gaze collided with his. "You do?"

"Every day. I pray for the whole team."

Of course. The team. But he included her in that. "Thank you." She hesitated, then, "Friends like you guys—or at least these guys— are what I've longed for, searched for, prayed for. My whole life has been one competition after the other. The only goal was to knock down the person in front of you so you could step on them to get to the next best thing. Even my brothers. While they've protected me in one sense—they've done their brotherly duty when it came to guys—in another sense, they've done nothing but compete with me for Dad's approval. Knock me down and show how tough they were."

"Knocking you down showed their toughness?"

The disbelief in his voice made her shrug. "I know. I don't mean literally knock me down—much—but insult me or take me down a peg. Keep me in my place, in other words."

"That's verbal abuse."

"Yeah. It is."

"And they all do it?"

"Not now. And Mom kept them—and Dad—in line the first four-teen years, but after she died and Dad lost his job, Dad would lay into the guys and they would take their anger and frustration out on me. So . . . past wounds still ache. It took about five years of counseling and moving out of the environment to understand there was nothing wrong with me—and honestly, it's not my brothers' fault either. They were victims as much as I was. In other words, it wasn't me, it was him."

"There it is again," he muttered.

She raised a brow at him, and he shrugged. "That phrase is always going to remind you of her, isn't it?"

"Eh, one day it won't." He shook his head. "I really thought she might even be the one. In my head, I know it was her issues that broke us up, not mine. Mostly. But getting burned hurts. Makes you leery."

Boy, did it.

"I meant to ask you how you knew her name," he said. "I don't remember mentioning her to you."

She shrugged. "I overheard you and Logan talking about her one night a couple of years ago when we were at Logan's birthday party. I think you guys had just broken up, and Logan told you not to give up, that the right person was still out there."

"I can't believe you remember that."

She did. Every single detail. Because she'd wanted so bad to give him a hug and tell him she'd never treat him like that. She cleared her throat. "Is that why you play the field now?" The words slipped past her filter before she could stop them. "Never mind. Don't answer that."

"Yes, partly, I guess."

"I said not to answer."

"I don't mind answering. I enjoy the company of women. Smart women. But there's the whole trust factor, right? I'm not looking for romance—at least not actively. If the right person comes along, then . . . well, we'll see." His eyes glittered. "But I'm not a player, Kenzie. I don't lead anyone on. Friends are fine, good times are fine, a little light flirting is harmless. But romance is dangerous, and I make it known real fast that I'm not interested in anything more than friendship if I know right off the bat they're not the one for me."

She nodded, her heart aching. So, that moment in the hospital was just a little harmless flirting. Lesson learned. She forced a smile to her face and tilted her head toward her office. "I'm going to grab my laptop and see if I can get in touch with Tabitha Lewis."

He looked a little taken aback at the abrupt topic change, but she had no desire to hear any more about how he wasn't interested in relationships or romance.

"And I'll grab my computer out of the car and start looking for Hamilton," he finally said.

"Meet in the den?" She was so proud of how steady her voice was when she really wanted to go have a good cry and let all the stress out.

"Yes ma'am." He headed for the door.

As soon as it shut behind him, Kenzie gasped and bolted for her home office. There, she shut the door and let the tears flow. But only for a short time. Finally, she pulled herself together, sucked in a deep breath, and cleaned her face in the bathroom. Thankfully, she didn't go all blotchy and red when she cried, and within a few minutes, she was satisfied there was no evidence of her little breakdown.

With a steadying breath, she grabbed her computer and headed out to the den area to act like nothing was wrong and she was fine.

But she wasn't. She wasn't fine at all.

Because with everything else going on, the last thing she wanted to deal with was admitting she was in love with Cole Garrison.

And she had no idea what she was supposed to do about that.

WHEN KENZIE WALKED into the den with her laptop in hand, Cole was already seated on the couch and scrolling. He had Esther working on finding Hamilton as well, but the man seemed to have dropped off the planet.

"Or was he paid to disappear?" he murmured.

"What?" Kenzie dropped into the recliner opposite him.

She sounded a little stuffy. "Are you okay?" he asked.

She sniffed. "Fine. Allergies, maybe. Lingering smoke inhalation. Whatever. It'll pass. Now, what do you mean? Who was paid to disappear?"

"Cliff Hamilton." He narrowed his eyes at her. Something was going on with her.

"What makes you say that?" she asked without looking at him.

"Because it's like he never existed. Two weeks after writing that report, he resigned and disappeared."

"So how do we find him?"

"We keep looking." He rubbed his chin. "Well, Esther is looking, but I know someone who works at the lab. Someone who was there before Tabitha got there."

"Who?"

"Sherry Templeton. I'll call her."

"How's that going to help?" She finally looked at him and there was a new distance in her eyes.

He frowned. What was that about? "She's been there forever," he said. "She was there when Hamilton was. Maybe she can tell us what the man was thinking and where he went."

"Okay, you do that and I'll try to get ahold of Tabitha." She rose, walked onto the sunporch, and shut the French doors behind her.

Cole could hear her muted voice on the phone before he even dialed Sherry, his contact in the lab. With one last lingering look at Kenzie, and a sneaking suspicion he'd upset her but she didn't want to admit it, he tuned into his call, realizing Sherry was calling his name. "Oh, sorry. I'm here. Hey, I have a question for you."

"Sure."

"It's an odd one."

"I work in a crime lab. I believe I've seen odd. Go for it."

"You've worked in the lab basically since it opened—"

"Careful now. You calling me old?"

"No ma'am, just that you were there when Cliff Hamilton was."

"Yep." Had her voice just gotten slightly guarded? "What about him?"

"Did he ever talk to you about his cases?"

"Of course. We talked to each other about them all the time."

"I kind of thought you would." He blew out a low breath. "See, here's the thing, Sherry. I need to talk to him, but I can't find him. Do you know where he went when he left the lab?"

"Nope."

Her answer was a smidgeon too fast. "Okay, do you know why he resigned?"

A sigh greeted his question. "Why are you asking all of this? That's all in the past."

"True, but sometimes the present and the past wind up colliding, and when that happens, you have to figure out why."

"You're talking in riddles, boy."

Only she could get away with calling him boy. And it had everything to do with the fact that she'd changed his diapers when he was an infant. "No riddles." He was tempted to fill her in but didn't want to put her in the position of having to keep secrets. And right now, he wasn't ready to announce the evidence until he knew who he could trust. "I just need to talk to him about a report he did. I think it's related to a cold case, and he's the best one to answer my questions."

"I took over his cases when he left, then passed them on to the new person who was hired after him."

"Tabitha Lewis, right?"

"Yes. So why not go to her?"

"Why'd he leave, Sherry?"

"He had his reasons."

"Sherry, I'm not in the mood to pull teeth. What were his reasons?"

"I'm not talking about it on the phone." Her voice dropped to barely above a whisper. "You want to meet, I'll explain a little more in detail."

"Name the time and place."

"Tomorrow morning at Cornerstone Café. Seven thirty."

"I'll be there."

Kenzie stepped back into the room. "Tabitha said she would look into the case and see if she could find out anything, go over the pictures of the car. You find Hamilton?"

"No, not yet." He told her about his conversation with Sherry.

Kenzie frowned. "You think she'd mind if I came?"

"I think it might be best if I handle this one alone."

She looked like she might want to protest, but instead nodded. "All right."

He glanced at the clock. "You ready to head to the lake?"

"Sure, but I can drive myself."

"I'm not sure that's a good idea. You're hurt, remember?"

"But I'm not taking any narcotics, so I can drive."

He frowned. "What's going on, Kenzie?"

She raised a brow at him. "Nothing. I'm just saying I want to drive myself in case I decide to leave early."

"If you want to leave early, I'll bring you back here."

"Cole . . ."

"Seriously, Kenzie, you have someone who's tried multiple times to take you out. I really think you shouldn't be alone right now."

She drew in a deep breath and closed her eyes for a brief second. "Fine. Just let me grab my bag and the potato salad from the fridge and we can go."

"Fine. I was supposed to bring a dessert. We'll have to swing through the donut shop."

"Donuts are always welcome."

Her flat tone carried back over her shoulder as she disappeared down the hallway in the direction of her bedroom. "What is her problem?" he muttered. Then sighed. He wasn't stupid. He knew what her problem was. Him.

He was definitely a problem.

He'd made it a point to let her know that relationships and romance weren't anywhere on his radar. It had shaken her. Most likely because her mind went to their little moment in the hospital.

A moment that had rocked his world more than he cared to admit. Shame engulfed him. He'd trivialized it when that was the last thing he wanted to do. And yet, he couldn't let himself fall for her. He refused. And if he apologized for that moment of weakness in the hospital, he might hurt her feelings even further.

Past hurts and treacherous green eyes were never far from the surface of his memories, and if he tried to talk to Kenzie about his conflicting emotions, he wasn't sure how she'd take it. So when they were in his 4Runner and on their way to the lake house, he turned the radio to his favorite country station and kept his mouth shut the entire forty-five-minute drive.

And so did she.

FOURTEEN

Kenzie tossed her clothes onto the twin bed in the lake house guest room and pulled on her swimsuit. She might not be swimming, but she could lounge on the dock in the zero-gravity chair with the best of them. Maybe even sleep if her friends would ignore her and not make her join in the conversation.

Not likely.

She turned, catching her reflection in the full-length mirror. Admitting to herself she was in love with Cole had been hard. So hard her nerves still shook. Thankfully, the shaking was all internal, but still . . .

She hated that it had taken him announcing he wasn't interested in romance to get her to face her feelings for the man. How dumb was that? She studied her reflection in the glass and knew that most men found her attractive. She was well aware that she wasn't magazine-model worthy—whatever that meant—but she had nice features and great legs, thanks to all of her running and biking. Not that she showed them off—it was also genetic. Her mom had had great legs too. And why did she remember that, but sometimes had to look at her mom's picture to remember what she looked like?

A huff escaped her and she turned to find Lainie watching her with a raised brow.

"Don't ask," Kenzie said.

"You have really great legs, you know that?"

Kenzie snorted, then laughed. "Yeah, I do."

"What were you thinking about so hard there?"

"I said don't ask." There was absolutely no way she was going to admit to Lainie she was in love with Cole Garrison.

Lainie crossed her arms and left that obnoxious brow raised.

Kenzie groaned. "Okay, but if I tell you, you have to keep it just between us."

"Sure. What?"

Kenzie pressed her fingers to her eyelids and let out a slow breath. "I realized I'm in love with Cole."

"You just now figured that out?"

Kenzie whipped her gaze toward her friend. "You knew."

"Of course I knew. One couldn't walk between the two of you without being worried one might actually acquire a chemical burn."

"Ha ha. That's funny." But not untrue. "The chemistry is there, isn't it? I'm not imagining it."

"You're not."

"Do you think the guys on the team know?"

Lainie tilted her head. "I don't know. You two have fought it so hard and so long now that . . ." She shrugged. "And let's face it. They're guys. They're not always in tune with stuff like that."

She had a point.

"What's going on?" Jesslyn asked from the door.

Kenzie and Lainie turned. Jesslyn looked beautiful, as usual. She carried her five-foot-eight-inch height well, and the bathing suit and wrap she wore complemented her in every way possible. She had her red hair pulled into a stylish ponytail while her green eyes sparked questions.

"Nothing," Kenzie said, "I'm just having romance woes." She didn't want to go into it with Jesslyn, as much as she liked the woman. To be honest, she was a bit intimidated by her.

Jesslyn shot them a friendly smile, but Kenzie thought she caught a flash of hurt in her eyes. If so, it was gone as fast as it had appeared. "Romance woes?"

"I'm just processing. What's up?"

"We're heading down to the dock and the water. You two coming?"

"We are." Lainie paused. "Who's we?"

"Cole, James, Kristine, and that new detective friend of James', Nathan something or other." She paused and a slight smile tugged at her lips. "He's cute. Steph and her guy just got here, with Dixon and Keegan right behind her."

Kenzie recognized the siblings' names. She'd only met James' brothers a few times, but they were fun guys. "Did Dixon bring his horse?"

"Of course." Jesslyn's laugh was genuine, so if Kenzie had hurt her feelings, she seemed to be over it. "He exercised him and put him in the barn. Said once he had Jericho taken care of, he'd join us on the dock. See y'all out there." She gave a little wave and sauntered off, her flip-flops snapping against the bottoms of her feet.

Kenzie let out a breath. "Why does she intimidate me so much?"

"Because she's perfect," Lainie muttered. "Always has been. Even back in elementary school."

"In my head, I know she's really not perfect, but she sure does come across that way, doesn't she?"

"Yeah, but don't judge her. You know her past."

"I do." Jesslyn had lost so much in a fire when she was five years old. She'd been spared only because she and Lainie had been spending the night in this very house. "I'm not judging, I promise."

Lainie linked arms with her. "Then let's go enjoy the rest of the evening."

COLE CHECKED IN ON THE TEAM and received positive reports all around. The team was always invited—even Butler—to join in the fun with the rest of the group since he, James, and Kenzie were regulars, but Buzz and Cowboy had decided to opt out, and Butler would never come because Kenzie was there.

Before he thought about how to fix his massive Kenzie-blunder, he called his dad's number, stepped off the dock, and walked down to the edge of the lake. The sand sucked at his flip-flops, and he kicked them off, hissing when the cold water closed over his toes.

"Cole," his dad said in greeting, "good to hear from you. What's up?"

"I had a question."

"Sure."

"I was talking with Ben King today and he brought up something about Gram and Gramps Garrison."

"What about them?"

"How were they part of some family feud that Kenzie's family was involved in back in the late 1940s, early '50s?"

His father let out a low breath that meant he was thinking. "Well, that was all before your uncles were born, and no one wanted to talk much about it, even though my brothers and I heard rumors and stories. Unfortunately, Mom died shortly after I was born. Your uncle Robert was twelve then, and Dad was overwhelmed with trying to keep up with a newborn and three other boys. From what I understand, if it hadn't been for some of Mom's friends in the church and Betsy King, things would have been really bad."

"I see. And what about her? Kenzie's grandmother? She was Gram Garrison's best friend. Couldn't she shed some light on all of this?"

"Maybe, but I'm not sure her mind works that great. She's got to be pushing a hundred."

"Yeah. Okay, well, do you mind doing a little digging to see if you can find out what the feud was about? I'm curious. This is part of my history, and these are my ancestors. I want to know more."

His dad chuckled. "Sure, son. I'll see what I can dig up."

"Thanks."

He hung up, slipped his flip-flops back on, and walked back to the dock. The food smells tantalized his nose and his stomach growled.

Kenzie was fixing a plate of grilled chicken, baked beans, potato salad, and corn on the cob. Everyone had brought something, and most had started with the donuts. He dropped into the nearest chair to wait for the line to die down a bit. And, okay, he wanted to watch Kenzie without her knowing he was watching. He really hoped that wasn't too stalkerish, but he needed to think. Hard.

Like how to apologize for being an idiot.

James sat beside him and popped the tab on a can of root beer. "You okay?"

"Fine. Why?"

"You seem to be a little morose."

"Morose?" Cole chuckled. "Where'd you learn that word?"

"School. Probably a couple of years before you got to that one since I was in the accelerated program."

"Ha ha. Such a comedian."

"Seriously, what's going on?"

"I don't date."

"Um . . . yeah, you do. Someone different depending on the day of the week."

"Aw, those aren't dates. They're just hanging out with people I enjoy spending time with."

"That's your interpretation. I'm sure if you checked with any of those women, they'd call it a date."

Cole sighed. "Maybe so."

"Come on, man. What is it?"

"I did something. Then I said something. And now I don't know how to make it right."

"You kissed her and apologized, didn't you?"

"What? No!"

"Then you almost did?" Cole fell silent and James' eyes widened. "You almost did? And *then* you apologized."

"No. I didn't apologize. I think I did something worse. I made it sound like the moment was . . . irrelevant or unimportant." He ignored James' soft groan and kept his eyes on the others gathered on the covered dock, laughing and chatting under the lights strung across the ceiling. Normally, he'd be right there with them, but today he just couldn't join in the fun.

So. Why had he come? He looked at his friend, who'd fallen silent. "Well?"

"Kinda biting my tongue right now," James said. "Give me a minute."

After James had decided to call the lake house his permanent home, he'd made some improvements. He'd extended and covered the dock and put an outdoor kitchen and serving area on one end. The flames from the grill danced in the darkness and the water lapped gently against the sides. A direct contrast to the waves of turmoil battling it out inside Cole's body.

"I need to know how to fix this, James. Without my attempts to do so backfiring on me and making it worse."

"Yeah. One question."

"Sure."

"*Was* the moment irrelevant and unimportant?"

Cole shut his eyes. "No."

"It got to you."

"It did. *She* did. Does. From the moment she walked into headquarters and claimed her locker, she's been getting to me. I've known her basically all our lives, but never once thought of her as anything other than Logan's baby sister. But now . . ." He paused and opened his eyes to look at his friend. "I'm in trouble. And not just because I crossed the line as her supervisor, although I'm ashamed to admit that I sort of did. And then messed *everything* up even further when I tried to backpedal."

"I know you, Cole. You'd never cross that line. At least not intentionally."

He appreciated the vote of confidence, but still . . . "I wanted to offer her comfort and, like I said, fumbled it royally. Unintentionally, true, but there it is. If it was anyone else under my authority and they'd done something like that, I'd call them out on it, tell them to apologize and make it right, and that's the plain truth."

"Then the only way to fix this is to be honest with her."

"I know."

"Great. Glad we got that all worked out." James patted his shoulder.

"Right. All worked out." Cole shook his head and rolled his eyes at his friend. "Thanks for listening even though I don't like your advice."

"My correct advice."

"Yeah, yeah."

"Now that I've solved all your problems, I'm going to get some food before I take the polar plunge in that frigid water. I suggest you do the same. Besides, it takes calories to apologize and do it right."

Cole directed a glare at his friend's back. James' knowing chuckle pulled a sigh from Cole, and he stood. He needed fortification before he talked to Kenzie. He knew that conversation would entail pulling his foot from his mouth while doing his best not to wind up swallowing it.

FIFTEEN

Eliza rolled over and the twin cot creaked. Two days ago, Dr. King hadn't been able to stop the therapy—how could they call it that?—and her head pounded like wild mustangs racing across the open land. The visual was beautiful. The feeling was not.

Her skull licked with residual flames and her body ached like every muscle had gone through an extreme workout. In a sense it had. She was quite surprised she'd survived. If she had to go through that again, she would surely die.

Her safe home was no longer safe and she had to figure out how to get out. A knock on the door stilled her. She had no energy to get up and greet whoever it was; however, when Dr. King slipped inside, she found the strength to sit up. "Where's William? Why hasn't he come for me?" Why wouldn't her mind work properly? The look in his eyes didn't bode well. "What is it?" she whispered.

"Betsy found William, remember?"

And just like that, a bolt stronger than any stupid therapy session zipped through her. "Is he coming to get me?"

He shook his head. "No, I'm so sorry, Eliza. You don't remember this conversation?"

155

"No."

"Betsy found William and he was in a horrific car accident. That's why you haven't heard from him."

"What? No." She stood and wobbled.

Dr. King hurried to her, grasped her arms, and gently lowered her back to the bed.

"He's dead?" she whispered.

"No, no. I'm sorry. I didn't mean to make you think that. He's alive, he's just injured."

"Oh." She pressed a hand against her racing heart. "Oh my word." The memories came crashing back into her brain. The therapy must have blocked them for a brief time. What else had it taken away? Eliza sucked in a breath, then gripped the doctor's fingers. "You must discharge me immediately. I have to go to him. I *have* to."

He nodded. "I knew you'd want to, and I've been doing nothing but thinking how to make that happen."

"Can't you just discharge me?"

"And have you go where? Back to your father's home?"

"No, of course not, but I do believe Betsy would let me stay with her." He hesitated and she frowned. "What is it?"

"Betsy would love for you to stay with her."

"You've talked about this?"

He nodded.

"What is it?"

"Your father went to Betsy's father and told him of your delicate constitution and that if somehow you were to be released and showed up at his home, he was to be notified immediately."

"And, of course, her father agreed. They're two peas in a pod. Thick as thieves."

"Yes, I'm afraid so."

She dropped her face into her palms. What was she going to do?

His gentle hand on her shoulder lifted her chin. "Don't worry, Eliza, I'm going to figure something out."

"Before my next treatment?" She grimaced.

His jaw hardened. "Yes, before that."

"I . . . I need to see William, Dr. King. I must."

He paused. "I must admit, I've been thinking of a way to release you without your father pulling strings to move you to another place. A place where you'd have no help whatsoever. At least here, you have me."

"I believe the Lord arranged for that."

"Exactly. Which means he's also arranged for me to help you. I've thought of going to the authorities, but I'm afraid I don't know who to trust in that department. Nor do I have any proof of any accusation I may levy."

"No, he has the police in his pocket. Not all, of course, but a lot."

"I thought he might. So, it comes down to this. How are your acting skills?"

She blinked. "What?"

"Could you pretend to be submissive, apologize to your father, promise never to see William again, and go home without letting on how you're really feeling?"

Eliza pressed her fingers to her lips as she thought. "For how long?"

"For as long as it takes for William to heal."

"I don't know. I just know I need to see him. I can't stay away while he needs me."

"Once he wakes up, I can get him a message. He can focus on healing and you'll be out of here, out from under the threat of more therapy that you don't need, but you must convince your father."

Could she? Did she have a choice? She'd been dodging her father for years, avoiding him and his abuse. The thought of William straightened her spine. "Yes. Yes, I can do it."

"You're sure? It could be very dangerous for you. If he truly tried to kill you once . . . He knows you, Eliza, and if he thinks you're faking—"

She lifted her chin another notch. "If that's what it takes to be with William, then I can do it."

He stood. "Very well. I've been communicating with your father since you were admitted, of course, and once I realized your situation and connected all the dots, I let him believe that he's convinced me you tried to kill yourself. I'll contact him and ask him to come see you so you can convince him. It will have to be his decision to allow you to come home."

"Yes, it will have to be his decision," she murmured.

Dr. King said his goodbyes and left her alone with the other empty bed. She still didn't have a roommate despite the overcrowding, and she wondered if that was her father's doing. Keeping her isolated, unable to tell anyone her story. Protecting himself. Keeping her from William.

A flicker of doubt sent a shudder through her. Could she do this? Convince him she'd seen the light, so to speak?

She pulled her journal and pen from under the mattress and wrote page after page, detailing everything. Not that she was likely to forget, but if she had to tell this story to anyone, she wasn't sure she'd be able to. And if she didn't live to tell it, then maybe one day, her words would find their way into the hands of someone who could tell it for her.

SIXTEEN

From the corner of her eye, Kenzie watched Cole and James fill their plates, wondering at the intense conversation they'd just finished. Part of her wanted to think it was about her and Cole but figured she was being silly. Cole had made it clear that she was nothing more than a coworker.

But there was a small part of her that wondered if that was true. The more she thought about it, the more she thought she'd seen something else in his eyes in that moment.

Something like fear.

He'd been burned badly by his ex-girlfriend. What if he'd just said all of that because he was afraid of what he actually felt for her?

She snorted. She was delusional.

No. Wishful.

"Hey," Jesslyn said, sitting in the empty seat next to her.

"Hey."

"You look very serious. What's going on?"

Well, she hadn't planned to make this evening all about her, but she didn't want Jesslyn to feel slighted again either. And maybe Jess would have some good insight into everything. "Other than someone trying to kill me, finding out more about the night my mom died, and a very complicated relationship with Cole?"

"Oh my."

"Oh, and don't forget the team doesn't really want me on the team, and I wonder if one of them is behind all the attempts to get rid of me."

Jesslyn blinked. "That's a lot."

"Yeah. It is. Sorry I dumped that on you. I seem to be doing that a lot even when I order myself not to."

"I'm honored you'd share, Kenzie. I know we really haven't had a lot of heart-to-hearts and I want to change that. The truth is, I was a little jealous when you and Lainie became friends so quickly." She glanced away. "I need to apologize for that."

Kenzie nearly fell out of her chair. "What? Jealous? I never would have guessed."

The woman let out a small laugh. "Well, thanks for that, but you probably noticed I didn't make a huge effort to get to know you, so again, I'm sorry about that and hope you'll forgive me—and give me another chance to get to know you better."

Kenzie reached over and squeezed Jesslyn's hand, then released it to pick up her candy bar from the table. "Nothing to forgive, but if you need the words, I forgive you. And while we're on apologies, I didn't mean to shut you out earlier. I had vented to Lainie and felt like I'd taken up enough time with my issues that I just wanted to get out here and enjoy the fellowship."

"And here I am insisting you go through it all over again. I'm batting a thousand tonight, aren't I? I'm sorry. Again."

Kenzie gaped. "No. Not at all. The last thing you did was insist. You simply asked. The truth is, I'm very focused on myself right now and need a distraction, so tell me about you. How's your work going?"

Jesslyn shrugged. "Some days it's a challenge, other days I feel like a hero."

"You mean like when you put away that arsonist who was burning down schools?"

"Exactly like that. Although I'm not sure why he thought burning down the schools was going to achieve his goal of overhauling the education system."

"It was a symbolic act."

Jesslyn smiled. "It was. He made no secret of the fact that he thought the whole system needed a revamp. I don't think he meant for anyone to get hurt, but someone died because they chose to work late." She sighed. "At least he's behind bars and can't hurt anyone else."

"Yes. Amen to that."

"I'm curious how it's going for you, working in such a male-dominated arena," Jesslyn said. She took a sip of her water and tilted her head at Kenzie. "Firefighting is too, but SWAT . . ." She shook her head. "That's a whole other ball game."

Kenzie sighed and let Jesslyn turn the conversation back to her while Lainie lit the firepit and James tossed a bag of marshmallows to the newcomer, Detective Nathan Carlisle. New, but not inexperienced. "It's funny you should ask that. That's been a hot topic ever since I was accepted." She broke off a piece of her Hershey bar. She liked s'mores. She also liked plain chocolate just as well. The sugary sweetness coated her tongue. "That was the happiest day of my life." She glanced at Jesslyn. "The day I got the news I'd be joining the team. Even better than getting into med school."

Jesslyn laughed. "I can imagine." Her eyes tracked Nathan, and Kenzie raised a brow that Jesslyn didn't notice. Then her friend blinked and turned her attention back to Kenzie. "And?"

Hmm . . . that was interesting, but she let it go. "Truthfully, it's also been the hardest thing I've ever done, next to going to my mother's funeral."

"Yeah." Jesslyn frowned. "I know about losing people."

"Your family," Kenzie said.

Jesslyn nodded. "It's the reason I do what I do. My family was murdered and the arsonist never caught."

"I heard. I'm so sorry." Kenzie cleared her throat. "I just recently learned my mother's death may not have been an accident."

Jesslyn straightened and her gaze sharpened. "What?"

Kenzie summarized, leaving out a lot of the details, but telling enough so Jesslyn had a good picture of the issue. "But we're not sure. It's just a theory I'm looking into."

"Let me know if you need any help. I don't know what I can do, but if I can do it, I will."

"Thanks." She drew in a slow breath. "Now, back to you. Not a lot of female fire marshals out there."

"No, but I don't get much grief about it. I'm respected in the field now, but I've been doing this a while. You'll get there, if you're not already."

"Oh, I'm not." She took another bite of chocolate. "I've worked my tail off to prove myself, but it just doesn't seem to matter."

"You're not giving up, are you?"

"Well, I can't say I haven't thought about it. Sure would be a lot easier, but quitting isn't in me. And besides, I'm good at it. I enjoy it when we're all working as a team and"—she thought about Micah and his family—"the rewards are great."

"You should be proud of yourself. I'm praying that the guys come around and the tension disappears."

"Thank you."

"Now, why haven't you and Cole spoken or even looked at each other since you got here?"

Kenzie groaned. "You noticed that, huh?"

"Hard not to."

"It's a long story. We had a little disagreement and are sulking—mostly me—but we'll both get over it and go back to behaving like adults before too much longer."

Jesslyn looked amused. Then she took a swig of her water and nodded toward the edge of the dock. "Looks like the polar bear plunge is getting ready to happen."

"While I'm very comfortable sitting here in my suit with the nice breeze and my warm cover-up," Kenzie said around another bite of chocolate. She touched her side, feeling the bandage under her suit.

"I'm very glad I'm not allowed in the water. It's cold. It was cold before the sun started going down and it's even colder now."

"Hence the stupid dare."

"At least it's not snowing this time." She shuddered. "I can't believe I did that one last year. Are you going in?"

"What do you think?"

"I think you picked working with fire for a reason."

Jesslyn laughed. "You got that right, but I wouldn't miss this for the world." She glanced at Kenzie. "Unless I had a wound that could get infected."

Kenzie smirked. "I'll be honest. I'm just using that as an excuse to stay warm."

"I don't blame you."

"But why don't you go show that hunky new detective what you're made of?"

Jesslyn simply raised a brow and shot Kenzie a mysterious smile before walking over to stand between Nathan and Lainie. Then she turned back to Kenzie and winked.

"One, two, three, go!"

The splashes and shrieks echoed, and Kenzie laughed like she hadn't in a very long time. When Cole hauled himself out of the water and onto the dock, shivering, his eyes connected with hers and he shot her a tentative smile.

She smiled back.

ONCE THEY WERE IN his 4Runner and heading back to Kenzie's home, Cole glanced at her from the corner of his eye. "You okay?"

"I'm fine. You thawed out yet?"

He shuddered. "I may never be warm again." He cranked the heat up a notch for good measure.

"You didn't have to do that, you know. Jump in. That's crazy stuff."

He was glad she was at least talking to him. It helped open the door to the apology he still owed her. There'd been no chance earlier when she was surrounded by friends right up to the end. "Who you calling crazy? You did it when it was snowing last year."

She chuckled. "I know. I'm teasing." Her phone pinged and she glanced at it. "Logan's texting. My grandma Betsy's birthday is next week."

"Man, how old is she now?"

"Ninety-seven and still pretty sharp." She glanced at him. "She doesn't talk much about the past but does mention your grandmother, Eliza, and how she used to visit her at the psychiatric hospital."

He laughed. "I can't believe Betsy met your grandfather there. Can you imagine what they used to say to the question, 'So, how did y'all meet?'"

Kenzie grinned. "Oh yes, she had fun with that one. And she also had stories about some guy who worked with my grandfather who used to hit on her."

"What? Who?"

She shrugged. "I don't know. She just called him Dr. Stephen. He was the director back then before my grandfather took over. He had a crush on her that turned into something of a stalking situation. Apparently, she had to really put him in his place and let him know she was in love with my grandfather and to leave her alone."

"Ouch. Poor guy. That had to hurt." Probably almost as bad as Tracy dumping him. "What happened after that?"

"I'm not exactly sure. Grandma Betsy kind of clams up after that. I don't think she likes to remember those days. She did ask me one time if I'd found the journal."

"What journal?"

"I don't know, and when I pressed her for more details, she just shrugged and said never mind, that it was probably lost."

"Interesting."

"I thought so, but I've been so busy working on renovating the house and pushing hard career-wise that I haven't had much time to think about it."

"Maybe you can ask her about it at the party."

"Yeah, maybe I will."

Cole hesitated, took a breath, then blurted, "Kenzie, I need to be honest with you about something."

Her gaze sharpened. "Okay."

"Do you mind if I come in for a few minutes when we get to your house?"

"Sure, that's fine."

It was dark. It was late. And he was so full of nerves that he had to call on all his training not to give in to them. Maybe he should have waited until a better time to do this.

But no. He wanted the air clear between them.

When they arrived at Kenzie's home, she unlocked the front door, turned off the alarm, and led him inside.

He shut the door and locked it. "Let's go through your house, make sure it's clear."

"Fine."

Because she knew as well as he did, an untripped alarm didn't necessarily mean someone couldn't get inside.

Together they walked through, clearing the main floor. He held up his hand at the entrance to the basement. "Stay here, okay?"

She nodded. She'd wait at the top of the stairs to make sure no one came to ambush them and would be there for help if he needed it. Cole made his way into the basement, stepping over the seventh step, and noted the window had been fixed—and covered with bars on the outside.

No one was coming back in that way without making a lot of noise.

The punching bag was still hanging from the hook and the weight system was organized, waiting for the next workout. He walked back up to the kitchen and found Kenzie leaning against the counter. "Clear down there."

"All good up here."

"Attic?"

"Follow me."

Cole fell into step behind her. She had a walk-in storage area off the utility room. "So, this is your 'attic,' huh?" he said.

"Grandma Betsy didn't like stairs. She tolerated the basement— mostly because she didn't have to go down there. She used it for storage, just like this room. When I moved in, the basement was full of all kinds of antiques and stuff that I gave my brothers first pick of. I kept a couple of things that I wanted, then sold the rest so I could get started updating the house."

"You've done a great job so far."

"Thanks." She shot him a smile, then looked around the room. His gaze followed hers. Boxes and bins were stacked along the perimeter of the room. A card table and chairs leaned against the wall opposite the door. A clothing rack went wall to wall, a variety of items hanging from it. She pointed to the oversize chair in the corner. "I keep thinking I'll pull that out and use it somewhere, but I don't want it in the den."

"Maybe the sunroom?"

"It might work there. I'm sure it needs a good cleaning and I'd want to recover it with something a little more my taste, but yeah. The sunroom might be a great place for it." She sighed. "But for now, it can stay put while I tackle the other stuff."

"It's a lot," he said, "but looks pretty well organized."

"It is, which will help because I have no idea what's here. I still have to go through all of it, figuring out what needs to be tossed, donated, and possibly kept. Maybe I'll do that with my few days off."

"Happy to help if you need it."

She raised a brow. "I might just take you up on it." She led him back to the den area, where she motioned to the couch. "You had something you wanted to talk about."

Wanted to talk about? Absolutely not. "I owe you another apology. That moment in the hospital wasn't me being a player, Kenz."

He wanted to get up and pace. Instead, he locked his gaze on hers. "As you know, Tracy burned me pretty bad."

"Tracy, yes, I know," she said.

The distaste in her voice almost made him smile. "Yeah. I liked her a lot. I'm not going to say I loved her, but I definitely cared about her. The truth is, she used me to further her own career and that hurt. Made me mad."

"And suspicious of me? Did you wonder if I'd use your friendship with my brother to get you to make things easier for me?"

"Maybe a little in the beginning, but as time went on and you were obviously determined not to accept any help whatsoever, it didn't take me long to realize you weren't like Tracy."

Anger flickered in her gaze, then fizzled. "No, I'm not. I'm glad you can see that."

"When it comes to . . . certain situations . . . I make light of those that get to me. Make it seem like they don't matter. When in reality, they matter more than I want to admit."

She stayed quiet for a moment. "So, you're saying when you almost kissed me in the hospital, it did mean something."

"Yeah. It did."

She blew out a low breath. "Thank you for admitting that. I didn't like the thoughts I was having about you when you said it meant nothing."

He winced. "I don't blame you for the thoughts. But I was also worried that it was a wrong move in the sense that I'm your supervisor. It could be construed as taking advantage of you. And I never want to put either of us in that position ever again. It's not fair to you at all."

She sighed. "I get it. You don't have to say anything else. It's all good. We'll just be coworkers and friends, all right?"

Relief and something else he refused to identify swept through him. "Right. Perfect. Thank you."

"That was really hard for you, wasn't it?"

"You have no idea."

Kenzie tucked stray strands of hair behind her ear. "Well, it's late and I'm ready to get some rest."

He knew a dismissal when he heard one. He glanced at his phone. "Officer Butte is here and watching the house. Get some rest and I'll call you after my coffee date in the morning with Sherry."

She nodded, walked to the door, and held it open. Cole walked through it, wondering why it was so hard to do so. He acknowledged the officer with a wave and turned back to Kenzie. "Night, Kenzie."

"Night, *friend*."

The slight emphasis on that last word made him wince, but she shot him a tired smile before she shut the door with a definitive click, then the deadbolt slid home.

SEVENTEEN

Kenzie *wanted* to sleep. She was tired, but sleep was a couple hours off and she now had time to circle back to her mother's death. She'd been avoiding thinking about it even while it was never far from her mind. She'd give just about anything to be at that meeting in the morning with Cole, but she promised to stay out of it, so she would.

She took out her phone and saw the string of text messages and groaned. Kristine, Lainie, James, Jesslyn, Allison, and Steph had all sent her messages asking if she was okay.

She tapped a response to the group.

> I'm fine. Cole just left. Now I'm going to start going through my grandmother's storage room because it's about time and I HAVE the time.

Or she could go put in some hours at the hospital, but her side was sore and she frankly just didn't want to. She hadn't had a moment to herself in a while, so some alone time might be a good thing.

> Want some help?

> I can come help.

> Help is just a text away.

169

She grinned at the responses and a wave of gratitude washed over her. She shot back a text to say thanks and she'd let them know. So this was what it felt like to have a community of friends, people who had her back and were concerned about her well-being. She'd hoped she'd find that with the guys in the unit. Hadn't really expected to in the beginning, but had hoped that by now they'd trust her and have her back.

Unfortunately, real life was different from the television shows that had women on their SWAT teams. The guys still didn't consider her an integral part of the team. No matter that she'd proved herself over and over. She glanced at her phone once more and took a deep breath. It didn't matter. As long as she had this group. That had kept her going more than once over the last six months.

She walked into the storage room and flipped the light on. "Good grief, Grandma Betsy, how'd you get so much stuff?" She set up the card table, grabbed the nearest box, and pulled the top off. Stuffed animals? From a hundred years ago most likely. Even if it was just thirty years ago, she wasn't touching them. "Ick." She slapped the top back on and carried the box to the outside trash can.

On the fourth trip, she paused. The trash can was just around the side of her garage wall, and each time she hauled stuff to it, she waved to her bodyguard. Except now, the officer wasn't there. She reached for her phone, only to remember she'd left it on the card table in the storage room. In the house with the alarm momentarily disarmed. "Great."

Her skin pricked and the hair on the nape of her neck bristled, just as goose bumps pebbled her arms. "Who's there? What do you want?"

Silence.

Then a slight rustle to her left in the shadows.

She spun to run back to the house. A hard arm closed around her throat, and she grabbed the forearm with both hands and stepped back to ram her hip into the person's midsection. He grunted and she bent forward, flipping him over her head. Her side protested, but she ignored it and he landed on the cement. She dove for him, her knee digging into his solar plexus. The sound that came from him wasn't pleasant, but she pressed harder—until he swung his right hand and something hard connected with her head. She cried out, falling away from him while stars danced in her vision. She managed to roll to her knees. A wave of nausea stunned her just long enough for him to place the barrel of a gun against her head. He dragged her to her feet and she froze, her back to him, the gun still there.

"What do you want?" She hated that the words came out on a strangled gasp.

"You gone. Quit the team or die."

She spun and stared into his masked face—and the barrel now lined up with her nose. "What?"

"Hey!"

The shout from across the street froze the guy for a millisecond, but it was long enough for Kenzie to grasp the wrist attached to the hand with the gun and shove it up. She brought up her knee, aiming to do as much damage as possible, but he twisted, shoved her back to the drive, and took off, disappearing back around the side of the house. Kenzie scrambled to her knees, her side throbbing, head pounding.

Where was her protection?

"Kenzie?" Mrs. Arnold, in her early seventies and clutching her pink bathrobe at her throat, hurried from across the street. "Are you all right? I called 911."

"I'm okay. Thank you." Kenzie pulled in a breath and winced at the pain in her side. Okay, she may have pulled one of her stitches.

"Who was that?" The poor woman trembled.

"I don't know. I'm going to file a police report. You don't have a video doorbell, do you?"

"No, but after tonight, I might consider it. Honestly, I don't understand what this world is coming to. Being attacked in your own drive."

"It's okay." Sirens sounded in the distance. "When the cops get here, can you give them your statement? I'll talk to them when you're finished."

"Of course."

"Thanks. Tell them to knock when you're done."

She ran—okay, *hobbled*—inside, hand pressed to her side, grabbed her phone, and tapped Officer Butte's number. "Yeah?"

"This is Kenzie. Where the heck are you?"

"Got a DV call a half a mile away—husband had a gun."

"Right. Thanks *so much* for letting me know."

"I texted you, Kenzie. I'm sorry."

"Right. And when I didn't respond, you couldn't call?"

"No, I was already at the— What's going on? Are you okay?"

She sucked in a steadying breath. "Yeah. I'm fine."

And she was. Other than aggravating her wound, a throbbing headache, and a blinding rage that continued to build.

But she was fine.

"Kenzie, I'm on the way back," Butte said. "When I got to the address, it was an empty lot in a new subdivision."

So, he'd been pulled off by the guy who attacked her. She had no proof, of course, but she still knew it. The guy couldn't have known her bodyguard would be the officer to respond, but being that close, he would have been the most likely to do so.

When she'd done everything with reporting the incident and everyone was finally gone, she locked herself in her house, armed the alarm, placed her Glock on the nightstand, and finally settled in her bed prepared for a sleepless night. She should call Cole and tell him what happened, but the thought of him coming over was too much to deal with. She'd fill him in tomorrow. Fury at the situation boiled with no outlet because she wasn't about to go downstairs for a workout.

Her attacker had been watching her home and she'd given him the opportunity to strike. She'd figured with the officer watching, the guy wouldn't be so bold as to strike and she'd be safe.

She wouldn't make that mistake again.

SATURDAY MORNING Cole walked into Cornerstone Café and spotted Sherry at the far corner table. She'd parked herself against the wall, her eyes on the door. She wore a floppy hat, sunglasses, and a dark red dress. He checked his phone, thankful for no SWAT calls, and slid into the booth opposite her. "Hey."

She pulled the sunglasses off, but kept her head tilted down. He glanced above her head. The camera wouldn't pick her up the way she'd jammed herself against the wall with the floppy hat. There would be footage of her walking to the table, but with her hat and shades, no one would be able to tell it was her. She followed his gaze. "That's the only camera in here that works. Overheard the manager tell that to someone who had her wallet lifted from her purse last time I was in here."

He nodded. "All right, wanna tell me why all the cloak-and-dagger?"

"Wanna tell me why you're looking into a twenty-year-old *closed* case?"

"Because I have three reports and one of them is doctored. I believe the other two are the real deal. The first shows DNA in the stolen vehicle used in an accident that killed Hannah King and paralyzed Ben King. The other shows that the brakes on the former chief of police's car were cut. The doctored one says no such thing and the cause of the accident wasn't due to any kind of mechanical failure, but rather was human error."

She paled. "How did you get them? Why do *you* have them?"

"They were sent anonymously to the chief. He gave them to me. I have them because he wants me to look into the accident that he's believed all along was no accident. Now, who could have given him those documents?"

"Well, you obviously thought it was me."

"Let's just say you were on the list as one person who *could* have done it, not necessarily who actually *did* it."

She sighed. "Well, I did."

"Why the secrecy? Why not just tell Ben what you know? You had to realize this would come back to you."

"I was willing to take the chance."

"Where's Cliff now?"

She licked her lips. "He's dying. Pancreatic cancer. He said he had only one regret and this case was it."

"So he wants to set the record straight before he dies."

Sherry nodded.

"I need to talk to him."

"Cole, he's probably already gone. His wife texted me three weeks ago and said he didn't have much longer. Days, maybe. We arranged to meet. She gave me the files, told me what was going on, and made me promise not to try to find Cliff or tell anyone anything. I was to deliver the package to Ben King and go on about my life like that wasn't a blip on my radar, because if anyone found out I knew what Cliff knew, then I could be in danger."

"Because the person responsible is still out there."

"Yes."

"Did Mrs. Hamilton say who it was?"

"No. And yes, I asked. She said Cliff refused to tell her, that she was safer not knowing."

He sighed and rubbed his eyes. "All right, so this means that someone cut the brake line, Chief King ran the stop sign, and Mrs. King, Kenzie's mom, was murdered and someone attempted to do the same to the chief." He took a sip of the coffee she'd ordered him. "Somebody went to a lot of trouble to make this happen, and somebody else went to a lot of trouble to cover it up. I want to know who those somebodies are."

"Well, I can't help you there, I'm sorry. I thought Cliff and I were good friends. I never thought he'd do something like this, but he did. Then ran."

"Which means he was scared. Scared he'd get caught or just plain scared of the people who asked him to hide evidence of a murder."

"Probably both."

"Yes. Probably." He sighed. "Tell me this. Do you know anything about Shady Talbot and his role in the accident?"

"I assumed he stole the car and crashed it. I knew who he was from the media surrounding his case."

Then someone had doctored the results of the alcohol blood level test for the chief and . . .

And what? Who hated him so much to go to all that trouble?

"Then Shady was found dead of a drug overdose while awaiting trial for murder," Cole muttered. "Which isn't suspicious because he was definitely an addict, but how in the world did he make bail?"

"I don't know, but the fact that he did is as shady as his name."

"Yeah." His phone buzzed and he glanced at it. Carl Butte, the officer on Kenzie's home. "Sorry, I need to take this."

"Of course."

He swiped and held the phone to his ear. "Hey, Carl, everything all right?"

"That's what I was trying to find out. I got called off King's home last night to a fake DV report. Got there and it was an empty lot in a new subdivision. Kenzie called wanting to know where I was. She sounded shook but insisted she was fine. Turns out she reported an assault during the time I was gone."

"You left and you didn't let her know?" He almost shouted the words and several patrons looked in his direction. Sherry slid lower in the booth.

"I texted her, man, but I guess she didn't look at her phone."

Cole got a grip on his emotions. "Didn't think to call her?" The question came out between gritted teeth, but at least he'd lowered the volume.

"No time. I was already pulling in by the time the text went. When I realized it wasn't a legit call, I was about to call her when she called me first. I was gone a whole ten minutes."

"And we all know it takes a lot less time than that to kill someone."

"Yeah. All I can do is say sorry and be thankful she's all right."

"I know you are. I'm just bent out of shape about what could have happened. Thanks for filling me in."

He hung up with Carl and looked at Sherry. "I've got to go."

"Sounds like you have a friend in trouble."

"I do."

"Is it related to this thing with Cliff?"

"I don't know. I don't see how except through the link with Shady, which might just be a coincidence." He frowned. But was it? "This thing with Cliff is new, but enlightening." He stood and placed a twenty on the table. "I got this. Thanks for meeting me."

"Will you let me know what you find out?"

"Of course."

He left and hurried to his car, then aimed himself toward Kenzie's home.

EIGHTEEN

Kenzie pulled her fifth box of the morning from the wall, set it on the card table, and removed the top just as the doorbell rang.

She hurried from the room and checked the side window next to the front door.

Cole.

When she opened the door, he glowered at her. "You didn't think to call and tell me that someone attacked you last night?"

"Good morning to you too." She stepped back and he entered.

"Forget the good morning stuff. You got attacked last night."

"I did." She led him into the den and took a seat on the couch.

He dropped onto the opposite end, his scowl deepening by the second.

"I'm fine. I fought him off with the help of a neighbor's yell."

He closed his eyes for a second, rubbed a hand down his face, and let out a low breath like he was searching for patience. "All right. I get it. I'm glad you're okay. Why wouldn't you call me?"

She stood and paced to the mantel and back to the sofa. When she returned to the mantel, she spun. "I would have, but it shook me. Bad." She pressed a palm to her temple. "I just wanted to process it. Butte was back so I felt like I could sleep. If you'd come over, it just would have added stress to the whole matter." He flinched and she sighed. "And that didn't come out right. *You* wouldn't have added stress, but me having to talk about it and relive it and—"

She wouldn't have slept much because he would have insisted on staying and she just couldn't have dealt with his presence last night. But she wasn't saying *that*.

"And what?"

"Nothing." She waved a hand in dismissal. "Never mind. I'm just still . . . rattled, I guess." She cleared her throat. "I . . . uh . . . left one detail out of the police report that I need to tell you."

He frowned. "Okay."

"He spoke to me before my neighbor scared him off. I asked him what he wanted, and he said, and I quote, 'You gone. Quit the team or die.'"

Cole's scowl fell away. He raised a brow and leaned back. "Whoa."

"Yeah. So, who wants me off the team so bad that they'd threaten to kill me?" She pressed a hand to her side. Gently. "Attack me in a market? Break into my house and shoot at me?"

"I have someone in mind, but I . . . don't want to admit it."

She raised a brow at him. "Butler?"

He sighed. "Yeah."

She nodded and pressed her fingers to her lips, thinking. "Then I want proof it's him. Irrefutable proof."

His eyes narrowed. "How do you propose to get that?"

"I don't know. Follow him, I guess. I've still got a few days off, thanks to my attack, to figure this out. I'm going to use them for that."

"What about your training for the triathlon?"

"Really?" She pointed to her side, then her head. "You think that's even a priority right now?"

"No. Sorry. You're right. But if it is Butler, I don't want to see you get in over your head." He hesitated. "I'll help you."

She raised a brow. "Why? I can handle him. I've handled him for the last six months."

"No," he said. "This is different. If he's really able to bring himself

178

to commit murder, then it's not a fair fight. You need someone to watch your back."

As much as she wanted to protest, the pain in her side and the ache in her head said that wasn't the best option. "Okay. Fine." She didn't have the bandwidth to think through all the ramifications of spying on one of their own, but if he was a potential killer, then all the team rules and codes went out the window. "When do we start?"

He sighed and looked at his phone. "Today. He asked for the morning off. Said he had a family thing he needed to take care of."

"What if he does?"

"What if he doesn't?"

"All right. Fine. The team is down to basically nothing. Who have you got responding to calls?"

"I've alerted the second string. They know they're on standby. If we get a call, I'll go. Magic Man was on today anyway. Cowboy and Greene both said they're ready to get back to work."

She frowned. "Not sure Greene has the *green* light from his doctor yet." She smirked. "See what I did there?"

"Not funny."

"It was. Kinda."

"Not even a little."

"Hm. Fine. Can you fill me in on what Sherry had to say?"

For the next few minutes, Kenzie listened. With each passing word, her heart sank and a desperate need flared to know why the information was covered up and by who. "How do we find out if Hamilton is still alive?" she finally asked.

"I don't know. I don't even know if we should. He sent the information to right a wrong but didn't send the name of the person responsible, which means he's scared of the backlash that could come from it."

"His family."

"Yeah."

"But they're all under the radar, right? I mean, you looked for him and couldn't find any of them even with your various resources."

He nodded. "Any luck with Tabitha?"

"No, actually, I haven't heard back from her. Let me shoot her a text and see where she is on that."

"You mean you actually remember how to do that?"

She wrinkled her nose at him but refrained from sticking her tongue out. "Talk about someone who's not funny."

"Sure I am."

"Only in your own mind."

"Rude."

She snickered, then sobered, but was glad they were back to being sparring . . . what? Friends? Coworkers? Well, whatever it was, she was glad the awkwardness seemed to be gone. She sent the text to Tabitha. "I'm just going to get ready and then we can tail Butler."

"I'll find his location." He pulled his work phone from his pocket.

"You're going to track his work phone? That seems . . ." Wrong. A breach of trust. But . . . necessary.

He raised a brow at her. "I don't like it either, but if he's the one doing this, I'll do whatever I have to do to stop him."

She nodded. "I know."

"And if it's not him, I'll apologize."

"Then give me fifteen minutes and we can go."

Kenzie was ready in twelve, but she paused to check her wound one more time and was satisfied that it seemed to be healing well. No sign of infection and no busted stitches from her violent encounter. She examined her eyes in the mirror. Any sign of her inward turmoil? Nope.

Good. She was ready to go. Maybe. Deep breath. Let it out slow. Now she was ready.

Maybe.

"Ugh!" She spun from the mirror and marched out of her bedroom and down the hall to find Cole still on the couch in the den, head back against the cushion, eyes closed. She paused while the breath whooshed from her lungs and she simply watched him. And for one magical moment, she let the past and all of her suppressed feelings wash over her. Then she grabbed them and stuffed them back into the little emotional box labeled "Cole—Do Not Open" and cleared her throat.

He blinked, then rubbed his face. "Sorry, it's been a while since I've had a good night's sleep."

"It's okay. Glad my couch is comfortable enough for a catnap."

He rose. "It was, and now I feel good as new."

"You find Butler?"

"Yep. He's at Freedom Franks and Burgers."

"Oh, I love that place. I haven't eaten yet. I want a freedom frank."

"For breakfast?"

She looked at her phone. "For an early lunch." She waved to the door. "After you. I'll arm the system."

COLE HEARD KENZIE'S PHONE ping just as they turned into the parking lot of the restaurant. He chose a spot at the back when he spotted Butler's truck near the entrance. "I'm going to slip in through the kitchen and see if I can spot him in the dining room without him seeing me," he told Kenzie. "Want to try and do the same from the front?"

"Yep." She started for the door.

"Hey, Kenz?"

She turned, eyebrows raised. "Yes?"

"Keep your phone handy, I might need to text you."

"It's always handy." But she patted it in her back pocket, checking to make sure it was there, and he smirked before heading to the back entrance.

He'd been in the restaurant numerous times and was even on a first-name basis with the owner. The team often came here to unwind after a stressful day. Or even a not-so-stressful one. So it wasn't surprising that Butler would choose this restaurant to meet someone for a meal.

Cole slipped into the kitchen and found Mrs. Polly at the stove like always. She turned, sweat beading on her smooth dark forehead. "Cole?"

"Hey. Sorry. Just taking a little shortcut. I need to look into the dining room and check on something without that something seeing me."

She frowned and placed her hands on her slender hips. "Okay. Go on." He never failed to wonder how someone could own a restaurant and cook like her and still weigh a hundred and thirty at a max.

He walked to the door that would take him from the kitchen into the dining area. A waitress balancing a tray filled with steaming burgers, fried chicken, and the famous freedom hot dogs swept past him. The aromas lingered behind her, and his stomach growled.

Once she was through, he caught the door before it could swing shut and peered out into the room. The tables were full, with customers in the waiting area just inside the front door. Butler sat in the second booth to the left of the hostess station. Opposite him was another man, but his back was to Cole. He texted Kenzie.

You see them? You recognize the guy he's with?

Three little dots appeared.

No, and I can't move without him seeing me.

All right, how about that early lunch?

What? You're serious?

We're here all the time. You go on in and grab a table. I'll head back and make an entrance in the front door to meet you.

Um . . . okay. So we're just having lunch and we just happen to run into Butler and his buddy. Do I have that right?

You're brilliant.

Okie doke, heading in.

He whipped back through the kitchen and stepped through the front door just in time to see Kenzie being led to a table. He followed, glancing left at Butler's table, and finally got a glimpse of the other guy.

And whoa. Oscar Woodruff?

He slid into the booth, still unnoticed by either man deep in conversation. *Serious* conversation. "To the exclusion of all else" kind of conversation.

"Wonder what that's all about?" Kenzie murmured.

"It's like you read my mind."

"It's not so hard to do sometimes."

The waitress took their drink order and left. He glanced at Kenzie. "You flashed your badge at the hostess to get bumped to the front of the line, didn't you?"

"Guilty. Told her we were watching someone. Someone who was not dangerous or a threat in any way, just someone we were keeping an eye on. She was thrilled to help."

"Someone who wants to help a cop? That's refreshing."

"Her father's a cop."

He smiled.

"What?" she asked.

"How do you do that?"

"Do what?"

"You're like best friends with her from the time it takes to walk from the hostess station to the table."

"Not best friends exactly. She just volunteered the information when I told her what I needed."

"Everyone talks to you." He eyed her. "Why is that?"

She slid a glance at Butler's table, then reconnected with him. "Not everyone."

"Yeah."

"You see who he's with."

"I do."

"I thought he quit law enforcement for personal reasons a few months ago."

"Yeah." Cole rubbed his jaw. "He did, but he's coming back. It was more of a sabbatical than a quit."

"Oh, okay, I'm glad to hear that." She narrowed her eyes at him. "What is it? Tell me."

"You know how I said the SWAT position was between you and another guy?"

"Yes."

"Oscar Woodruff is the other guy."

NINETEEN

Kenzie sucked in a hard breath just as Butler looked up, his eyes landing on hers. He flinched and immediately swung his attention to Cole.

Anger flashed across his face for a brief second before it was gone, and he stood to make his way over to their table. "Garrison. King."

"Butler," Cole said. "This is a surprise."

The man flushed. "I didn't lie about a family emergency. You know Woodruff is like a brother to me. He's having a tough time"—his accusing gaze landed on Kenzie, then flicked back to Cole—"and asked me to meet him. ASAP. I told him I could meet him here since it's not too far from HQ. I was going to take the rest of the day to visit my dad. He's not doing so great either."

Cole frowned. "You never said anything."

Butler shrugged, looked at Kenzie, then away again. "I try to keep my personal and professional business separate. Talk to you later, okay?"

"Sure."

Kenzie kept her mouth shut. Butler walked back to his table, and Cole rubbed his chin. "Well, that went better than I thought it would."

"But?"

"But I find it odd he took half a day to meet with the guy who was your competition for the SWAT position."

"You think he's trying to get rid of me on behalf of Woodruff—out of some sense of loyalty to a friend who got beat out of a job he wanted?"

"I won't say it didn't cross my mind."

The waitress reappeared and they gave their order.

Kenzie sat back. "Now what?"

"Well, we keep an eye on Butler for sure. In the meantime, I have a little project I'm working on."

She raised a brow at him. "What's that?"

"You might think it's stupid," he hedged. The look of uncertainty on his face floored her.

"Why would you think that?"

"Past experience," he muttered, then shrugged. "Okay, so . . . uh . . . I want to give Micah and his buddies a basketball court."

"Oh." Past experience? Had to be Tracy. "A basketball court?"

"Not what you thought I was going to say?"

"No, but that's a fabulous idea."

He blinked, then a slow smile curved his lips. "You really think so?"

"Yes, so why do you have that silly smile on your face?"

"Silly?"

"Or something. Regardless, why the smile?"

"I don't know. I guess I just didn't know what you'd think about that. I'm going to have to pay for it myself out of pocket, but it's something I want to do."

"I can pitch in some." She could always wait to replace the plumbing in the guest bathroom.

He frowned. "I didn't tell you that to get money out of you."

"Didn't think you did. It's a great cause and I'd love to be a part of it."

"Really?"

"Of course. The team probably would too, if you asked."

"I hate to ask them since they've already given for the groceries. I don't want them to feel obligated—or pressured in any way."

"So, ask them privately and give them permission to say no."

He pursed his lips. "Not a bad idea. You mind if I get this started?" He held up his phone.

"Go for it."

Their food arrived and Kenzie enjoyed the savory flavors while they discussed the logistics of how to replace the court without a ton of expense. "I got it," Cole said. "There's a guy in my church who does reno stuff. I'll check with him."

The excitement in his voice made her smile, and her eyes lingered on his face while he was focused on his phone. Longing, swift and sharp, pierced her and she swallowed a gasp. *Stop it. He's not for you.* But she couldn't help the little question that snuck into her subconscious. *Why not?*

Just as she washed the food down with a swig of her tea, her phone pinged with a text from Tabitha. "Well, she's no help."

Cole looked up. "Couldn't find anything on Cliff?"

"No. Said all of his old files are in the document room and look to be in order. Even the accident file is there."

"So he made a copy of everything before filing the false report."

"Which doesn't help much, does it?"

"Nope."

Butler chose that moment to slide out of the booth and wave to them. Woodruff looked over and saluted Cole. His eyes landed briefly on Kenzie, and he gave her a short nod with a faint frown. Then he aimed himself toward the door.

"Wow," she said. "He didn't look too happy."

"Nope. And neither is Butler if the look on his face is any indication." He eyed her. "What are you going to do the rest of the day?"

She tossed enough cash to cover her meal and a generous tip onto the table and stood. "We're going to follow them."

He added more cash and joined her. "My thoughts exactly."

They hurried out of the restaurant and climbed into Cole's 4Runner. "Where'd he go?" she asked.

"Not sure." Cole checked his phone and frowned. "He cut off his location."

"What? Well, that's not sketchy at all."

"What is he doing?" Cole mumbled the words under his breath, and Kenzie didn't bother answering.

"You think he knows we tracked him to the restaurant?"

"A guilty person would wonder."

"And a guilty person would turn off his location."

Cole sighed, cranked the vehicle, and pulled out into the street. "We'll try this way, heading back to headquarters. I want to give him the benefit of the doubt. All of this 'evidence'—or whatever you want to call it—is circumstantial. There could be a reasonable explanation behind it all."

"Like he's in an area without a signal?"

"Yeah. He said he told Woodruff to meet him at that location because it was close to HQ, but why did it matter if he was taking the rest of the day off?"

"Maybe taking the rest of the day off was a last-minute thing?"

"Hm. Maybe."

A motorcycle whipped past them, the rider leaning into the wind.

"If I didn't want to find Butler, I'd pull him over," Cole said. The 4Runner shuddered and tilted, then Kenzie heard the thwack of a flat tire rotating against the asphalt. "Ugh, seriously?" Cole groaned and pulled to the side of the road. He got out and Kenzie joined him. They stood there, staring at the flat. "I hate to admit this, but I have no idea how to change a tire."

She choked. "What? You can't be serious."

He shrugged. "I've never had a flat before."

She couldn't help it—she gaped.

He laughed. "I'm sure I can figure it out, I've just never had to before."

Kenzie shook her head. "Okay, the tire is underneath the car so you have to get the tools out and use the doohickey to remove the spare. Then you take the other tire off, put the good tire on, and drive to a service station, where they either patch the old tire or you spend a fortune on a new one."

His lips quirked into a sideways smile. "Thank you, Google."

He grabbed the tools from the small storage area in the rear. Once he had the two pieces of the thin rod put together, he turned and opened his mouth to say something. Kenzie saw his eyes widen and he dove for her.

Cole's shoulder caught her in her midsection. Pain arced, but she also heard the crack of a high-powered rifle and the shattering of glass just as she hit the asphalt.

"Get under the car!"

Still gasping for breath, she rolled under the 4Runner and Cole dashed behind it.

Kenzie finally managed to fill her lungs. "I'll call 911!" She pulled out her phone. "Shots fired," she said, then rattled off their location. "Officers need backup. Now!"

Behind her she could hear Cole speaking on the phone as well. She waited for the next shot, hyperaware that the bullet had been meant for her, and if Cole hadn't tackled her, she'd most likely be dead.

She scooted to the other side and came up next to Cole. "Backup's on the way."

"I called too."

"What tipped you off? What'd you see?"

"A motorcycle parked just a little ways ahead with no rider. It looked very out of place to me, especially since it looks like the same one that buzzed us. Then there was a flash beyond the tree line. It spooked me."

"Well, I'm very grateful you were spooked."

She peered around the back of the 4Runner just in time to see a figure, rifle strapped to his back, dart to the motorcycle and hop on.

It wasn't going to work, but . . . "Stop!" The engine roared and

Cole ran past her, aimed his weapon, then lowered it when the bike rounded the next curve.

COLE SPUN TO RUN BACK to Kenzie. She leaned against the 4Runner and pressed a hand to her side while the other hand still gripped the phone. "They're on the way. I gave the direction he was traveling, so we'll see. They're sending a chopper."

"Good. How's your side?"

"Painful, but not ripped open or anything. I'm good."

"Sorry I had to hit you so hard. I didn't mean to, I just reacted."

"Don't worry about it. I can recover quickly from this pain. Might not get the chance with a bullet."

"Right." He walked to the rear of the vehicle and squatted next to the tire. "It's cut. Big enough to let the air out pretty quick, small enough to allow us to get away from the center of town."

"The guy on the motorcycle obviously followed us from the restaurant," she said, her eyes narrowing. "Butler has a bike."

"Yeah, but I doubt he'd use his own to try and commit murder."

"True, but he knows how to handle one. And he has access to a high-powered rifle."

"So do a lot of people."

"True."

"Look, I'm not saying it wasn't him, I just . . ."

"Want to give him the benefit of the doubt."

"Yeah."

She pursed her lips. "Fine. I get it." She brushed the debris from her jeans as backup pulled in behind them.

Thirty minutes later, they were in the back of a squad car, heading toward Kenzie's home. James had promised he and Cowboy would bring Cole a rental—another 4Runner, please. In the meantime, Cole had no plans to let Kenzie out of his sight from now on. "I think you should lay low. Work on your father's cold case. But stay out of sight."

She stilled and kept her gaze on the window. Then, when he thought she wasn't going to answer, she turned. "Would you do that?"

Would he? Probably not.

"He was definitely aiming for me, wasn't he?"

"I'd say so."

She narrowed her eyes. "I'm not quitting. At least I don't want to. I don't want to give him the satisfaction."

"I get that. Though if you quit, and he knows it, he may have what he wanted and disappear."

"Never to be heard from again? I don't think so. I want him. I want to look him in the eye and tell him he doesn't get to be the killer bully."

He could see her doing just that.

"And what's to say that he'll stop coming after me should I concede? I mean, it's not like he's going to keep his word and leave me alone if I quit."

"Very true."

"But I don't want to be a danger to others." She sighed. "Have you talked to the commander?"

"He said it's up to you."

She hesitated with another long silence that lasted until the officer pulled into her drive. Then she turned to Cole. "I want to ask the team what they think."

"That could really go either way, Kenz."

"I know, but they have enough to worry about with the job itself. And I know that I can be a distraction all by myself. But if I'm a bigger distraction than usual—simply because they're afraid each time I'm with them that they're going to be attacked by the person after me, then . . ." She bit her lip. "I can't do that to them without running it by them. And I think it needs to come from you. They'll be honest if they don't have to look me in the eye."

He nodded. "All right. Let's get inside and I'll give them a call."

TWENTY

Once they were inside, the officer pulled around to the front of her home and took up guard duty. Kenzie went to the kitchen while Cole went to the den and placed a call to the team. She really didn't want to hear the conversation and was mentally preparing herself to take an extended leave until the guy was caught.

While he spoke via what sounded like a Zoom call, she put together a snack of cheese and crackers, tuna, ham, turkey, and crostini. It would hold them until they could order in some decent food. Like steak and potatoes.

He stepped into the kitchen just as she put the charcuterie board on the table. "Looks great."

"I don't cook a lot, but I can make a mean board." She shrugged. "I needed something to do while I waited to hear my fate."

"The guys said they didn't want you to quit. That you should stay where you are and fight back."

She stilled, her eyes on his. "And you had no influence over that decision?"

"None. Told them you said it should be up to them."

"And you were able to get ahold of Butler?"

"He answered my call, surprisingly enough. Guess being the boss

192

still pulls some weight. Anyway, he was on board, believe it or not. Reluctantly, and the last one to agree, but he did."

"Hm. Well, if he's the one trying to kill me, I can't see him going against the team and looking too obvious."

"He's been very vocal about how he feels about you on the team, so this just makes me wonder what he's up to. But at least with him close by, we'll be able to keep an eye on him."

"I suppose."

"So, that's settled. What's next?"

"Cleaning out the storage room and ordering a pizza?"

He nodded. "We'll get enough for James and Cowboy too."

"Perfect."

When the guys got there, the pizza arrived seconds later, carried by Kristine. When Lainie and Jesslyn and the new detective, Nathan, joined them, Kenzie smiled. She should have known. This was what they did for one another. What they'd done for Lainie when she'd needed it and now they were doing it for her. She had her people, and that knowledge finally sank in. It was almost more than she could process. So she smiled through the threat of tears. "I don't even know what to say."

"I do," Cole said. "Who wants to bless it?"

Once they'd stuffed themselves on pizza, Cole shot Lainie and James a sideways look. "Anyone up for a game of Scrabble?"

Kenzie's eyes widened and she groaned. "Why would you even bring that up? You know she'll win. She studies the dictionary."

"Oh, I don't know. I think she's been too busy planning a wedding to worry about all that."

Kenzie looked at a radiant Lainie and grinned. "All right, I'm in. Jesslyn?"

"Why not? We can team up and work together. I'm on Lainie's team."

Laughter rang out and Kenzie pulled in an emotional breath. She really needed to get herself under control. What in the world was wrong with her? She never cried. Crying had gotten her mocked by her father and brothers. Crying never solved anything. But happy tears? Maybe that was okay.

She glanced in the direction of the storage room and decided that it could wait. She'd rather play Scrabble, even though she'd probably get beat.

As though her thoughts were prophetic, she leaned back two hours later and threw her hands up. "I give. Lainie is still the champion."

"Hey," James protested. "I helped."

She laughed. "If you say so."

He kissed his fiancée's forehead and grinned. Then turned serious. He nodded to Cole, and Cole nudged Kenzie. "Can we talk in the sunroom?"

"Sure."

Kenzie followed them, ignoring the questioning looks from the others, but over his shoulder, Cole simply said, "Business for a moment."

Jesslyn shot her a thumbs-up and the others aimed themselves toward the kitchen. Kenzie knew it would be spotless in no time.

"What's up?" she asked.

"I spoke to Commander Hill and we have a plan," James said.

Oh boy. "Okay."

"Your house is the new HQ if you're up for it."

"Um . . . sorry, what?"

He laughed while her mind spun. "We're going to base the on-duty unit here out of your house. That way you're protected at all times. If we get a call, the off-duty guys will be here within minutes."

"But . . ."

"We'll keep everything—well, most everything—in the basement. Cole said it was secure. No separate exit, but it won't take us long to put one in."

She gaped. "You want to put a door in my basement?"

"It'd be a good safety feature to have regardless."

"Uh, okay. Yeah, that would be fine." She frowned. "And you're sure the guys are okay with this?" And what if it was Butler who was out to do her in? She'd be letting the fox right into the henhouse. She searched Cole's gaze.

"Keep your enemies closer," he said.

So. He was thinking the same thing. And as long as she was careful, it could work. She nodded. "All right."

"Great, I'll get it set up. It won't be official, of course. There's nothing that goes on record about this, but we'll hang out here, and when we get a call, we'll respond."

"And having Dolly outside will be a big deterrent to anyone who might decide to attack you here," James said.

"Right. Dolly." She laughed. "Okay then. I guess we'll see how this works out."

TWENTY-ONE

LAKE CITY STATE HOSPITAL
OCTOBER 1947

Eliza paced the small room, her mind spinning, her lungs near to bursting. Her father was coming today. According to Dr. King, she could very well go home in just a few hours if she could convince her father that she'd seen the error of her ways and was ready to be the good daughter he expected her to be.

Anger flared and she shoved it away. "Think of William," she whispered. "Think of William."

A knock sounded and she bit off a nervous screech. Heart pounding, she waited for the door to open. Betsy slipped inside.

Eliza ran to her friend and wrapped her in a hug. "How did you get in here?"

"It helps to have friends in high places."

"You and Dr. King are getting awfully close, aren't you?"

Betsy blushed. "We are." Then she scowled. "I just need that awful Dr. Stephen to leave me alone. He is constantly making excuses to see me whenever I come visit. He even showed up at my home the other night."

"What?"

"He did." She pulled Eliza to the bed and they sat. "He wanted to court me, and I told him I could never go out with someone who allowed things to go on in this place like he does. The conditions are atrocious, and I told him so."

"What did he say?"

"He left in a hurry, but said . . ." She bit her lip.

"Said what?"

"Nothing. It's not important."

"Betsy, what did he say?"

"He said you had it very good in here, and that if I didn't want that to change, I'd learn to be a bit nicer to him."

Eliza gasped. "He didn't!"

"He did."

"What did Dr. King say about that?"

"I haven't told him. Yet."

"But you will, right?"

"If necessary."

"I've noticed I have it better than others," Eliza said. "It's so overcrowded, and I don't even have a roommate like everyone else."

Betsy shuddered. "Be glad. I can't believe some of the things I've seen. I've talked to some of the other patients and it's terribly tragic. Someone needs to do something. These people are treated ghastly and it's not a bit their fault they're here."

"I agree. I think my father paid for me to be alone in here. I've also noticed that every time I try to talk to or make friends with another resident, a staff member is quick to intervene and engage me in conversation or try to distract me. He's paying to keep me isolated and from talking much." She twisted her fingers together. "He's afraid I may say something about that night."

"Well, he couldn't pay to keep you from George—er, Dr. King."

"No, of course not. But he thinks he has Dr. King in his pocket." She bit her lip. "He doesn't, does he?"

Betsy gripped her fingers. "He does not. George is an upstanding and wonderful man. He cares deeply for the patients here and has even gone toe to toe with Dr. Stephen about everything from the nasty food to the insufficient care. Dr. Stephen is not too fond of George for bringing him to the attention of the board."

"But you are," Eliza said with a slight smile. Goodness, what would she do without Betsy's regular visits? She'd go absolutely mad and be here forever.

Betsy glanced at the little gold watch on her wrist. "I've got to go. I can't let your father catch me here."

Eliza embraced her friend once more, and Betsy slipped out as silently as she'd slipped in. Eliza dropped onto the bed, pressed her palms to her heated cheeks, took a deep breath, and forced herself to put the memories from the night her father tried to kill her from her mind. And William. The thought of him alone, possibly wondering where she was, squeezed her heart nearly in two.

She grabbed her hidden journal and pen and started writing, desperate to get her thoughts down, mapping out what she'd say, how she'd say it, and dreaming of being reunited with the man she loved.

Ten minutes later, the door opened once more and Bart Crane stepped through. He was six feet tall and had developed a slight paunch in the three months she'd been gone. His hair had thinned and he had more wrinkles around his eyes and mouth. She stood and faced him, then dropped her eyes to the floor. It would be easier to lie if she didn't have to look at him. "Hello, Father."

"Eliza. Dr. King says you're ready to come home."

"I am."

He walked toward her and she refused to shrink from him. "Why?"

She stilled. "Why what?"

"Why do you want to come home?"

Confused, she remained silent, unsure what she was supposed to say to that. "I . . . I . . . it's my home."

"What about what happened the night that landed you here? I can't go through that again."

She bit her lip and forced herself to look up. To meet his gaze and furrow her brow. "I'm sorry, Papa." She nearly gagged on the childhood nickname she'd used for him for years, before reverting to the more formal "Father." "I don't really remember that night." She lifted her wrists and looked at them as though thoroughly befuddled. "They said I tried to hurt myself, but I don't want to do that anymore. Doesn't that mean I'm ready to come home?"

"I see." He cleared his throat. "Very well. I have a young man who I want to introduce to you. Are you willing to dine with him and consider him as a possible beau?"

Eliza suppressed a shudder. *You can do this. Do it for William.* "I . . . I mean, if he's willing to consider me after . . ." She waved a hand at the room.

"He doesn't know about this, and you'll not speak of it. Once we're gone from here, this place and everyone in it ceases to exist. Is that clear?"

"Yes. Of course. I have no wish to rehash this nightmare." She swallowed the bile at the back of her throat and went to him to wrap her arms around his waist like she used to do as a child. Before she knew what a monster he was. "Thank you, Papa," she whispered.

His hand rested on her shoulder before he set her away from him. "I brought you some clothes and personal items." He opened the door and pulled in a bag from the hallway. "Take this and make yourself presentable and we will get out of here. I'll be waiting just outside. And hurry. The smell is enough to make someone with the strongest constitution gag."

He left and Eliza let her shoulders fall. Tears gathered and she wanted nothing more than to throw herself on the bed and weep. But now she had a part to play. A script to follow until she could find a way to get to William.

Be strong, my love, I'm coming.

TWENTY-TWO

PRESENT DAY

Cole shut his laptop and rubbed his eyes. Three quiet days had passed since they'd implemented the plan, and Kenzie seemed to be feeling back to normal. They'd had two legitimate calls in the three days, and Magic Man had taken the call that was over two hours from Kenzie's house. They'd alternated "bodyguard duty" for Kenzie and it had worked well. No attacks on the team had occurred, but Cole wasn't ready to drop his guard. He just didn't know where to look next. The guy was lying low, which was good. But not.

At least they'd all been able to work on other cases they had to stay on top of outside of their SWAT duties. Cole had made great progress on several and thought he'd be closing them out before too long.

Unfortunately, that didn't include Kenzie's father's cold case, and the man had been about as accusing and belligerent as one could be. Kenzie had finally quit looking at her phone. More so than usual.

"You're thinking hard there, my friend," James said around a bite of a chicken biscuit. Cowboy and Greene had ridden up the road to a fast-food place and returned with breakfast.

"Just can't believe how quiet it's been."

"You trying to jinx it?"

"I don't believe in that and neither do you."

"Nope, l don't."

Footsteps pounded up the stairs and Butler joined them at the table, grabbing two of the biscuits from the plate. "All the weapons are clean, I changed the oil in Dolly, I've even shined my boots." He sighed and leaned back to stare at the ceiling. "Can we get any more bored?"

"Be grateful for it and work on the cases stacked on your desk—or laptop."

"I've done that too, of course. Closed three of them with about a hundred phone calls and sent officers to make the arrests. Where are the other guys?"

Greene and Otis chose that moment to come in the front door after a short run. Otis headed straight for his water bowl while Greene grabbed a bottle of water from the fridge and three biscuits from the plate.

Kenzie walked in, looked around, took a deep breath, and did a one-eighty. Cole rose and followed her into the sunroom—the only unoccupied space in her house. She sat on the wicker sofa and pulled her knees up to rest her chin on them.

He shut the door behind him. "How are you feeling?"

"Antsy. 1 have too much protection. He's not going to make a move with all of you here. The hospital is wondering when I'm going to come back to work and 1 don't have an answer, which sits well with no one. I haven't left my house in three days and I'm about to climb a wall."

"Well, you got most of the storage room cleaned out and we hauled everything off for you. So that's progress, right?"

She shot him a small smile tinged with weariness. "Yes. True. I just have a few more boxes and my grandmother's trunk to go through."

And she needed a distraction. "Well, the next call is yours if you want it. You're officially back on duty."

Her eyes widened. "1 want it."

She said it so fast he laughed. "Okay then, it's yours." He turned serious. "But you're right. He's not going to make a move as long as you're holed up here. We'll take all the precautions we can, but you're going back to work."

"Thank God," she whispered.

"In the meantime, you want to go get the rest of that room done?"

She looked up and wrinkled her nose at him, and his mind snagged on how cute she was. Then he struck that thought away immediately. He would not notice the fact that she was cute, attractive, funny, highly intelligent—

"Sure, why not?"

"Right. Let's do this."

They walked back into the den to find Buzz on the couch. If he couldn't go back to work yet, he was going to be a bodyguard. Butler had joined him and the two were playing cards. Cole smiled. Kenzie might not realize it, but the team had her back whether she wanted it or not. He glanced at Butler. Well, most of the team. Butler had been cool to Kenzie and hadn't mentioned the lunch with Woodruff, but he'd basically kept his distance and had little interaction with her. If he was trying to kill her, he was biding his time.

The thought did not comfort him. "Kenzie's back in the rotation, guys. Next call is hers."

Buzz gave them a thumbs-up. Butler sighed.

"I'm going to help her in the storage room a bit, then we can figure out the rest of the day." He followed Kenzie into the storage area and smiled. "It's almost empty. What will you do with the space?"

"I'm not sure yet. I'm thinking about moving my workout room up here and turning the basement into a little Airbnb or something now that I have the separate entrance you guys put in. It's already got the bathroom down there and space for a small kitchenette." She shrugged. "Just a thought."

"That's a great idea."

She walked to the trunk and ran a hand over it. "This was Grandma Betsy's. When we moved her out, she brought me in here and said she'd put some stuff inside that I might find interesting. I just haven't had a chance—or made the time, really—to go through it."

"You want to do that while I tackle this box?" He set the nearest one on the card table.

"Sure."

She flipped the latch on the trunk and lifted the lid.

KENZIE LOOKED into the trunk and drew in a soft breath.

"What is it?" Cole asked.

"Her wedding dress. It's in plastic and perfectly preserved." She ran her fingers over the pearl-covered front.

He walked over to look down. "How awesome. Now you don't have to go buy one."

She shot him a look. "Um, I wasn't looking for one."

His cheeks went red and he huffed a laugh. "I didn't mean now. One day, though. Don't you want to get married?"

She wasn't going there. "Maybe. I don't know. When I was a teen, I told my mother I was never getting married for a lot of reasons. Not much has changed since then."

"You're kidding, right?"

She tapped his chin to close his mouth. "Stop. Why do you look so stunned?" When he didn't answer, she frowned. "Why? Do you want to get married?"

"Yep. Sure do."

"What happened to you're not looking for romance?"

"I still have dreams like anyone else. I just . . . have to get past some stuff. Doesn't stop me from enjoying an evening out with someone." She paused. "Tracy really did a number on you, didn't she?"

"Yeah." The flush in his cheeks faded and a sadness she'd never seen before flashed across his face. "I hate to admit it, but she did. I know not everyone is like her, but it's hard letting your guard down after something like that." He shrugged. "I just have to figure out how to trust again. I think the right person will help me overcome that." He smiled. "But yeah, I'd like to get married, have a family.

Just don't know if or when that will happen. Doesn't stop me from wanting it, though."

"With the right person."

"Of course." The look in his eyes sent her heart thudding, and that was the last thing she needed. Right?

But she had to admit the thought of Cole married to someone other than her made her stomach hurt. She cleared her throat. "Well, I wish you luck in the hunt for the right person." She went back to the trunk and spotted an old book. "Speaking of a hunt. Look what I found. It's a journal. Maybe my grandmother's?" She let it fall open carefully, noting the pages had yellowed and become brittle with time. But they were perfect and still readable. "Wow. I can't wait to read this."

Her work phone pinged. Cole's did too. He grabbed it. "We've got a call." He raised a brow. "At the abandoned mental hospital."

She set the book on the card table for later. "Let's grab the gear. I'm ready."

With Cowboy at the wheel of Dolly, they left her home and headed toward the hospital. Butler groaned. "I hate places like this."

Kenzie shook her head and bit her tongue.

"Okay, folks," Cole said, "looks like drug dealers have moved into the hospital and there are reports of shots fired. Officers are en route, we're simply backup in case of trouble."

They left the main part of Lake City and headed up the mountain road. Cowboy took the turns tight and with a skill Kenzie envied. Her medical kit was tucked under her feet and her weapons loaded and ready to go should she be called to use them. Today there was no heckling, which she found interesting, but she wasn't about to question it. Her side still ached but had healed enough that she was confident it wouldn't slow her down much. If at all.

By the time they arrived, officers on the scene had surrounded the place. Cowboy parked at the edge and all but Kenzie climbed out. Cole was already in touch with the chief of police, Rav Badami, who was on-site. He walked over to the man, and Kenzie could hear

Cole through the comms as she grabbed her medical kit and stepped out of Dolly. "Any contact?" he asked.

"No. We're going to let you breach at this point. We can't find any sign of life and definitely no shots fired. At least not at us."

An instant breakout of goose bumps pebbled her arms. "Cole, this doesn't feel right. Feels like last time. This is an ambush. Tell everyone to take cover. Take cover!"

Her team moved, officers scrambled, and her shout ended in a spate of gunfire from the building.

"Return fire and cover us," Cole told Badami. "Team! As soon as the gunfire from the building stops, go!"

Bullets from the officers' weapons peppered in the direction of the shooter, who ceased firing, and Cole led the way through the main entrance of the hospital.

Kenzie had taken cover inside Dolly, ears tuned to what was happening in the building, eyes scanning the outside. The hospital was spread over a thousand acres, but the main building where the action was taking place was just ahead. It curved into a wide U-shape with the covered drive. On either side of the drive, the overgrown courtyard sprawled. In its heyday, it would have been quite a sight. Today it was falling apart and looked like it was destined to be a battle zone.

She saw a figure. "There! Movement in the window on the third floor, second room from the end." She grabbed her weapon and exited Dolly. The figure pulled away from the window and ran to the next room. Then the next, glancing out the window each time. "Keep going, he's headed for the east wing exit, I think. Who's on the blueprints?"

"I've got them up in here." Badami's voice came through the comms. "Officers are moving to cover that exit."

Kenzie darted in that direction as well since she was closer. She ran across the broken drive and toward the fire escape on the side, stopping to peer around the corner just as the door opened and the figure started down. "Freeze!" She stepped out and took aim. "Drop your weapon now!" He was almost to the bottom when he vaulted over the wrought iron railing and hit the ground with a thud and a yell, his rifle skidding from his fingers. He rolled to his feet as the other officers closed in behind Kenzie. She leapt up and rounded the bottom of the stairs to go after him. "Get the rifle!" She threw the words over her shoulder to the officers behind her, then turned and yelled, "You! Stop!"

He ran faster. Naturally. The rest of the team was coming in from different directions, but she was in the lead and she really wanted to get this guy now.

But he had a motorcycle waiting. She recognized it as the same one the shooter who'd punctured Cole's tire had been on. "No!"

But he was already riding toward the back of the property. "He's heading north," she said. The brick wall that used to run the perimeter was spotty now, broken in many places, but he wasn't going for that. What was he doing? Surely he'd have an escape route planned, but he seemed to be driving in a random pattern through the grounds that had become an overgrown jungle. A chopper roared overhead, sweeping the area.

Kenzie stopped running to watch the shooter, but when he took a sharp right turn, she sped up again. "He's turned now. Going east again." The chopper banked at her words.

And then the guy—and the motorcycle—disappeared.

"What in the world?" She skidded to a halt.

"What is it?" Cole asked, racing up next to her.

"He just vanished. Dropped into the ground. I don't even hear the bike anymore."

Together, joined by the others who'd caught up with them at this point, they followed the motorcycle tracks until they stopped amid the thick, overgrown bushes. "There." She pointed. The ground gave way to a sloping drive that led to a tunnel. "Seriously?"

Cole shrugged. "Let's go." They descended into the place, Maglites leading the way in the darkness.

Kenzie grimaced. "I hate this kind of stuff. Dark places, tight places. Places with no exit."

LYNETTE EASON

"When was this hospital built?" Greene asked.

"Early 1900s?"

"It's an air raid shelter," Cole murmured. "Probably had the ramp for the gurneys."

"I think I remember hearing about this," Kenzie said. "They built it after Pearl Harbor. No one knew if they were going to be next."

Cowboy stepped around her. "It's huge."

"Would have to be," she said. "They had over two thousand patients back then."

"Well, it's big," Cole said, "but not that big. There's no way they would have fit everyone in here even if the ones who cared fought to do so."

"No," she said, her voice soft, "but the staff would fit. Not sure why they'd build a ramp if they weren't going to save the patients, though."

He blew out a low breath. "Yeah. I can't believe all of the caretakers were bad, but it seems like patients were really low priority."

"Overcrowding, experimental treatment. The stuff nightmares are made of."

They hurried through the shelter until they came upon the motorcycle leaning against the wall. A crude exit had been dug through the wall, slanting up, then with a ladder leading to the top, allowing the shooter to climb out. "Well, that's not original to the structure," Cowboy said from behind.

"Nope, but maybe Otis can track him down now that the guy's on foot?"

Greene nodded. "The bike can be the scent article." He pointed and Otis's ears pricked. "Otis, scent."

The dog went to the bike and did what he did best. He barked once, then padded to the ladder, his nose up and quivering.

"All right, everyone," Greene said, "guess we're going up." Man and dog climbed.

Once Otis and Greene were up top, Kenzie turned to Cole. "I guess we are too."

"After you."

Kenzie climbed and pulled herself out of the shelter to find herself on the other side of the fence and next to a road.

Otis was pacing, sniffing, and searching. He took off east and Greene followed behind him. "Guy's on foot," Greene said through the comms. "I don't know if we'll catch him, but I'll follow as far as Otis'll take me."

"We're right behind you," Cole said. They all trailed Otis down the road, loping along while the dog zigzagged his way into the old cemetery across the street from the hospital. The dog finally stopped and sat, looking at Greene for his next command.

"The guy's gone," Greene said. "He must have had transportation stashed around here. Another bike or a car."

"Or a driver waiting to pick him up."

Butler raked a hand over his head. "I've about had enough of this guy."

Kenzie looked at him and raised a brow. "I know the feeling."

COLE DIDN'T KNOW WHAT TO THINK. Obviously Butler wasn't the shooter in this instance, but it didn't mean he wasn't working with someone.

Like Oscar Woodruff?

They finished up at the scene and headed back to HQ. While Kenzie's home was a fine place to wait for a call or to work on a current case, HQ was more convenient if they could use it.

But all the way back, Cole couldn't get the thought out of his head. Butler and Woodruff working together to get Kenzie off the team?

It made sense, unfortunately, but he had no proof, and a lunch meeting between two men known as friends didn't a killer make.

With his thoughts still spinning, he walked into the kitchen to find Butler, Cowboy, and Greene sitting at the table, snacking on chips and sucking down water. "Everything okay?"

"She's got to go, Garrison," Butler said, thumping his water bottle onto the table. "Can't you see that? Her first day back and we're dodging bullets at another fake call. All because she won't back down."

"Would you?" Kenzie asked, stepping into the kitchen.

The room went silent.

Butler flushed, but his eyes glittered. "Yeah. Yes, I would if it meant my leaving was for the good of the team."

Cowboy choked and Greene snorted. Butler turned his glare on each of them, then back to Kenzie.

Kenzie studied him. "No," she said, her voice low, "you wouldn't."

He stood up, stepped forward, and jabbed a finger at her. "Now, look here—"

She swatted his hand away and planted her fists on her hips. "No, *you* look here. You're many things, Butler, but you're not a coward. And you're not a quitter. You have the support of this team and they'd make sure you didn't *have* to quit."

Everyone went still once more. Even Cole wondered where she was going with this.

"That's my point." She drew in a shuddering breath. "I may not like you, but you're my team member, and believe it or not, no matter how you treat me, I'll have your back. And if you could put aside your snark and your prejudice, and whatever else is going on inside you about me being in this position, then you might see that accepting me would be a lot more advantageous than working so hard to be my enemy."

The silence was so thick, Cole was tempted to try the whole "cutting it with a knife" thing just to see what it looked like.

"Hear me out," she said, her voice low, almost vibrating with the intensity of the feeling behind her words, "because I'm only saying this once. If I quit, he wins. If you convince me to quit, you *help* him win." She lifted her chin another notch. "I was under the impression that this topic had been dealt with, that you guys wanted me to stay—or if you didn't *want* me to, you were at least okay with it. But apparently that's not the case. So . . . here's my compromise. If the majority of you feel like I'm putting you all in danger, then I'll take a leave of absence until this guy is stopped. But know this. *I'm not quitting or giving up my spot permanently. Ever.* And nothing you say or do will change that. I'm here for the long haul. Accept that and move on and we might finally be a real team." She looked each man in the eye, ending with Cole. "You can let me know what they decide."

"I can give you my vote right now," Butler said. He turned his scowl on Cole. "You and I both know the position should have gone to Woodruff. She stole it from him and I'm never going to get over that!"

"Shut up!" Cole's shout reverberated and everyone froze. He curled his fingers into fists at his side, ordering himself to stay in control. "Just shut up. You've crossed the line and this is going in your record."

And once again, the room fell silent with Butler glaring at Kenzie. The other men had dropped their eyes. "I'm going to make a couple of phone calls and get my things," Kenzie said. "I need a decision before I leave."

She swept out of the room and Cole crossed his arms, looking at each member. His gaze lingered on Butler, who looked away, a tinge of shame in his eyes. That little bit of remorse gave Cole a fraction of hope.

"Think about what she said and text me your thoughts," Cole said.

Greene shook his head. "Don't have to. She's right and I'll say it here in front of everyone. I don't need any anonymous, snowflake junk. We told you we were fine with her on the team, but I don't think we really were. At least not unanimously. But that girl's got more guts and stubbornness than anyone I've ever met. I like her and I respect her. I vote she stays and we start acting like the team we're supposed to be. That includes you, Butler." He stroked his dog's head. "Now, Otis has business to do. We'll be outside." He clicked to Otis and they headed out the back door into the fenced area behind HQ.

Cowboy nodded. "Ditto what Greene said."

Butler scoffed. "You've got to be kidding me."

"No, not kidding you," Cowboy said. "The division in this team isn't because of her. It's you and your attitude and it's time someone told you that. So, man up, grow up, and let's pull together to help figure out who's trying to kill her. We owe her that."

"We don't owe her squat," Butler said.

Cowboy looked at Cole. "Maybe he's the one who needs to go."

Butler flinched like the man had punched him in the face. "Really?"

"Really." Cowboy's instant—and cold—response obviously took Butler aback. Cole didn't think he'd ever seen the man at a loss for words like he was at that moment.

"While you two work this out," Cole said, "I'm going to call Buzz, James, and Magic Man, fill them in, and get votes. They're still at Kenzie's house holding down the fort and making sure it's a safe place for her. You know, acting like team members would act. So I'll see you all back at her place in a bit."

He left the room and went to find Kenzie.

He searched the living space, the conference room, the computer area, and finally stopped outside the women's bathroom and heard what sounded like crying coming from it. He knocked. "Kenzie? I'm coming in."

"Go away."

"Not a chance." He found her on the bench next to the row of stalls trying to stem the tears. "Aw, Kenz."

He dropped beside her and she swiped her face. "I'm fine. I'm not usually a crier. I just had to let it all out."

"Nothing wrong with crying. I've done it a few times in my life."

She gave a short chuckle and a final sniff. "You shouldn't have told him to shut up."

"I would have told him that, regardless of who he was firing off at." He slid an arm around her shoulders, disregarding the fact that it was probably a bad idea. "Kenzie, the guys are supporting you. They admire you." He told her their responses. "And they mean it this time. It's not just lip service."

"But not Butler." She sighed.

"I think even he may come around if he wants to stay on this team."

"Assuming he's not the one trying to kill me?"

"Yeah."

Another sigh shuddered through her. "I hate giving in to a bully," she whispered. "Butler or the guy causing all of the problems. And if they're one and the same, then . . ."

"I know." He pulled in a breath and dropped his arm. "How'd you like to go visit Oscar Woodruff?"

"And ask him if he's working with Butler to get rid of me?"

"Great minds think alike."

TWENTY-THREE

While Cole drove the rental 4Runner, Kenzie relished the fact that her team had voted for her to stay and stand up to the person trying to force her out. Butler, according to Cole, had scowled and pouted, but hadn't raised any more objections.

Then Cole had called Oscar and asked to see the man ASAP. He was off duty and visiting with his father at Harmony House, the independent living home the man had moved into two months ago.

They parked and made their way to the recreation room to find Oscar and his father engaged in a game of chess. Kenzie blinked at the sight. When Oscar's father served as chief of police, she'd had pretty regular interaction with him until he resigned last year. He'd aged ten years since she last saw him. "How old is Oscar's dad? Same age as mine, right?"

"Not sure. Late fifties, early sixties?"

"And he lives in an independent living home? Interesting."

"Only requirements to live here are that you're fifty-five years old and have the money to pay for it."

She sighed. "I asked Dad about living in a place like this, thought he might be more comfortable, feel more secure, and he nearly bit my head off. Said I was trying to stick him in a home so I didn't have to deal with him anymore."

He sucked in a hard breath. "Kenzie, that's a terrible thing for him to say."

"Yeah, it was pretty terrible to hear. Especially since it wasn't true. I was just worried about him being in that house alone so much. Even though Logan still lives with him, he works long hours. The nurse is only there part of the time, and I thought it would be best if Dad could be around other people. He didn't think so."

"I'm sorry."

She shrugged. The elder Woodruff moved his queen. "Checkmate, my boy."

Oscar laughed. "You're still the champ, Dad." He glanced up and spotted Cole, then his eyes widened slightly when they landed on Kenzie, but he waved them over. "Dad, you remember Kenzie King and Cole Garrison?"

The man went still for a few seconds, then he narrowed his green gaze on Kenzie. "Ah yes, Kenzie King. Of course I remember you. You look more like your mother every year." He paused. "In fact, the resemblance is stunning."

She hoped she concealed her slight flinch. "Thank you."

"It's been twenty years and I still can't believe she's gone some days."

"I know the feeling."

"You know he stole her from me, don't you?" He laughed.

"What?"

"She and I dated before she fell hard for your dad. It wasn't anything too serious, just a couple of dates before we realized we weren't meant to be together. I'd already met my Lydia, Oscar's mother, so I wasn't too upset about it. How's your father doing? Been a while since I've seen him."

"He's doing as well as can be expected." Which wasn't great, now that he thought his wife had been murdered, but she wasn't about to blurt that out. "I could tell him to come by and see you."

The man smiled. "That would be nice. I'd like to see him. We were so competitive in our younger years that it would be great to catch up without all of that between us."

214

"I'll let him know."

Oscar stood, effectively ending the small talk. "Want to walk out to the courtyard and find a place with some privacy? It's hard to talk around here without listening ears. The ones that can still hear anyway." He shot a wry smile at his father, and the man rolled his eyes, waving them toward the door.

"I've got to head to my physical therapy appointment anyway. Stop by and say goodbye before you leave." He grasped his walker and pulled himself to his feet, then shuffled away, looking more like a man twenty years his senior than someone in his early sixties.

Oscar led them outside into the warmth of the afternoon sun, but the breeze was brisk and Kenzie shivered, thankful for her long sleeves and vest. "What happened to your dad?" she asked, not yet ready to get to the point of their visit. "I know he took over the position of chief of police when Bernard Jackson was killed and it was a rough transition, but Dad—all of us really—figured he'd be in that job until they forced him out."

"We all thought that, but . . ." Oscar sighed and scratched his head. "Last year, Dad was in a skiing accident. Blew out his knee. Between surgeries and physical therapy and . . . more, the job got to be too much for him. He finally had to take a leave of absence about six months ago, which turned into . . . this." He waved a hand at the building behind them. "I couldn't believe it when he said he wanted to move in here, but here we are."

"So, the accident was almost a year ago."

"Yeah. He was doing really well, bouncing back and making progress. He even seemed to be thinking better."

"Thinking better?"

The man's lips pursed. "Dad lives in the past more than the present, and I've been worried about dementia or Alzheimer's, but then the accident happened and . . ."

"And?" Cole asked.

Oscar sighed. "He really wanted me on the SWAT team. When that didn't happen, I think it broke his spirit a bit. He just kind of started going downhill, living in the past more, not being as active. Just sad, I guess." He shot Kenzie a sad smile. "But don't think anyone blames you. You deserve the spot."

Well, that took the wind out of her sails. "Uh, thanks."

Cole cleared his throat. "Look, I'm going to have to disagree with you there. Butler has made it clear he doesn't think Kenzie should be on the team. Has he said anything to you?"

Oscar looked away. "All right. Yeah, he's mad she was chosen over me. And he's filled me in on the incidents where someone has tried to hurt—"

"Kill," Cole said.

The man blinked. "Uh, yeah. Kill Kenzie. But he didn't have anything to do with that." His gaze hardened. "And if you think otherwise, then you need to take that up with Butler." Oscar spun on his heel and headed back inside the building.

Kenzie let out a low breath. "Well, that was a bust."

"Maybe. If he's lying, he's good at it."

"If he can help kill someone, lying's probably second nature."

"COME ON," COLE SAID, leading her back to the car. "We'll head back to your place and—" His phone buzzed. "It's Sherry."

She raised a brow. "Maybe she's heard something about Cliff."

"Only one way to find out."

He swiped the screen and put the phone on speaker so Kenzie could listen in. "Hi, Sherry. You're on speaker. I'm here with Kenzie King." He drove away from the assisted-living home and headed toward Kenzie's house.

"Hi, Cole. Kenzie. I just wanted to let you know two things. One, I think someone's following me. And two, I found out that Cliff passed away a week ago."

He exchanged a concerned glance with Kenzie. "Do you think you're in danger?"

"I don't know. I just think someone's watching me. I'm not changing up my routine or acting in any way suspicious as far as I can tell, but I have to admit, it's making me a little nervous."

"Do you need to take a leave of absence and disappear for a while?"

She laughed. "Well, if someone's keeping an eye on me, seems like that might clue them in real quick."

"Agreed, but I don't want anything to happen to you either."

"I know. I appreciate that, but I just wanted you to be aware. Just in case."

Just in case. He grimaced. "Any word on Cliff's wife?"

"No. She sent the text from a burner. I'll admit I tried to trace it. But by then, the phone was disconnected and probably in a trash can somewhere."

Cole pinched the bridge of his nose. "All right. Thanks for letting me know. Stay safe, Sherry. Call me day or night if you need to."

"I will, dear boy. Thanks."

Cole hung up and turned into Kenzie's drive. She blinked at the vehicles in front of her home. Cole chuckled. "Looks like the guys are putting their words into action."

"I don't see Butler's vehicle."

"He's still stewing. Let him."

He followed her inside, and after she greeted the others—and thanked them for showing up—she walked to the storage area and looked around.

"Want to finish this room while we have time?" Cole asked.

She walked over to the journal she'd left on the table. "Actually, I think I just want to curl up in that chair there and read this for a bit."

"Well, I vacuumed it, so you shouldn't have an allergy attack by sitting in it."

She laughed. "I know. Thanks."

He nodded. "All right then. Let me know if I can do anything to help."

She studied him, her eyes soft and . . . secretive. The look dug into the very heart of him and he forced himself not to squirm. "Kenz?"

"I was just thinking. Thank you, Cole, for everything. For standing by me and supporting me—and just . . . doing all things right."

He thought about that moment in the hospital. Not quite all things.

She smiled as though she could read his mind, settled herself into the overstuffed chair, and opened the book.

He turned to leave her alone when she gasped. He spun. "What is it?"

She held the book up. "This isn't my grandmother's journal, it's yours."

"What?" He joined her to look over her shoulder.

Kenzie pointed to the inside cover and he read, "'This journal belongs to Eliza Crane. Please return if found.' Huh. How about that?"

"Your grandmother must have given it to mine, and she kept it all these years." She handed it to him. "I guess I'll give this to you then."

He took it and ran his hand over the cover. "Let's read it together. I'm sure she mentioned your grandma Betsy in it."

Her eyes smiled. "That would be awesome."

He grabbed a chair from under the card table and pulled it around next to her. "All right, let's see what Granny E has to say." He opened the book to the first entry and began reading.

1947. I don't even know where to start. Everything is so fuzzy at the moment, but I feel like if I don't get the thoughts out of my head, it may explode. I've been here at the hospital for two days now and I'm truly living my worst nightmare. The only consolation is that Betsy came to see me and snuck in this journal and pen. I can't say how wonderful it is that she knew I'd need this in order to survive. The screams from last night still echo in my mind. The poor lost souls who cry out for help that is nowhere to be found. So, how did I get here? Why am I here and how do I get out? Please, Jesus, comfort me. I'm terrified.

A tear slipped down Kenzie's cheek and she swiped it away. "That poor woman."

That poor woman had been his grandmother, and his heart pounded in sympathy at all she'd gone through at the hands of the man who was supposed to love and protect her. "Nobody knew how to deal with mental illness back then," he murmured.

"Not sure a lot of people know how to deal with it today."

"True."

"And besides, she wasn't really mentally ill, was she? I remember Grandma Betsy saying Eliza's mind was just fine. It was her father who was the sick one."

"Yeah, but he sure made it seem like she was." He shook his head. "It's hard to believe this was less than a century ago. Seems like it should be much further in the past. Want me to keep reading?"

"Sure."

Nurse Alice is one of the nicer ones here. She apologized for cutting my hair so short in order to get rid of the lice. Who knew an infestation could happen so fast? But they took out the old bed and brought a new one, so maybe Father is pulling some strings even though he's the reason I'm here. I thought I'd have to sleep in crowded conditions, but I'm the only one in the room. Again, probably Father's doing since most every other room is packed to the brim. I doubt he's doing it out of love. Maybe appearances? But he's not telling anyone I'm here, so . . . why? I guess I'll have to figure that out later. The thing that concerns me most is that they tell me I tried to kill myself. But that can't be true despite the wounds on my wrists. I don't want to die. I want to get out of here and find my William and start a new life. But how, when my father holds all the power?

Kenzie looked up at him. "Wow. William was the man your grandmother married, so it seems like she did get out eventually, but in the meantime, wow. It sounds bad."

"Yeah," he whispered.

"Your great-grandfather had a lot of pull, didn't he?"

"From what I understand, he had everyone in his pocket. There wasn't a soul in Lake City who didn't owe him a favor or two."

"And so he could pull strings with the state hospital where he locked up his daughter."

"Sounds like it."

His phone buzzed and chimed, then Kenzie's followed along with the other phones all over the house.

A call.

"Where to this time?" she asked. She shut the journal and set it on the table, pulling her mind from the past to focus on the present.

"The warehouse district. A former employee with a grudge and a gun. Officers are on scene."

"Great. What happened to giving us a heads-up and we plan out everything? All of these last-minute calls are unusual."

"That's because most of them have been fake."

"True."

"This one sounds legit. Let's go."

Kenzie grabbed the journal, and then they were out the door where the others were waiting in Dolly. Seconds later they headed out of Kenzie's neighborhood and to the warehouse district. It sounded larger than it actually was. In total, there were five buildings on the edge of Carson Lake, the second largest lake in Lake City. Local police already had the place blocked off and were standing by. Badami and the same team that had been at the hospital were there again. Cole's phone buzzed and he glanced at it. His sister. She'd have to wait. He hurried over to Badami, well aware this could be another ambush situation. "Any communication?"

"Yeah. There's definitely a guy in there with a semiautomatic. He's got four workers held in the main office, but he won't let us talk to them and he hasn't made any demands yet."

"Name?"

"One of the workers said it could be Charlie Matthews, a former employee who was recently fired, but they're not sure because of the mask."

220

"Negotiator?"

"Ten minutes out. I called another SWAT team from Asheville. They're being choppered in. Not taking any chances with this one."

Cole waved to James. "Cross, you got this? King can go inside with us while you work out here."

James stepped forward. "Yep. Get him on the phone, will you?" James had training as a negotiator, and while Cole wasn't thrilled with pulling Kenzie from the safety of Dolly, he also knew she could do the job.

Butler didn't even roll his eyes at the statement.

Badami dialed as James settled the headset over his head, and Cole motioned to Kenzie to join the team. Through the comms, they'd be able to hear James and the gunman.

"I don't want to talk, man, I want justice."

"I know you do," James said, his voice soothing, but firm, "but we have to talk in order to figure out what we can do to make that happen."

"They need to suffer," the man said softly. "They need to be scared of what's going to happen, what's to come."

"Why?"

"Because they didn't care that he'd be homeless. And terrified. So now they're just getting a little taste of their own medicine before—"

"Before what, Charlie? Can I call you Charlie?"

The chuckle was raspy. "Sure. Why not?"

"What's to come? What do you have planned?"

"That's for me to know and you to . . . *not* find out until much too late."

Cowboy went ahead, with Greene and Otis on his tail. Kenzie stayed behind them, while Cole and Butler brought up the rear.

"Get us out of here!" The female voice screeched through the comms and Cole flinched. "Please, help us! He's crazy! He's going to blow us all up!"

Shots fired in rapid succession from inside and screams echoed seconds later.

TWENTY-FOUR

"Is everyone all right?" James' calm voice came over the comms. "Why are you shooting?"

"Because this wasn't supposed to happen! It's messing with the plan and I have to think. But I can't think with your constant yapping in my ear. So shut up!"

James fell silent. And Kenzie knew he was simply letting the man talk, think things through, and hopefully, give him something to work with. "I . . . I need to get out of here." A harsh breath exploded in her ear. "I need a car. Bring a car and I'll leave. I won't hurt anyone and I'll leave. Leave it at the back door with the keys in it and running."

"Don't believe him!" The high-pitched shriek echoed. "He's going to kill us all!"

"Shut up! Shut up! Or I'll finish you off right now!"

Oh, please listen to him and be quiet, Kenzie silently begged the terrified woman. Sobs reached her, but no more screams. And no more bullets.

James continued to talk with the man, promising him the car, asking for a bit of time to get it, while Kenzie clamped down hard on her nerves and clutched her weapon. She took a deep breath and stepped into the warehouse to find row after row of shelving with items organized neatly, making them easy to find and ship. Everything from dishware to clothing to Christmas trees.

She was right behind Greene and Otis, and she pulled up short when Otis barked and sat, refusing to go farther than the three feet just inside the door.

Greene frowned. "He doesn't like something."

"What?"

"I'm not sure. He's never done this before. What is it, boy?"

Greene started to step forward, but Otis circled in front of him, blocking his path.

"Stop," Kenzie said. "Trust him."

"Yeah."

"Cowboy," Cole said, "get eyes on this guy for me. You may have to work around the outside to the window. If I remember the blueprints correctly, the office is glassed in on the side facing the warehouse and there's one window on the exterior wall. You should have access out there."

Cowboy hesitated, his eyes on the dog, then lifting to Greene. "You done any explosives training with him?"

Greene stilled, then nodded. "Yeah. Some. Just for fun."

"Looks like your fun might be paying off." His eyes scanned the warehouse. "One of the hostages said something about blowing them all up. I don't like this."

Kenzie didn't either, but what choice did they have? They were one man short and the other team had yet to arrive. "Do we wait on the others?" she asked.

A burst of gunfire from somewhere straight ahead answered that question. Cole huffed. "We need eyes. Now. Cross, update on hostages?"

"No one is hurt at the moment. He's just angry and shooting at the wall, but I don't know how much time we'll have before he kills a hostage. I think he's capable."

"Understood." Cole frowned.

"They've made the assumption that this is Charlie Matthews, but

I'm not so sure. He keeps ranting about how they took his job—not *his*, but someone he knows? Maybe? It's not exactly clear."

"Okay, keep trying to get more info and we'll see what we're dealing with here." He looked at Cowboy and the man nodded.

"Going for eyes," Cowboy said. "I'll let you know when it's up."

"No," Kenzie said. "Let me do it. This place may be booby-trapped. You're the explosives expert and you have the tools. You're needed here."

She met Cole's gaze, and he gave a reluctant nod with a glance at Cowboy. "She's right." Then back to her. "Go."

Kenzie broke off and exited the warehouse. Cole would be able to use his phone to see once the camera was in place, as would the ones in the command vehicle. Now she just had to find the right spot to put it.

And make sure she didn't trip any explosives on her way to doing it. But, if the building had explosives inside . . .

"I need a dog out here," she said. "I need to make sure there aren't any explosives around the perimeter. It's concrete, though, so I'm relatively sure I would spot something if it was there."

"There's no time," Cole said. "Badami and Cross say the guy is escalating. It's now or never, King."

"Then I guess it's now."

"Be careful."

"Always."

She stepped with precision, putting one foot in front of the other, scanning the area. She didn't have the level of explosives training that Cowboy did, but she had the basics they all had and could spot a wire or laser just as easily as the next person. She could have a robot come in, but that would take time. And she wasn't sure the hostages had the time.

"Why are there only four workers inside?" she asked. "Where's everyone else?"

"He let them go," James said. "According to my source here, the four who are with him are Margaret Tomlinson, Garth Kittridge,

Jenny Bowman, and Trixie Brown. Margaret is a supervisor who does a lot of firing. Garth is a new worker, only on the job for a few weeks. Jenny and Trixie walked out of the bathroom after the others were released from the building. Trixie saw the gunman and ran back to lock herself in the bathroom and called 911. He threatened to kill one of the other hostages if she didn't come out, so she did, and that's when the dispatcher lost contact. The other workers agree that if it's not Charlie Matthews, he has some kind of connection with the place. Said everything felt personal."

"Great," she whispered. "Lots of anger then."

"Loads."

"What do we know about Charlie? Experience with explosives?"

"Yeah. Just learned he used to do demo for a construction company."

"Fabulous."

He went silent for a moment and she continued on, rounding the building. The window was just ahead on her left. She held the tiny camera and approached, eyes still looking for any kind of tripwire. Finally convinced there was nothing, she placed her back against the wall and raised the camera to the corner of the window. The blinds were pulled, but all she needed was a crack of an opening. Bit by bit, she twisted the camera near the edge of the bottom blind until she could see just inside the office on the screen of her phone.

"Second SWAT team is on the ground," James said. "Sniper setting up position."

"And we've got explosives in here," Cole said. "Cowboy's taken care of two. No idea how many more."

"Get out of there," James said, and Kenzie's heart plummeted. They had to get the hostages. Her work phone pinged with a text from Tabitha Lewis. It had to be about her mother's case. She ignored it but made a mental note to check it as soon as everything was under control here. She tilted the camera slightly and finally got a good look at the gunman.

"Guys, he's got on a vest full of explosives. If he detonates it, no one in this building is walking away."

She heard James sigh. "Thanks, King."

"Hostages are side by side on the wall perpendicular to the window wall."

"So, all together."

"Yeah." She screenshotted the picture on her phone and sent it to the team. Then she took another angle and another. "Who's our sniper?"

"Gabe McClane," a deep voice said. "Got my thermal scope on. If I can light him up, I can take him down that way."

"He's got a bomb strapped to his chest," she said. "He's sitting behind the desk. Rifle is laid out in front of him. His hands are resting on it and he's staring at the phone on the desk. I don't see a dead man's switch. I'm guessing he can detonate the bomb with his phone or"—she zoomed in as close as possible and snapped a close-up of the explosive—"he has the switch attached to the device. I can't tell. Hostages are sitting quietly. Their hands appear bound behind them. Oh wait. He's moving. He's standing and . . . he's taking off the vest."

"What?"

"Don't do anything. McClane, you might want to stand down. I don't know what will happen with the bomb. If it's on a timer or if he has to actually detonate it. Cross, give me a sec to see what he's up to."

The team and other local law officers waited.

"Okay," she said, "he's got the vest off and is laying it on the desk next to the rifle." She licked her lips. "McClane, do you have a shot?"

"Negative."

"Detonator?" Cole asked. "Kill switch?"

"Still can't see one. He's got his phone. Badami, is there another exit out of there? Through the bathroom attached to the office? He's headed that way. Bomb vest is still on the table. He's got the rifle with him. McClane?"

"Negative. No shot."

226

"Breach!" Cole said.

"No!" Kenzie had stopped panning the camera at the entry door to the office. "He's got it wired. If you open it, it blows."

"Stand down! Stand down!"

Kenzie released a slow breath. She turned the camera back toward the bathroom just in time to see the shooter's feet disappear into the ceiling. The hostages couldn't see him from where they sat, and if she hadn't caught the glimpse of him climbing from the sink into the ceiling, it would have appeared that he'd just vanished. "He's going up," she said. "He has an escape route. Once he's out, I can't say a hundred percent, but I have a strong gut feeling he's going to detonate the explosives. Where does the ceiling go? Badami?"

"Blueprints don't show anything. Cross is asking."

"Ask faster!"

"King," James said, "the worker I've been dialoguing with says he doesn't know anything that could be an escape route for the guy that could be in the ceiling, but if it's Charlie Matthews, they suspect he'd been living in the warehouse for a while before he was fired. They could never prove it, though. Never found any real evidence of it. Just said that he was always there. First one in the building and last one to leave. If it's him. No one can confirm his identity."

She could see Cowboy outside the office door, trying to get a good look at the device. "I don't think you're coming through that door, Cowboy," she said. "You're going to have to disarm it from the inside."

"I'm thinking the same thing. You guys work on catching him before he sets this thing off. We're going to scan the ceiling and see if we can locate him."

The chopper roared overhead, and Kenzie backed up, trying to figure out where Charlie planned to exit. Surely not the roof. If he'd been living in the place, he'd know every nook and cranny. He'd have hiding places, escape routes, a place to keep whatever things he might have. And all of that would be in the building.

Then again, he was prepared to blow it all up, and the only reason he hadn't yet was because one hostage had gotten a 911 call in before he could execute his plan.

But he had a way out.

So where was it?

COLE'S WORK PHONE vibrated with a call, most likely Mariah and an emergency with Riley. But right now, family matters had to be on the back burner. His phone vibrated again with the voicemail.

"The guy is in the ceiling," Kenzie said via the comms. "I'm coming to join you. Bomb squad needs to get into the office from this side of the building."

"Bomb squad is on the way, King," James said. "Everyone needs to get away from the building."

"Cross, we've got to keep him in the building," Kenzie said. "As soon as he escapes, he's going to blow it. Like I said earlier, he doesn't want to die. He's not going to detonate those bombs until he's well clear. He's away from the hostages, so they're no longer in danger of being shot, just blown up if he slips away."

"In other words, the hostages can wait. Catching this guy can't."

"Exactly."

"Then let's get him. Explosives dog is here. Otis can sit this one out while the trained one does the rest of the work."

It took Kenzie less than ten seconds to join them, and Cole motioned for the new handler and his dog to lead the way. They kept their thermal glasses locked on the ceiling, looking for anything that emitted heat while moving forward with the permission of the dog.

"There," Butler said, pointing. "That could be him."

"It's definitely a large heat source," Cowboy said. "And it's moving. I'd be willing to place my bets on it being him."

"How's he walking across the ceiling like that?" Kenzie murmured. "He must have laid down some kind of flooring."

"Well, he's headed toward the back of the building, so that means we are too. Keep him in sight and let's see where he comes out."

With the warehouse ceiling being one big open area, following him wasn't hard.

Until he disappeared. "Northwest corner," Cole said. "We believe he has some kind of exit."

"Negative," James said. "He's not out here."

Cole scanned the ceiling and the area where the man disappeared. "We've lost eyes on him. Any progress on the explosives?"

"Bomb squad is now inside the room. Hostages are secured but not out of the build— We got him. Suspect is running!"

"Back door!" Cole's shout propelled the team out of the building, and Cole spotted the man heading for the loading dock. "He's got a boat docked there! Cut him off."

Law enforcement closed in. The man turned, rifle held at his waist.

"Put the gun down! Put it down now!" The shouts echoed.

The man hesitated, then lowered the weapon to the ground. "Don't shoot. I don't want to die." He straightened and held his hands away from his body. He'd removed his mask and Cole blinked. The guy was seventy if he was a day.

"On the ground, face down!"

Cole and the others stopped, then lowered their own weapons while the officers cuffed the guy, then hauled him to his feet. Beside him, Kenzie let out a low breath. "Well, that ended well."

A sharp crack echoed and the suspect jerked, blood flowed from the wound in his forehead, then he hit the ground.

"Sniper!" Kenzie's shout sent people running for cover. "McClane? Was that you?"

"Negative! Searching for him now."

Officers dragged the body of the man behind a vehicle. Then a loud explosion rocked the earth and they all went to their knees.

Cole spun to see the side of the warehouse blown out—the side where the office window had been. But the rest seemed to be still in one piece. "Hostage situation update?"

"All hostages safely extracted. Looking for the sniper now."

He looked back to see officers hovering over the suspect. "Check his pocket for a cell phone! Someone find the shooter!"

"When he went down, he detonated it somehow," Kenzie said. "Didn't he?"

"Yeah." Cole shook his head. "Or the sniper did."

"I'm going to grab my kit and see if anyone is hurt."

"Cross, any wounded?"

"None reported as of the moment," James said.

Kenzie nodded and took off for her bag anyway.

Cole looked at the others. "Find this guy."

For the next thirty minutes, they joined in the search while two choppers roared overhead and law enforcement swarmed the area.

Finally Cole radioed the team. "He's gone. Let's round up and get our reports done." The others would keep searching, of course, but Cole was quite sure the guy was long gone.

His personal phone buzzed once more. He let out a low breath, snagged the device from his pocket, and slapped it to his ear. "Yeah?"

"It's Riley," his sister said on a sob. "She fell off her bicycle and needs your blood. She's already had loads from the hospital, but they're almost out due to some kind of shortage and they think she's got some internal bleeding they can't find and they're talking surgery and they only have a pint of your blood left. They have a rush order in to process whatever you can give—" Another sob. "I'm sorry," she whispered. "Can you come?"

"I got it, Mariah. Tell them I'm on the way."

He filled the others in, and Kenzie met his gaze with a nod. "If I could give, I would."

"I know. Thanks."

Cole looked at James, then locked eyes with each of the other members of the unit. "Keep Kenzie safe."

They nodded. All except Butler, who let his eyes slide from Cole's. James scowled at the man, who sighed and said, "Don't worry. She'll be fine. Go."

Cole darted to one of the officers to grab a ride. They headed out for the hospital with lights and sirens, and he found himself at the entrance in record time. "Thanks, man," he said to the officer and raced through the doors.

He went straight to the triage desk. "Hi, Monica, I'm back for Riley."

"I was told you would be. Follow me. You have the room to yourself today."

"Thanks."

As much as he wanted to go see Riley and give her a hug, the faster they got started with his donation, the faster it would get to her. He rolled up his shirtsleeve as he walked. It would take a couple of hours to get the max they'd allow him to give, but he had his phone and he could catch up on whatever he needed to catch up on.

Not that he could remember what that was at the moment.

Once he was settled and hooked up to the appropriate tubes and machines, including an IV to pump fluids since he was slightly dehydrated, he called Mariah and let her know he was there. "How's Riley?"

"Stable at the moment, but the doctor says that could change at any second."

"Tell her to hang on. Her Cole-y juice is coming."

"Thank you, Cole. I'm sorry I called you so much. I know you were probably working. I was just terrified."

"It's all good. I'm here now. We'll get Riley fixed right up, and then she can tell me all about her adventure."

"Oh, it's been an adventure, all right. I've got to go, Cole. I'll come see you if I can."

"You focus on Riley. I might take a nap." He hung up and pulled out his phone. As if a nap was anywhere in his future. He texted James.

At the hospital. You got Kenzie in your sights?

I do. We're just now leaving the scene and heading back to HQ.

Okay, great. Keep an eye on her. I don't think this
guy is finished with her.

We got it covered. You focus on helping Riley.
Offering up prayers for her too.

Cole knew his friend wasn't just spouting platitudes. He'd really
be praying. And Cole couldn't thank him enough.

Another text from James.

Dead guy's name is Eric Matthews. He's Charlie
Matthews' father.

Any more info?

He was seventy-two years old and lived at
Harmony House.

Harmony House?

Yeah.

Thanks.

Harmony House. The same place Oscar's father lived. No way was
that a coincidence. He tapped a text to Commander Hill request-
ing more information on the man and if he had any connection to
Oscar. He'd be interested in questioning the staff to see if Oscar had
ever met with the man.

He leaned his head back and shut his eyes. While he waited on
Hill's response, he tried to work through the next steps in Ben King's
case.

And said a few prayers for Kenzie's safety. And Riley's.

TWENTY-FIVE

Eliza tucked the pen into the journal, then slid both items under the mattress. Her father had brought her home and straight to her room. Where he'd locked her in.

She'd heard the deadbolt click into place before she'd even set her bag on the bed. Heart thudding, she ran to the window and threw the curtains back.

Bars and sunlight greeted her.

"Oh, dear Lord, have I made a terrible mistake?" she whispered. Had she exchanged one prison where she at least had access to Betsy and Dr. King for another cell with no hope of escape or a friendly face?

How was she to get to William now?

A knock on the door and the click of the deadbolt spun her around. A woman with a basket of food and a glass of water entered. She set everything on the floor just inside the door, then stepped back without a word to lock Eliza in once more.

In the distance, she heard the telephone ring twice, then cut off.

She sank onto the bed, refusing to cry. This was just the beginning. Her father didn't trust her in spite of bringing her home. It dawned on her that he was afraid of her. Well, afraid of what she might say.

Somehow, that gave her the strength to straighten her spine before she slumped once more. What if she didn't get the chance to say it?

Well, if she didn't get the chance to say it, she'd just have to write it. Thankfully, her father hadn't searched the small bag with the very few items she'd had at the hospital, and she'd managed to get her journal and pen home.

She itched to write, but what if someone entered before she could hide it and caught her? They'd take it, she had no doubt. And read it.

And there was no one in this household she wanted reading the words in her book.

So she'd wait, see how the schedule panned out over the next few days, and then plan her escape.

Another knock and the door opened once more. This time her father stepped inside. "I've just spoken to Dr. King. He'll be by to see you tomorrow."

Hope sprouted and relief flowed, but she kept her expression neutral. "All right. What time?"

"Nine in the morning."

"Very well. Thank you."

His brow furrowed and he studied her for a moment longer before backing out of the room.

She heard the click of the lock, but this time it didn't bother her as she was already looking forward to the good doctor's visit. Maybe he'd already have a plan and she wouldn't have to come up with one.

She could only pray that he'd really show up and that he'd bring Betsy with him.

TWENTY-SIX

Kenzie stepped through HQ's door and went straight for her locker, then the showers. She usually waited to get home to shower, but Dolly was her ride and the guys would be with her. So she'd have more privacy here than her home. Which was weird.

When she exited, she went to the kitchen to find the team gathered around the table, laptops open and working on their reports.

She grabbed hers from her bag. If they were going to work, she might as well get her stuff done and out of the way as well.

James walked into the room rubbing his chin, looking at his phone. She could hear Butler in the other room having a low-voiced conversation on his phone. She wished she could hear what he was saying.

"What is it?" Cowboy asked James.

"Badami said Charlie had definitely been living there," James said, "and had been for a while. The bomb took out a nice chunk of the building, but the ceiling was mostly still intact. He'd built an entire network of tunnels and ways to navigate through the ceiling. He had to do it that way in order to not set off any of the motion sensors in the warehouse—and keep his key card from setting off alerts every time it was swiped."

"So, where is Charlie now?" Cowboy asked.

"Not sure. They're trying to track him down. The latest word is when he was fired, he started living out of his car, then moved to the ceiling once he got it the way he wanted it."

"And no one noticed the little exit he carved into the side of the building."

"Nope. He did an excellent job with that. Worked construction with his dad, so it wasn't hard for him at all."

"And somehow," Kenzie said, "this is all connected to me. Someone set him up—or convinced him the whole thing was a good idea for whatever reason—and got us there with the intention of blowing us all up."

"The connection is Harmony House," James said. "And Oscar. And we need to anticipate that Oscar's said something to Butler, so be prepared for that."

"Great. Another reason to hate me."

"Hopefully, he'll realize we're just doing what he would do. Following the evidence and chasing down all the clues."

"I'm not holding my breath."

"I guess I can't blame you for that. So . . . time for another conversation with Oscar." He looked at Kenzie. "In the meantime, you ready to head home?"

"No."

"What?"

"Cole—Garrison's—at the hospital giving blood for his niece. I think I'd like to go keep him company for a bit. Should be safe enough if we alert security to keep an eye on his area."

James smiled and nodded. "He'd probably appreciate that. We'll both go."

"Aw, you just want to catch a glimpse of Lainie."

He grinned. "I'm not even going to try and deny it. Come on. My Jeep's out back. The guys can follow to make sure all goes well in getting there."

Kenzie frowned. "I hate to inconvenience them like that."

"Not an inconvenience at all," Cowboy said. "Let's roll, guys."

Butler walked into the kitchen, tucking his phone into his pocket. "I've got something to do, sorry. I'll catch up with you guys a little later."

Kenzie sighed and kept her scream of frustration tucked away. Would she never win him over? He left in a hurry, and she seriously considered following him. If she'd had her own vehicle, she might have done just that, but . . . she didn't. And there was no way she could demand he stay without either looking like an idiot or tipping him off that she suspected he—and Oscar—were possibly behind the attempts on her life.

She waited for James to finish a phone call—sounded like he was talking to his dad—and then followed him to his Jeep.

Dolly fell in behind them and they started the trek to the hospital. In the meantime, she pulled the journal from her bag and opened it to a page near the middle.

I'm home. I'm out of that horrid place, but I've exchanged one terrible prison for another. At least this one has hot water and clean sheets, but it's still a prison. I do hope I'll be able to pretend well enough and long enough to convince Father to let me have visitors. I doubt Betsy will be on the approved list. However, Dr. King will come. I know he will. This is all his idea and while part of me is terrified he'll abandon me, another part of me knows he's a good man, a godly man, who sincerely cares that my father tried to murder me.

Kenzie gasped and James shot her a look. "You okay?"

"Yeah, just learning a lot about my family history—and Cole's. I knew our families were entwined all the way back to the late 1940s, I just didn't have all the details. Reading them is fascinating. And shocking."

She flipped the page.

Dr. King came to see me today. I knew he would, but it was an incredible relief to see him in the flesh. Betsy wasn't allowed to come, but he slipped me a note from her. They're engaged! But the best part is, they have a plan to get me out from under Father's thumb and into William's arms. If only it will work.

"We're here," James said.

Kenzie snapped the journal shut and followed James inside.

COLE WOKE WITH A START, the feeling that someone was watching him sending a rippling shudder through him. He looked around but only saw a figure in a lab coat putting something in his IV. Wait, what?

"Hey, what are you doing? I just gave blood. I'm not here for anything else."

"Just flushing the IV with saline before I take it out," the man said. He sounded familiar.

A strange lethargy started to work its way through him.

"No. This is wrong. Stop." But the words came out weak, slurred, and darkness approached the edges of his vision. He grabbed his phone and tapped a message to the first person his messages app opened to.

Drugged. Fake doc. Need help.

With a shaky finger, he hit send, then lost his grip on the phone.

"Don't worry," the figure said, turning back to Cole and capping the syringe, "I know exactly how much to give you. You'll wake up in a few hours."

"But—"

"You've been a huge thorn in my side, Detective Garrison. It's past time that I remove it."

"Who are you?" He could barely get the words out even as he tried to force his eyes to stay open to see the man's face.

"All in due time. We'll have a nice chat when you wake up because

238

I need you to do something for me before you die. But for now, I've got to be clever and get you out of here."

Cole struggled to watch, to take in every detail.

The man shrugged out of the white lab coat to reveal a blue-and-green transport T-shirt many in the hospital wore. The bed started to roll and panic grabbed at Cole. He was helpless. Couldn't move, couldn't call out for help. Nothing.

Riley. She needed the blood. *Please, God, get that to Riley.* And then he gave in to the drug that pulled him under.

TWENTY-SEVEN

Kenzie and the others entered the hospital and wound their way to the lab. The area for giving blood was across the hall. James laid a hand on her arm. "You go on in. We'll wait out here and take you home when you're done."

"You're not coming?"

"Cowboy, Greene, and Otis will make sure the area is secure and keep an eye on all the things. But I'll drop by after I find Lainie. I need to ask her a question."

"You could just text her, you know. She checks her phone a little more often than I do."

"Ha. I know that's right, but I prefer the face-to-face."

"Of course you do."

"You will too one day."

She rolled her eyes. "I already do. For everyone." She waved her work phone at him, briefly thinking she should check her personal one. "Get out of here."

James left and Cowboy took up residence near the exit, his positioning strategic in that it would allow him to see everyone coming through the front door, the side door that opened into the main part of the hospital, and everyone in the waiting room. Greene settled into a chair on the opposite side of the room and Otis dropped beside him, planting his muzzle between his massive paws. Kenzie smiled, grateful for the crew and wishing Butler would come around—assuming he wasn't the one trying to kill her—and made her way to the back where Cole would be giving blood. Once at the door, she pushed her way into the room to find three empty beds and a missing one.

She frowned and stepped back out to find a worker she recognized behind a counter, tapping on her laptop. "Hey, Delia, Cole was supposed to be here giving blood, but I don't see him."

Delia looked up, frowning. "Well, I got him settled and going on his donation. When I last checked on him, he was almost done. Looked like he was dozing."

"When was that?"

The woman glanced at the clock on the wall. "About twenty minutes ago."

"Is someone else on duty who would have disconnected him? There are two bags on the tray next to a plasma machine, but no donor bed."

"What?" She rose and followed Kenzie back to the room and gasped. "What in the world?"

"What's wrong?"

Delia's wide brown eyes met Kenzie's. "His drink and snack are still here." She walked over to hold up the package of cookies and the bottle. "He'd never leave these. He knows how important it is to keep his blood sugar up and rehydrate."

"I agree." Dread swirled and something on the floor against the wall caught her eye. She hurried over to pick it up. "This is Cole's phone."

She tried to open it, but the screen was locked. And required facial recognition. She had no clue what his six-digit passcode would be either. She checked her work phone. No messages there.

For some reason, she checked her personal phone.

And there it was. A text from Cole.

Drugged. Fake doc. Need help.

She didn't bother standing there in shock but took off running toward the waiting room. She found Cowboy, Greene, and Otis where she'd left them. "Follow me!" Otis barked and lunged to his feet while Greene and Cowboy did the same. "Where's Cross?"

"With Lainie, I reckon," Cowboy said.

"Text him and keep moving to security. We need to look at the security footage. Someone's kidnapped Cole."

"What!"

She rounded the corner and bolted toward the emergency department. The security office was right next to it just off the hall. She rapped her knuckles on the door, then pushed it open. "Jared, oh thank goodness you're here. Someone's kidnapped Cole right from the blood donation room. Couldn't be more than twenty-five minutes ago. Can you see if you can track him?"

Wide-eyed, the man spun back to his computer and pulled up the video from that area, and jumped to the time Kenzie had given him. They watched as Delia came in to check on Cole. Then within a minute after she left, another figure appeared. "There's the doctor coming in."

Kenzie shook her head. "No. His text said fake doc. See if we can get a look at his face."

The footage played and Jared groaned. "No luck. He knew how to hold his head so the camera wouldn't pick him up—at least not his face. Plus he has that surgical mask on. Dark hair, though." Seconds ticked past. "That's where he drugged him. Put something in the IV. Waited a little, took off the lab coat, and became an instant transport person." He clicked a few keys on the keyboard and switched cameras. "He rolled him out and toward the ambulance bay."

Kenzie looked at Greene. "What do you think about bagging that lab coat? Otis can use it as a scent article. Possibly." Maybe.

Greene nodded. "On it. I'll meet you at the ambulance bay."

"Oscar Woodruff wanted my position," she said. "I was warned to quit or else. Someone took Cole to get to me."

Cowboy eyed her. "What are you thinking? You think Woodruff had something to do with this?"

"I have no idea." What she wanted to know was where Butler had been all this time. But the man on the footage wasn't him. Wrong build, wrong hair color, wrong everything. But that didn't mean he wasn't working with someone else. "I need to talk to Commander Hill and we need to come up with a plan to find Cole. Can someone find Butler too? He should know what's going on." And she wanted to know where he was so she could keep tabs on him.

"Hang on, Cole," she whispered. "We're coming."

She and the others raced to the ambulance bay to find it busy, but no Cole in sight. "Whoever rolled him out here probably had a vehicle waiting."

"But Cole was unconscious," Cowboy said. "How would he get Cole into it? The man is big, and dead weight over two hundred pounds wouldn't be easy to handle."

"You're right." So how had he moved Cole? "What if he wasn't completely knocked out? What if he could walk a little or move when instructed?"

"That would make things easier, for sure," Greene said.

"There's got to be more security footage."

"We watched and never saw him actually come out here. What if he detoured to a different exit?"

Kenzie frowned. "Where?"

Greene pointed. "The morgue."

COLE OPENED HIS EYES AND GROANED, nausea clawing at the back of his throat. While he fought it, he registered he was lying on his left side on a comfortable mattress. The gurney? Yes, but he wasn't in the hospital anymore. Chills shook him and he pressed a hand to his head. "What—?" His throat rasped and he coughed, gagged, and stilled until the desire to be sick faded.

Once he thought he could, he rolled to a sitting position, caught his breath, then stumbled off the gurney to his feet, only to have to fall back onto the bed while the room spun.

"Okay, then," he rasped, his voice loud in the complete silence. "Easy now."

When the room stopped twirling, he took a moment to look around and noted he was in some kind of room about seven by fourteen. Two iron-framed twin beds minus mattresses were tilted and stacked against the opposite wall. A very dirty window let in just a glow of light. Morning? Afternoon? He had no idea. A tiny bathroom to his right with no door. Just a sink that now rested on the floor, and a toilet. No shower. And it stunk. The smell of mildew and dirt hit him. And he'd swear the odor of . . . stale urine? . . . hovered in the air.

A chair that looked like it belonged back in the late 1940s sat in the corner. There were restraints on the arms and legs and they looked new.

With all these details swirling in his head, he eased himself off the mattress once more, made sure his stomach was going to stay put, then walked to the door and yanked on the handle. He wasn't surprised to find it locked. Cole patted his pockets, looking for his phone. Again, not surprised to find it missing.

He moved to the window, whose curtain hung by threads. The pane was surprisingly still intact, but caked with so much dirt and grime that he couldn't see much through it. Then he spotted a sliver of clean glass, placed his eye next to it, and squinted.

He almost didn't need the visual confirmation to know where he was, what he'd suspected.

Lake City State Hospital.

And while he knew it was impossible after all these years, he definitely smelled urine and who knew what else had been left behind. Gross.

The lock clicked on the door and Cole scrambled to search for a weapon, but if he had to defend himself, he was going to be in trouble. Weak from giving blood and the drug that was still in his system, he was a hot mess. A toddler could knock him over.

The door opened and the man stood there, mask on his face, gun in his hand. Cole let himself fall back against the wall. His mind was still a blank as to how he'd gotten here.

Or who had brought him. *Fake doc.*

"Woke up a little faster than I thought you would in spite of two more doses," the man said.

That voice. Where did he know that voice from?

"Who are you?" He really hoped he wasn't going to have to engage in a physical fight because his muscles quivered like Jell-O.

"Someone who needs a favor."

"You could have spared us both all the drama and just asked." His head was splitting and he found it hard to keep his eyes open. He'd give just about anything to stretch back out on the gurney and sleep it off.

"Not this favor."

Again, the man's voice tickled Cole's memory, but he couldn't place it. "What is it?"

"You're going to call whoever you need to call, as far up the chain as you need to go, and tell them that they're going to get rid of Kenzie King and hire someone to take her place."

He stared at the dark eyes peering at him through the small eye-holes in the mask.

"And why would I do that?"

"Because if you don't, you won't live to see another day—and neither will Kenzie King or any of the others on your team. You've managed to protect her up to this point, but you and I both know eventually I'll succeed." His phone buzzed and he motioned with the gun. "Sit in the chair and strap yourself in. Legs first. Then one arm. I'll do the last one."

"No way."

"You can do it with or without a bullet in you. And trust me, I know where to put one so you won't die quickly. The without-bullet route will be much less painful for you. For a little while anyway."

Cole debated, then decided he'd have a much better chance of escape without the bullet wound. And this guy sounded like he didn't care one way or another. Cole sat in the chair and began to strap himself in.

His captor moved closer, and Cole noted the slight limp, but the man made quick work of rendering him helpless. "What now?"

"Now we get to work." He pulled a phone from his pocket, and for a moment Cole had hope that if he could get it, he could call for help. Another phone dinged and the man cursed, then dug in his other pocket, pulled out a smartphone, and looked at it. Another curse and he shoved the phone away, then tucked the first device into the other pocket. "Well, we're going to be a bit delayed. I have an emergency appointment to get to, then I'll be back."

"Why Kenzie? Why do you hate her so much? Want her off the team? Or dead?"

"Because she doesn't deserve the spot. For years, her family has taken what doesn't belong to them. I'm putting a stop to it once and for all."

Her family? "If Kenzie doesn't deserve it, who does?"

"You'll find out when I get back, but get ready to make some calls. It's time to make what I want to happen . . . happen."

He pulled out his phone to snap a picture of Cole, then he was gone. Cole leaned his head back, thankful for the headrest—and that the man hadn't pulled *that* strap around him, forcing him to stay in a position that didn't allow him to move his head.

He pulled on his arms, then his legs, but the restraints held tight. He was well and truly trapped.

TWENTY-EIGHT

They'd found footage of Cole being transferred into the back of a long black car. A hearse. Kenzie shuddered. Once it had turned out of the hospital parking lot, they followed it with traffic cams, then lost it when it turned down a back road. They'd called in reinforcements, got Cole's name and face on the news with pleas from the family to bring him back safely. Cole's parents and family had blown up the phones and rallied people to look for him.

Now it was early Thursday morning and she hadn't slept a wink. With whoever was after her being occupied with Cole, Kenzie felt confident the danger to her was minimal for the moment—not that there couldn't be someone else after her, but hopefully she could handle that. She didn't really have a choice. She paced the floor at HQ, thinking. Then grabbed a pen and paper and wrote down the day and time of each incident that was considered an attempt on her life.

She passed the paper to Commander Hill, who was on the phone with the FBI. When he hung up, she said, "I want to know where Oscar Woodruff was during each of those times."

"One thing we can do is cross-reference this with his work schedule."

She nodded. "That's what I was thinking. While you're doing that,

I'm going to call the assisted-living home where his father is and see if he was visiting him any of these times."

"Good idea." He shook his head. "I've known Woodruff and his father for years. I can't see Oscar being involved in this."

"I honestly can't either. Our families go back decades, but I also don't want to overlook the possibility. Let's just clear him and move on."

Hill pursed his lips, then nodded. "Harold was a pretty good chief of police." He shot her a smile. "Your dad was a great one, though."

A lump formed in her throat and she cleared it. "Sir, I've never asked you this before, but do you know anything about the night my mother was killed? Have you heard any rumors that my dad was drinking when he ran that stop sign?"

"Drinking? Your dad?" He scoffed. "No way. He never drank more than half a glass of wine at any social function we ever attended together. No matter how much they argued, he still loved your mom. He wouldn't have put her at risk by drinking and driving."

"Yeah," she whispered. "That's what I thought too."

"But?"

Should she tell him? Could she trust him? She looked into his eyes, saw nothing there but curiosity, compassion for her, and the desire to help. "But there was a cover-up." She explained what her father had told her and watched Hill's eyes widen with each word.

When she told him about the two reports—one describing failed brakes and one saying the brakes were fine—he nearly gaped. "Kenzie, we have to report this and figure out who was behind the cover-up—and who would benefit from your father stepping down as chief."

She nodded. "I know. The only person that really came to mind was Harold Woodruff, but he refused the position when it was offered to him and only stepped in when Dad's replacement was killed in that hunting accident." She sighed. "I've been trying to work this all out by myself, and I just don't know the people from back then. I mean, I can figure out their names and everything, but I don't know them. I need people who do know them to be working on this with me."

He blew out a low breath. "I knew Cliff Hamilton and his wife pretty well. It was a shock when he just up and left like he did. I always wondered if there was more behind that."

"Well, now you know."

The door opened and Buzz walked inside. Kenzie gasped. "What are you doing here? You should still be recovering."

"Cole's missing. I'm helping." His flat tone brooked no argument. "And . . . I know you want to know what's going on with Butler."

Kenzie raised a brow. "You know?"

"Yeah. He swore me to secrecy, though. But now that word is out he's a suspect in all that's been going on with Kenzie, thanks to his personal errands and such, I'm going to tell you. He's rude and he's a pain when it comes to Kenzie, but he's not trying to kill her. His sister is a single mom and she's been admitted to rehab for a drug addiction. Butler's been hanging out with his six-year-old nephew whenever he's had the chance. When I explained that he needed to come clean and let me tell you guys everything, he gave me permission to share and tell you that he's had an alibi for every attempt on your life. Including the home invasion. He was with his nephew each time. Butler sits by his phone day and night in case he's needed."

"What?" Kenzie sank onto the nearest chair, the news burrowing deep into her heart. "So, he's not—"

"He's not."

"All right then. Good to know." She only had a twinge of guilt at suspecting the man. Just a twinge. It faded quickly. "But that still leaves Oscar."

Commander Hill nodded at Buzz. "Thank you. And I'm glad you're here. We need all the help we can get."

"So," Kenzie said, "it sounds like our next move is to find Oscar. With backup, of course."

"Yep," Hill said, "but you're staying here."

"What? Why?"

"Because you're a target. This is the safest place for you. The building is secure. Nobody gets in without a key card. There are detectives and officers upstairs, so you won't be alone, and help is seconds away. We'll handle this. You stay put. Sleep on the couch if you want, but don't leave this building."

"But, sir—"

"I'm not arguing this with you. Follow my orders or face the consequences."

With a fire burning in her gut, Kenzie nodded. "Yes sir."

"Good." He looked at the team. "Get Butler if he's available and let's go. Crenshaw, you and Cowboy head to Woodruff's home and talk to him. Cross, Greene, Otis, and I are going to follow that back road where we last saw the hearse turn off, searching every home and structure that could possibly be a hiding place."

They left and Kenzie kicked the trash can. It clattered across the floor, then hit the wall with a solid thud. She drew in a ragged breath, then marched to the kitchen with her laptop. Just because she was trapped didn't mean she was helpless.

For the next hour, she worked and watched both phones—personal and work. Every so often a text would come through with an update on her work phone. Her personal phone, the one Cole had sent the "I need help" text to, stayed silent. Even her father had stopped sending her messages asking if she'd solved his case yet.

And then her personal phone buzzed. With a text from Amelia, Kash's girlfriend.

> Looking forward to seeing you and your plus-one
> tomorrow night.

She'd forgotten all about the promise she'd made to attend. She tapped a text back.

> Might not make it. Will let you know for sure by
> tomorrow morning. Will explain later. Emergency
> work situation.

No response. Not even three little dots indicating a reply.

She'd apologize later if she had to. Right now, Cole was her priority.

The back door to HQ opened and a short beep sounded. Slow, measured footsteps reached her. She frowned and placed a hand on her weapon. Then sighed. Only law enforcement personnel with a key card could get in.

But she rose to check the hallway and came face-to-face with Oscar Woodruff. Chills skittered across her skin, but she resisted the urge to leave her hand on her weapon. No sense in letting on that she didn't trust him. "Oscar. Hi. What are you doing here?"

He planted his hands on his hips. "Is it true someone kidnapped Cole and I'm a suspect?"

She sighed. "Yeah."

He frowned. "When? How?"

"Yesterday from the hospital. How did you know you're a suspect?"

"Butler gave me a heads-up. Said they were headed to look for me."

"So you came here?"

He shrugged. "I was on the way back to work after stopping off to see Dad at the home. He's been skipping his PT appointments, and I was going to make sure he went to this one. He was a little late, but we got him there. Butler called as I was getting Dad settled back in his room, and I told him I was coming here to talk to you and the others."

"They've already left."

"I see that." He sighed. "Why do you think I have anything to do with what's going on with you?"

Kenzie looked at Oscar. "Because Butler keeps saying you deserved to get my spot. He's angry on your behalf, what with you two being best friends and all. In fact, I thought maybe the two of you were working together to get rid of me." Might as well lay it all out there.

251

Oscar blinked at her. "Wow. That's really quite . . . unbelievable. So, you think I had something to do with the attempts on your life because I was ticked that I didn't get the spot on the team?"

It did sound asinine when he put it that way and said it with that tone, but people had killed for less. She shrugged.

"And going after Cole?" He scoffed. "Why Cole?"

"I don't know!" Frustration grabbed at her. She *wanted* Oscar to be the guilty one. She *wanted* him to admit to everything. Then it would be over. But looking at him, she wasn't convinced it was him. "Fine! If it's not you, then who? Do you have any idea who'd do this to get at me?"

"No. And it's not Butler either. He's got his own issues to deal with."

And an alibi for every attempt on her life. The guy was just a jerk when it came to her. Not a killer. "We know about his sister. I don't think it's him anymore."

"But you still think it's me." He shook his head. "I don't know where Cole is, but I'll definitely help find him. I've got my gear in my car."

Kenzie bit her lip. If he had anything to do with Cole's disappearance, he was doing an excellent job of hiding it. But she didn't want him out of her sight until they either found Cole or figured out for sure if he had anything to do with the attempts on her life. But she wasn't leaving the building. Not if she wanted to keep her career. "I'll call Commander Hill and let him know you're here, and he can make the judgment about what you should do next."

He shook his head. "I'm not waiting on him." His gaze flickered. "Kenzie, were your parents having marital issues when you were a teen?"

"Why would you ask that?"

He shook his head. "I just remember Dad saying the chief couldn't focus on his job while his marriage was in turmoil."

Kenzie flinched. "Well, I was just fourteen, so I'm sure I didn't see all there was to see or know all there was to know. But I don't have time to worry about that at the moment. If you're not the one trying to kill me, then I need to focus and figure out who is." Not that she believed him just because he protested his innocence, but . . .

"Then I'm going to get out of here and join up with the others."

Kenzie scowled. "I recommend you call Commander Hill first and clear that with him. Let him know where you are. Just my advice, but you do what you want."

While he did that, Kenzie shot a text to the man, letting him know Woodruff was there and asking if it would be okay to let him join them. They'd be able to keep an eye on him, and if he knew something about Cole's whereabouts, he might let it slip.

The commander responded with a thumbs-up.

Oscar disappeared down the hall and she heard the exit door open. Well, if he was trying to kill her, he'd certainly passed up an easy opportunity. It wasn't Oscar. So, who was it? Kenzie went back to her laptop, pulled up all her dad's cold case information once more, and started reading. Mostly because she kept drawing a blank on who could want her off the team and why. It was probably something very simple, but without all the information, she couldn't put it together and that terrified her.

Because if she couldn't figure it out, she might lose Cole forever. Then she stilled. The door had opened again. "Oscar?"

The squeak of a shoe on the floor behind her was her only warning. She started to turn when something landed on her skull and sent her tumbling from the chair.

Pain radiated, and for a moment she couldn't move, could only gasp in air and try not to puke. Then the barrel of a gun pressed against the base of her skull. "Get up and walk out if you want to see Cole Garrison again." The low, raspy voice was obviously an attempt to disguise it, but it sounded familiar. "So, it *was* you! I don't believe it."

He laughed. "Get up and walk out the door and get in the passenger seat. If you try to fight me, I'll just kill you and be done with it."

"Then why don't you?" Because he needed her for something.

"Go. Now."

If it would get her to Cole, then fine. She allowed him to shove her toward the exit. Once they were at his vehicle, a large Buick sedan, he motioned her to the passenger side, and she noted that he was being very clever about avoiding the station's cameras. Head tilted, gun held low, hand on the small of her back. He opened the passenger door for her and waited for her to get settled. "Seat belt," he said in that low whisper voice.

She strapped in while doing her best to ignore the throbbing in her head. "Don't suppose you have a bottle of Motrin on hand."

He hesitated. "Glove box. Now, I'm going to walk around and get in the driver's seat. If you try anything foolish, know that Garrison will die."

"How do I know he's alive right now?"

"I guess you'll just have to take my word for it, but you're alive because I need something from him first."

And she was the motivation for Cole to provide that.

All righty then.

"And that little bomb at the warehouse? That was nothing compared to what's planted around Cole. Now, get your pills if you want them while I walk around."

She raised a brow but fumbled for the latch and found the bottle. She also gave the glove box a quick scan to see if there was a registration or insurance card to confirm the man's identity, but didn't see one. Two protein bars, a bottle of water, a phone charger, but nothing to confirm that this was Oscar.

She shook out four pills and put the bottle back while her brain processed that her captor had something to do with the warehouse incident. But for the life of her, she couldn't come up with the connection. "Oscar, how did you—"

He laughed. "I'm not Oscar." He shut the door and walked—no, limped—around to the driver's side and slid behind the wheel.

And it hit her where she knew him from.

TWENTY-NINE

CRANE MANOR
NOVEMBER 1947

Eliza adjusted the headband and let her fingers trail down the earrings she just slipped on. The dress was new, purchased by her father and tossed into her arms with orders for her to wear it that night. He'd arranged a dinner party, and she was to convince Edward Hampton that she would make the perfect wife for him. She'd heard of the Hamptons, of course. Everyone had heard of them. They owned half the city.

They were also slumlords, and her stomach turned at the thought of smiling the night away at the man. But she'd do it. For William.

It had been four weeks since she'd come home from the institution. Four very long weeks of pretending, lying, acting . . . praying. And this morning, it had all paid off. Her father had told her she'd be expected to attend the dinner party and meet the man he'd chosen for her to marry. A wealthy man from a wealthy family. Old money, as he called it.

Her only contact with the outside world up to this point had been Dr. King, who'd snuck messages from Betsy—the only thing that kept her sane and encouraged her to pull on her strength to keep up the facade. He'd promised her they had a plan to reunite her with William, who was making great strides in his healing and was desperate to be reunited with her.

With one last breath and glance in the mirror, she went to her door, surprised when the knob twisted. Someone must have unlocked it while she was in the shower.

Eliza made her way down the hallway, following the path to the dining room. The large table dominated the area and it had been set to impress. The kitchen staff busied themselves, making sure everything was just so, and didn't even look up at her presence. Voices from the parlor across the hall beckoned, and reluctantly she made her way toward them.

Please let this work.

The prayer slipped from her even as she curled her lips into the smile she'd practiced all day.

"Ah, there she is," her father gushed. "Come meet the Hamptons." He began the introductions and motioned toward the young man hovering next to his mother. "And this is Edward."

Eliza turned her smile to Edward. "Hello. Lovely to meet you."

"And you." He inclined his head and his dark green eyes flickered with kindness and curiosity. He was a handsome man, and while she wasn't drawn to him like she was William, she was able to relax and hope the dinner wouldn't be a complete nightmare. He held out his arm. "May I escort you in?"

"Certainly." She slipped her hand into the crook of his elbow and caught her father's approving look. One day not too long ago, she would have relished that. Now, she just averted her gaze and turned her attention to Edward.

As time passed, Eliza couldn't help the anxiety that grew. She was supposed to get Edward to suggest a walk outside, which would allow her to slip away as soon as his attention was elsewhere. Dr. King and Betsy would be waiting nearby to take her to William.

When dinner was over, Eliza caught the subtle nod Edward's father shot his way. She pretended not to notice.

Edward cleared his throat. "It's such a pleasant evening. Would you like to stroll the gardens?"

And just like that, her anxiety eased. "What a wonderful idea. I'd love to."

"Fabulous," her father said. "I'll turn the lights on so you can see well in the dark. We'll just be in the parlor while the two of you get to know one another."

They both slipped into their overcoats and gloves, because while it was a lovely night, it was still chilly. Then Eliza let Edward take the lead.

With her hand settled in the crook of his elbow once more, they stepped outside and began a slow walk along the lighted path.

"The gardens are lovely even this time of year," Edward said. "And your father was very clever to put lights in so you can enjoy it after the sun goes down."

"Father has workers year-round who do their best to keep it up to par. He loves the outdoors and often strolls it when he can't sleep at night. Hence the lights." Her gaze swept the area as though taking in the sight. She had to get to the edge of the property near the wooden fence that led to the horse pasture. There she would slip between the slats and make her way to the back of the pasture to the road where Dr. King and Betsy would be waiting.

"Eliza, can I ask you something?"

She turned, surprised at the seriousness in his tone. "Of course."

"I'm not one for games and small talk, to be honest. You and I both know what our parents are aiming for in this introduction. What are your thoughts on it all?"

She bit her lip, desperately searching for the right words.

"Ah," he said, "I've caught you off guard. I'm sorry. Let me just say that while I find you to be quite charming and beautiful, my heart belongs to another."

A small laugh escaped her and she pressed her gloved hands to her lips. "Oh, I'm so sorry. I don't mean to be rude, but that's so good to hear."

His eyes lit up. "Really?"

"Yes. My heart belongs to another as well and I'm supposed to . . ."

"Yes?"

Should she trust him? Dare she? The last time she'd felt such an inclination to trust a man had been with Dr. King. And he'd saved her. "I'm supposed to meet with friends who are going to take me to him. It's a very long story, but my father has basically been keeping me a prisoner in that house. And tonight is my chance to escape."

He studied her, and for a moment, she wished she could take the words back. Then he offered her a gentle smile. "Then let me help."

THIRTY

PRESENT DAY

Cole clenched his fists and tried not to scream his rage at his unknown enemy. But that wouldn't help, so he focused on escape. The straps might be new, but the chair itself was not. However, no amount of searching had found a weak spot in the wood.

Next plan.

Since his head wasn't restrained, he was able to lean over and work the buckle with his teeth.

But the strap had been pulled tight, the position was awkward, and he had to take breaks to catch his breath. The blood donation and the drugs had taken it out of him, and he needed food to replace it. He recognized low blood sugar when he felt it. He'd made the mistake of giving blood once before without bothering to eat the crackers and drink the juice they offered him. He hadn't made that mistake again.

Until now. Not that it had been his choice.

He finally managed to get the buckle undone without breaking any teeth, worked the small section of strap backward through the buckle, then yanked his arm up to free it.

Sweat poured from his temples and he gulped in a breath while weakness stole through him. He'd give just about anything for a

Snickers bar right now. Once he was free of the chair, he sat for a moment, trying to gather the energy to find a way out.

KENZIE RODE, fingers clasped while her captor drove with his left hand, right hand holding the weapon against his thigh. She wondered if she could grab the wheel and crash the car to get away. But then what might happen to Cole if she died or was too injured to get help? At least if they were together, they could figure a way to outsmart this guy. "How did you get into HQ?"

He laughed. "It helps to have access to a key card one can duplicate. I was able to snag Oscar's and make a copy. I've had it for a while, figuring it would come in handy one day. Today was the day."

"This is all because you wanted Oscar on the team, isn't it? He was the number two candidate and I beat him. If you get rid of me, you think he will be hired."

He stilled. "You shouldn't have let me know you figured out who I am."

She sighed. "The mask might be an attempt to convince us that you'll let us go when you have what you want, but you and I both know there's no way you can do that."

He was silent for the next few minutes, then he turned onto a side road and pulled under the cover of a thick blanket of trees. When he stopped, he yanked the mask off.

Harold, Oscar's father, glared at her, then turned his attention back to the road. "You're too smart for your own good."

"Does Oscar know?"

"Of course not! He's so straight, he'd never approve of this. In fact, he'll probably never understand that I'm doing it for him. I'm sick of your family always taking what's ours."

Kenzie frowned. "What are you talking about?"

"It started with my father, Stephen Woodruff. Your grandfather got him fired and was hired to take over the hospital. Your father was chief of police, the mayor's choice, but when I asked him for feedback as to why I didn't get the position, he consoled me with the fact that if it hadn't been for Ben King, I would have been the one in that office. Even your mother chose King over me. Dumped me as soon as she could and went to build a life with him. When I told my father about it, he was furious. That's when I learned all about your grandmother. She'd done the exact same thing to my father. And then you . . . you steal my boy's chance to live his dream." His hands flexed around the wheel. "It was just too much. Too much. I had to do something again. Stop the cycle once more."

A cold chill started in her gut and spread through her limbs. "What do you mean, do something again? Stop the cycle once more?" But she had a feeling she knew.

"It doesn't matter." He aimed the weapon at her. "Now, climb out from the driver's side after I'm out."

"No. Not until you explain."

He shuddered and swallowed. "Things happen for a reason."

"You set my father up, didn't you? You had the brakes cut? You threatened Cliff Hamilton to falsify the documents?" She pulled in a ragged breath. "You killed my mother," she whispered.

"She wasn't supposed to be in the car!"

"But she was!"

"And there was nothing I could do about that."

"But that evidence combined with my father's injuries gave you the opportunity you'd been waiting for."

He shrugged.

"But you didn't take the offer of chief when it was up for grabs. You let someone else take it."

"I had to. How would that look if I'd just jumped at the chance?" He shook his head. "No, I knew my time would come, and four months later, after a tragic hunting accident, it did."

Kenzie stared. "You had him killed, didn't you?"

He opened his car door, started to get out, and paused. Then he looked at her with a cold grin. "I've always been a very good marksman."

Once he was standing by the car with the door open, she hesitated. Was he going to kill her now that he'd confessed it all?

"Out!"

She kept her hands where he could see them and did as ordered, climbing over the console to the driver's side.

He motioned with the weapon. "Around to the back. Get in the trunk."

"Harold, I'm cooperating. Why make me get in the trunk?"

"Now!"

She walked to the back of the sedan, and he pressed the button on the fob. The lid lifted.

"Boy, you sure had everyone fooled into thinking you were just a harmless old man, didn't you?"

He snorted. "Who's going to suspect an old guy with a bum knee who uses a walker or a cane to get around?" He pointed to the empty trunk. "Get in."

She didn't think he was ready for her to die just yet. He'd kept her alive this long because he needed her for something. And she needed to find Cole. She climbed in and shifted to sit upright while, with one hand, she pulled her work phone from her back pocket. She gave it a shove all the way to the back of the trunk, hiding the motion by stretching out to lie down.

Harold held out a hand. "Give me your phones. Both of them. If you fight me, I'll simply knock you out and search for them."

"I only have my personal phone. I didn't have time to grab my work one before you were ushering me out the door." She didn't bother to fight him and handed over the personal one, praying he wouldn't search her for the second one. He studied her for a second and she thought he might pat her down.

"Show me your pockets."

She did so, doing her best to keep her body in such a position as to hide the other phone behind her. Finally he grunted and turned his attention to the device she'd given him. Instead of tossing it to the ground and stomping on it, he turned it off and tucked it into his pocket. "Turn over on your stomach."

"What?"

He pulled a zip tie from his pocket. "Turn over." Again, she obeyed and let him bind her hands, praying he didn't notice the phone.

Then he slammed the trunk lid, enclosing her in darkness. The engine roared, and after a few jerks and bumps, they were on smooth road once more.

Kenzie didn't bother to try to break the zip tie. She simply wiggled through her arms until her hands were in front of her, all the while thanking God for the spacious trunk. It was difficult, but it could have been worse. Then she rolled with her hands outstretched, searching. Her fingers grazed the device and she snagged it.

How much time did she have? *Please, God, just . . . help.*

She dialed Commander Hill and it went straight to voicemail. He must be on his phone. She hung up and dialed James.

"King?"

"Yes, listen, Harold Woodruff kidnapped Cole and me. I'm in the trunk of his Buick navy-blue sedan." She rattled off the license plate. "I don't know if it's his car or not. Track my phone now. Also, find Oscar Woodruff. You may need him to talk his father down." She could hear him murmuring to someone about tracking her phone. "I don't know where he's taking me, but—"

The sedan stopped and the engine cut off.

"—we're here," she finished on a whisper. That had been a short ride. "Don't talk. Just find us." She left the phone on and, unable to shove it in a pocket or anywhere else Harold wouldn't notice it, she pushed it to the back of the trunk once more, praying he wouldn't see it when he hauled her out.

The lid popped and she blinked at the sudden brightness. Then climbed from the trunk with Harold's help. He looked at her hands now in front of her and just grunted. "Flexible little thing, aren't you?"

She ignored him and looked around. "Lake City State Hospital?"

Well, it made sense. No cameras, no one around to question his presence. And lots of rooms to keep someone prisoner in.

He escorted her through the broken front door, and Kenzie saw that it hadn't changed from the last time she'd been there.

She stepped carefully over the broken tile and dodged the skittering rodents with a shudder. Her hands ached, but her foremost concern was Cole. And so she willingly followed, praying the team would arrive before it was too late.

COLE STEPPED BACK from the window when the door opened, and a hard shove sent Kenzie careening his way. He caught her when she stumbled and she spun, planting herself in fighting stance.

Cole flinched. "Harold Woodruff?"

The man's eyes flared slightly when he saw Cole had escaped the chair, then he scowled. "Surprise, surprise. Don't get comfortable. I have to hide the car, then I'll be back and we'll get down to business."

The door shut behind him and Kenzie whipped her gaze to Cole. "Are you all right?"

He nodded. "Yeah. You?"

"A headache, but nothing major." She held up her hands. "I don't suppose you have a knife on you."

"Sorry. You don't have any sugar on you, do you?"

"Uh . . ." She patted her pockets and came up with a mint. "Just this."

"That'll help if you don't mind." He took it.

"Feeling weak from the blood loss?"

"Yeah. And the drug, I'm sure. I don't know what he hit me with, but it was a doozy. Knocked me right out. I remember him coming into the room, but the rest is kind of a blur." He sucked on the mint, not knowing if it would be enough to perk him up or not, but he had to try.

"I managed to call Cross," she said, "so help is on the way."

"Oh, thank God."

"They should be here soon. In the meantime, I know you've gone over every inch of this place. Any luck finding a way out?"

"Maybe. The bars are old, but the window is stuck. I tried to break it, but you wouldn't believe how thick that glass is."

"If he was planning to keep you—or me—here, he might have replaced the original."

"Maybe, then dirtied it up so it wouldn't stand out or look too clean." He shuddered. "I hate to think of the people locked in this room with no way out. What if a fire happened?"

"It did in some places," she murmured.

"Yeah."

She went to the window. "Where are they?"

A chopper zipped overhead, and Cole breathed a little easier. "They're coming."

"I'm going to look for a weapon while I fill you in on everything Harold told me in the car. He's responsible for the car wreck that killed my mother."

"What!"

"Yeah, and somehow the guy from the warehouse and Harold know each other—"

"They were both residents of the home."

"Oh . . . well, that makes more sense then."

"And there is nothing to use as a weapon unless you can find a sharp piece of tile or something. I even tried pulling the toilet out of the floor, but no go. You'd think the floor would be rotted enough and it would come right up. Apparently concrete doesn't rot like that." He couldn't help the petulance in his tone. He was peeved he hadn't found something that could be used to defend himself. And Kenzie.

She huffed a short laugh. "You think?"

The door slammed open and Harold stepped inside, his weapon held in front of him, eyes hard and slightly frantic. "How?" He glared at Kenzie. "You tipped them off. How?"

"It doesn't really matter at this point, does it?" she asked. "Come on, Harold, it's over. The chopper is here and the others are seconds behind. You're not getting out of here."

"Then neither are you two."

Cole stepped forward, wishing the returning weakness would go away. The mint hadn't been enough. "What do you want me to do, Harold? Let's get this over with."

The man tossed Cole a phone. "It has one number in there. The mayor. Call him and tell him that Oscar is to have the next position on the SWAT team."

"Harold . . ." Cole almost felt sorry for the man. He was defeated and refused to admit it.

"Call him!"

"You know this isn't going to work! Even if I tell him and he agrees, it's not going to hold up after all of this is finished!"

The weapon shook and tears slid down the man's cheeks. "It will! We came up with a plan. He failed. I won't. Make the call!"

"What plan?" Cole asked.

"Matthews and I. We planned it down to the last detail to get justice for our sons. Charlie and Oscar."

"Let me guess. You two got to talking and hatched this whole plan."

"Yes. And when he told me what happened to his son, I told him what happened to mine, and we came up with a plan."

"Get rid of me," Kenzie said, "and Oscar would have a very good chance of replacing me."

"So simple," Harold said, confusion in his eyes. "But nothing went according to plan. And I didn't want to kill Eric"—he jabbed the weapon at her—"but you just wouldn't die!"

"Dad?"

The voice came from down the hallway. The footsteps. Lots of footsteps.

His team.

"Harold," Cole said, "it's time to put the gun down. You're surrounded with no way out. Give it up before Oscar loses his father."

"He's lost me anyway," the man whispered. "I've done things I never would have thought possible." He looked at Kenzie. "Until you."

"Dad, please!" Oscar stood in the doorway, Cross next to him with his weapon drawn.

Harold swallowed, then settled the barrel of the weapon under his chin.

"No!" Kenzie's yell accompanied her forward motion. She slammed herself into Harold and they both hit the broken floor. The gun skittered and Cole went after it while someone jerked Oscar back. But Harold rolled after the weapon and managed to beat Cole to it. He curled his fingers around the grip and lifted it, aiming at the door as the team poured into the small room.

Harold fired just as Cole tackled him, yelling, "Don't shoot him!" But they would if it meant saving him or Kenzie.

It wasn't necessary. Harold had given up. He lay still, breathing hard and staring at the far wall.

"Butler!" Kenzie's shout echoed, and while Cowboy took care of securing the prisoner, Kenzie held her hands up to Cross and he sliced through the zip tie with a knife. She scurried to Butler, who was sitting and pressing on his thigh while blood spewed between his fingers. "I need a medical bag! Someone, get me a bag!" She looked at Cole. "Give me your T-shirt." Cole yanked his shirt over his head and tossed it to her. She turned to Cross. "I need the knife."

He gave it to her, and she cut a strip out of Cole's shirt, then handed it to him along with the knife. "Cut more strips. Anyone got a pen? Anything? I need to make a tourniquet if that bag is going to take too much longer to get here."

Someone handed her a pen and she fashioned the tourniquet, pulling it tight just above his wound. Butler's jaw was clenched and his face pale while he breathed in through his nose. "Where are the paramedics?" she asked. "He needs something for the pain."

"They're coming."

She glanced at Butler. "The bleeding is slowing. You're going to be okay." She tied the other strips around the tourniquet to soak up the excess.

"Feeling a little lightheaded."

"Yeah. That's normal. Just hang in there. What's your blood type?"

"A negative."

"Got it."

Cole started to volunteer to donate if the man needed it, but Kenzie's narrow-eyed glare told him that wouldn't be a good idea. Still woozy, he agreed with a nod.

"And someone get Cole a protein bar and a soda or some orange juice. Before he was taken, he gave blood and is about to pass out. If you can find the Buick, there are two bars in the glove compartment."

"On it," one of the other officers said.

Paramedics finally entered and Kenzie raided their equipment for everything she needed.

Cole turned his attention to Harold Woodruff and Oscar. The older man stood with his head dropped to his chest, defeated and trying to look invisible.

But Cole had questions.

The officer returned with two protein bars, a bottle of water, a ham sandwich, and a cold Coke. When Cole raised a brow, the woman shrugged. "I brought my lunch today. You need it more than I do."

"Thanks." While he started scarfing, the officer pulled a phone encased in a clear evidence bag from her pocket and handed it to Kenzie. "Found this tossed near the Buick. When I turned it on, I realized it was yours. I know it's evidence, but there are probably a lot of messages on there you might need to check."

"Thanks. You're right." She tapped the screen and lifted the phone to her ear.

With the food in his system, Cole's energy started to return and he took in a grateful breath.

Once he was deemed fit to be transported, officers left with Harold in tow. He'd be arrested and taken to the hospital for an evaluation, then the legal process would ramp up in earnest.

Buzz approached. "I get off my deathbed to come save your sorry self, and you didn't even have the grace to get out of the way and give me a shot."

"Sorry about that," Cole said.

Buzz scowled. "Seriously, I didn't have a shot when Kenzie tackled him and y'all were rolling all over the place."

"I know, man. It's all good."

He shook his head. "Harold Woodruff. Can't believe it."

"None of us can."

Buzz left, and Cole looked at Kenzie, taking in her scuffed appearance, flyaway hair, flashing eyes, and jutting jaw. She'd never looked more beautiful. "Kenzie?"

"Yeah?"

"I think I've fallen in love with you."

Her eyes widened and her jaw dropped slightly before she snapped it shut, then stepped up on her tiptoes to place a kiss on his cheek. "Let's talk later."

THIRTY-ONE

"Let's talk later?" Kenzie whispered the words as she stepped out of the HQ shower. *Really? Let's talk later?*

She was an idiot. The man had said he had fallen in love with her and she—

Yeah, an idiot.

When she walked out of the dressing room thirty minutes later, Cole was waiting. Thankfully, he was alone, but he raised a brow at her. "'Let's talk later'?"

She groaned. "I'm sorry."

"I don't want an apology. I want . . . well, not for you to say it if you don't feel the same, but at least acknowledge that we have something between us. If we do. Or if it's just one-sided, then—" He bit off the words and shut his eyes. "And I really need you to say something, so I'll shut up."

She went to him and wrapped her arms around his waist. "Cole, you took me by surprise. I almost wasn't sure I even heard you correctly and wasn't sure how to respond."

"I see."

"No, I don't think you do."

"Then help me out here."

"Okay, since you've taken the first brave step and laid your feelings on the line, I guess I can do no less. The long and short of it is, I've been in love with you for a long time." At his swiftly indrawn breath, she smiled and shrugged. "But you've always seemed out of my reach. Or league or whatever. And then you were crazy about Tracy, then you were my supervisor, and I couldn't give the impression that I was flirting or seeking any kind of special treatment."

He nodded. "I know. I was in the same predicament of being your supervisor and avoiding the appearance of giving you any special treatment. Then I realized my attitude might be encouraging the others to keep you at arm's length and so . . ." He shrugged. "Well, you know."

"Yeah."

"You know, for a while I thought Logan might have been the one targeting you. I didn't want to think him capable of it, but you and your brothers are so competitive, I have to admit, it crossed my mind."

"Crossed mine too, but don't tell him. He'd be so hurt. And mad."

"I'll take it to the grave."

"Not anytime soon, please."

His eyes softened and dropped to her lips. "No, not anytime soon. I really want to kiss you."

Heat crept into her cheeks. "And I wouldn't protest, but not here."

"Nope, not here."

"Should we head to the hospital to check on Butler?"

He cleared his throat and stepped back. "Good idea."

Once they were in her car and headed down the road, Cole glanced at her. "So, what happened with the whole triathlon thing? You still planning on competing?"

She laughed. "No, I'm afraid that one's on the back burner. All of my training has gone sideways." She shrugged. "It's okay. There's always next year."

"What about if we train together for next year?"

"You'd do that?"

"Sure. Why not? It'll be fun."

She raised a brow. "You hate running."

"I do not. I mean, it's not my favorite thing to do, but hate is such a strong word." He sighed. "Okay, but I'll make the sacrifice to be with you."

"Hm. Well, that's sweet, but I'm still not sure 'fun' is the right word."

He grinned at her. "Guess we'll find out."

Twenty minutes later, they walked into the hospital and made their way to Butler's room, only to pull up short when they found the door propped open and Oscar Woodruff at his friend's side.

Oscar stood and sighed. "I'll come back later."

"Don't leave on our account," Kenzie said. Oscar hesitated and Kenzie looked at Butler, who was watching them with a frown. "How are you doing?"

"I hear I'm alive, thanks to you." Red crept up into his neck. "I'm also aware I owe you multiple apologies."

"Accepted. Can we let it go and work together in the future?"

He met her gaze and nodded. "Yeah."

"Good." She smiled, then turned to Oscar. "Just to make it clear, I—" She glanced at Cole. "We don't hold you responsible for anything your father did, so there's no need to feel uncomfortable around us."

Relief and gratitude flashed across his face. "Thank you for that. I truly had no idea—" He pressed his lips together and shook his head. "I knew he had his issues. He always has. Always wanted what others had and was bitter about it when he didn't have it. But . . . I just . . . I don't know. I never saw this coming, that's for sure. He's, uh . . . here at the hospital getting evaluated, then he'll be transferred to the jail. I'm just so confused about all of this that I don't even know what to think."

"Do you know the story of our grandparents and their history with the mental hospital?"

Oscar frowned. "Not really. Dad used to mumble about what a raw deal his father got when he was let go as the director, but he never gave me details. I do know that your grandfather took over and was there until the place was closed. Grandpa Stephen married my grandmother, Hettie Smith, when they were older. I think she was like in her early forties when my dad was born, and she died shortly after, making him an only child. As am I."

Kenzie nodded. "I've been reading Cole's grandmother Eliza's journal. Your grandfather, Stephen Woodruff, lost his position to my grandfather, Dr. George King. And then lost the woman he fell in love with—my grandmother Betsy—to my grandfather. Apparently, he never got over that. Then when my father beat your father out of the chief of police position, things really heated up, and your father, influenced by the bitterness of his father, found a way to get the position."

She took a deep breath and wondered if she should stop, but Oscar, although white-faced and tight-jawed, waved for her to continue. "I might as well hear it all."

"So," she said, "when he learned that the SWAT position was between the two of us and I got it, well, it sent him over the edge."

Oscar dropped his head into his hands. "I'm so sorry," he mumbled around his palms. "He's the reason your mother is dead. He hired that guy, Talbot, to mess with the brakes on your dad's car and then wait at the stop sign as backup." Oscar swallowed. "When Talbot was out on bail, he went to collect what Dad owed him for doing all of that, and Dad killed him."

Kenzie exchanged a startled glance with Cole. "He just told you that?"

"Yeah. They let me ride with him to the hospital since he was so agitated, and my presence seemed to calm him. And make him way too chatty. He confessed everything in spite of me trying to shut him up and get him to wait for his lawyer. He's even the one who stole the evidence and set your dad up to take the fall so he could get the job."

Kenzie nodded. "Yeah, I knew about all that. He mentioned it after he grabbed me."

Sorrow and regret creased his features and he shook his head. "I'll turn my resignation in first thing in the morning."

"Wait, what?" Kenzie said. "Why?"

"Dude, no," Butler said at the same time.

"Well, I'd think that's obvious. People will never look at me the same."

"This will pass," Cole said. "You're not responsible for your father's actions."

"Any more than I am," Kenzie said. "My father may not have done what everyone accused him of, but he wasn't exactly a likable boss."

"The Dictator," Oscar said.

"Exactly."

The man rose. "I'll think about it. I need to go see if they'll let me visit with Dad before they take him to a cell. I've already got his lawyer on standby, so we'll see what he has to say." Oscar looked at Butler. "Again, I'm sorry, man."

Butler nodded. "I am too. For you. For your family. For all of it. I'll be in touch."

Oscar left and Kenzie glanced at her phone. "Well, we hate to run, but my grandmother's ninety-seventh birthday celebration is in an hour."

Butler nodded and locked his eyes on hers. "Thank you, King. I can't say it enough." He swallowed, then cleared his throat. "You're a good example of what a real professional is. I was a jerk and definitely not a team player or professional by any stretch. I really am sorry."

"And you're forgiven. I'm glad we can move forward from here."

Once she and Cole were back in her vehicle, she buckled up and laughed. "I kind of obligated you to go with me to my grandmother's party. You game?"

"I'm happy to go with you."

She smiled. "I'm happy about that."

He returned her smile.

"I've got to swing by my house first."

"Sounds good. My car's still there."

After a brief stop at Kenzie's house, Cole followed her directions to the assisted-living home where her grandmother lived. It was a step up from the one Oscar's father had been in and had a private room where families could celebrate their loved ones without having to take them from the facility.

When Kenzie walked into the room followed by Cole, the first person to notice them was Logan. He raised a brow in her direction and she shrugged. He grinned and she groaned. The teasing was coming.

Cole must have caught the look because he turned his gaze on her, then slid an arm around her shoulders and tucked her next to him.

"What are you doing?"

"Getting it over with."

"What?"

"Your whole family is here. Now we can just make it known we're a couple and move on."

"Oh."

He tensed. "Unless you'd rather not."

She rose on tiptoes to kiss his cheek. "I'd rather."

He relaxed. "Good."

HE'D RATHER TOO. He'd rather have her alone and in his arms, but that wasn't to be just yet.

Soon. Patience.

Once her family realized they were a couple and congratulated them, the attention focused back on her grandmother.

Kenzie let out a slow breath. "Well, that was painless."

He laughed. "I think I might be insulted."

"No, it's just . . . they've mellowed, I guess."

Her brother Kash walked up to them with a beautiful woman on his arm. Kenzie smiled. "Amelia."

The woman kissed Kenzie's cheek, then stepped back and gave Cole the once-over. Approval glinted in her eyes. "I assume this is your plus-one for the dinner party tomorrow."

"He is." Kenzie made the introductions.

"Excellent choice," Amelia said. "Very nice to meet you, Cole."

"And you," he murmured.

"Come on," Kash said to Amelia. "Let's go see if Paul has a plus-one he's bringing to the dinner."

They moved on with a little wave, and Kenzie squeezed Cole's hand. "I want to get my grandmother alone at some point and ask her about the journal and why she's had it all these years."

"Get in the back of the line and be the last one. You'll have more time."

Kenzie followed the advice, only to have her father roll up to her. "Hi."

He cleared his throat. "I . . . uh . . . suppose I should have said this before now, but I'm glad you're okay."

"Thanks, Dad."

"And you've given me something I haven't had in a very long time." He pulled in a breath. "Some peace."

Kenzie hesitated, then leaned over to hug him. He wrapped his arms around her and squeezed. "I'm glad," she whispered.

"Yeah. So don't be a stranger. You know where I live." Then he rolled away, and Cole stepped forward with Kenzie to face her grandmother.

The woman smiled, the creases in her cheeks and forehead and around her kind eyes making her look like an ancient, wise confidante.

Kenzie knelt in front of her and took her hands. "I found the journal, Grandma Betsy."

Her eyes softened. "Have you read it?"

"Some of it. But, honestly, I'd rather hear how you and Grandpa George helped Eliza escape."

"Such a long time ago."

"I know. And Cole wants to hear too."

Grandma Betsy turned her attention to Cole and let out a shaky breath. "You look like her, you know."

"So I've been told."

"She's been gone for such a long time, but I still miss her every day."

"Tell us about her, Gran, tell us about the night you helped her escape and find her way to William. And then we have a story for you."

"Oh, how intriguing."

She leaned forward and squeezed Kenzie's hands while Cole held his breath. "Well, Eliza's father was determined she was going to marry the man he'd picked out for her, Edward Hampton. They were in the real estate business and had loads of money. Eliza really expected him to be an arrogant so-and-so, but that young man was as kind and gentle as they come. The truth was, he had his heart set on someone else too, and they had a little discussion about it. George and I were just on the other side of the horse pasture when Edward and Eliza came walking up to the car. She introduced Edward to George and me, and we wound up being friends for the rest of our lives. Edward did wind up marrying his true love. But anyway, that night, Eliza got in the car and off we went to see William. They were married the next day at the courthouse and lived with his family until they could afford the deposit on an apartment. It wasn't too much longer that their first child was born." She smiled at Cole. "Your uncle Daniel." She spread her thin, wrinkled hands. "And the rest, as they say, is history."

"And my great-grandfather, Eliza's father, just let her go?" Cole asked.

"Cut her off without a penny but had a heart attack and died before he could change his will or be held accountable for his attempt to kill Eliza."

"That's quite the story, Grandma Betsy," Kenzie said.

"It is that for sure. Now, tell me yours."

An hour later, Cole led Kenzie from the building and to his vehicle. At the passenger door, he turned her to face him. "Now?"

She grinned. "Now."

"Thank God." He lowered his lips to hers and pulled her closer, so grateful she was alive and warm in his arms. She wove her fingers into his hair and tugged. And that was that.

No, not just yet. The kiss lingered and the air in his lungs seeped out, his knees went weak, and his stomach turned flips while his heart burned with a love that almost scared him.

He really should let her go.

And he would.

In another minute.

Once he had the feel of her lips memorized so that it would last him until morning. Then he remembered he was driving her home and could kiss her good night. He let her go and stepped back.

She stared up at him, a slightly dazed expression in her eyes. He didn't dare feel smug about that at all, as he was sure he mirrored the look. "Well," he said and cleared his throat.

"Yes. Well."

"That was—"

"If you say nice, I will literally punch you."

He laughed. Then snorted. And laughed again. "How about smoking hot?"

"That works."

"I think we should go now."

"Absolutely."

THIRTY-TWO

ONE WEEK LATER

Kenzie dressed in sweats and a T-shirt, then pulled a hoodie over that. The weather had turned decidedly colder, but today was a special day and Cole was coming to get her in less than five minutes. His church contacts had come through, and while she'd seen pictures of the new court, today was the day they'd get to hang out and shoot hoops with anyone who stopped by.

She pulled her hair into a ponytail, slipped into her tennis shoes, and met Cole at the door two seconds after he rang the bell. He leaned in for a kiss and she gladly returned it. Then he grinned down at her. "Ready to get stomped?"

"At basketball? I have three very competitive brothers, remember?"

"Oh yeah." He frowned. "Okay, you're on my team."

She laughed and swept out the door while he locked it behind them. The drive to the trailer park on the other side of town didn't take long. They passed Micah's home and pulled around to the new basketball court.

"Stands out like a shiny new penny," Kenzie said.

"Yeah. I just hope they'll take pride in it and help care for it."

She nodded to Micah. The young teen was pushing a broom across the concrete court. "I think there's hope."

"Yeah."

When Micah saw them, he leaned the broom against the fence and trotted over to them. His sister Randa followed, coming right up to Cole and grabbing his hand. "We ate all the M&M's. You got any more?"

"Randa!" Micah was clearly scandalized by his sibling.

Cole laughed. "Not today, kid, sorry."

"It's okay." She skipped away to grab one of the fully inflated basketballs and toss it at the kid-height hoop that had been installed on the side.

Micah shook Cole's hand and shot Kenzie a shy glance. "I can't believe y'all did this for us."

"You deserve it."

He ducked his head and shuffled his feet. "You two going to play?"

"As soon as the others get here." Cole nodded to the teens heading their way. "You spread the word?"

"Yeah. Figured if most of them liked playing on it, they'd help keep others from tearing it up."

"Good strategy."

"Thanks."

"We have a few friends coming too," Kenzie said as Jesslyn climbed out of her Chevy Traverse and waved. James and Lainie arrived, followed by James' new partner, Nathan Carlisle, and then Buzz, Cowboy, Greene, and Otis. Butler had texted his regrets. He was still recovering from getting shot.

"Is that Oscar?" Kenzie asked.

"Yeah, I invited him. He gave a good bit of money to the project once he heard what we were doing."

"I don't mind at all."

They all walked onto the court, and Micah grinned, made introductions, then aimed the ball at the hoop and let it soar.

When it swished, everyone cheered and he clapped his hands.

"That's what I'm talking about. Everyone divide into teams and let the games begin!"

Cole, being the tallest one there, easily made the tip-off to Kenzie, who dribbled the ball and passed it to Jesslyn. Jesslyn handed it off to Nathan, who took the shot but was blocked by one of Micah's buddies. He grinned at the ribbing that followed, and Kenzie couldn't help notice Jesslyn's gaze followed him—at least until she realized what she was doing.

For the next three hours, they played and got to know the residents of the trailer park. Some were more friendly than others, of course, but all in all, Kenzie was glad the rapport had been established and could only pray it made a difference in the way they viewed law enforcement in general.

When it was their turn for a rest, Cole pulled Kenzie aside. "You ready to have our first real date?"

"Not all gross and hot and sweaty like this. Not on your life."

He laughed. "I mean after showers and a change of clothes."

"Where are we going?"

"You up for a swim in the lake?"

"You're out of your mind."

"I'm kidding. How about a picnic and a boat ride? Cross said I could use his anytime."

"Now you're talking."

He pulled her close for a kiss. Moments later, he stepped back and looked down at her. "Sorry, was that gross?"

"Hmm . . . I think you need to kiss me again for an accurate assessment."

He did so. Sweat and all. Then lifted his head and laughed. "I think I'm going to like doing life with you, Ms. King."

"The feeling is mutual, Mr. Garrison. Gross kisses and all."

Turn the page for
a sneak peek at the next book
in the Lake City Heroes series,

SERIAL BURN

COMING SOON

ONE

Deputy State Fire Marshal Jesslyn McCormick surveyed the charred remains of the building that used to house a thriving church community—*her* church community. It had burned all day yesterday, and firefighters had worked tirelessly to put the blaze out.

This afternoon, she'd been able to do her walk-through with the structural engineer and established a safe path from one end of the scene to the other while she'd examined and collected what she could. It had been enough.

Now she stood in silence, helmet on the ground beside her, gloves tucked into her protective coat pockets, working hard to contain her devastation at the tragic sight. And even harder to control her tears at the thought of sweet Mr. Christie, a member of the cleaning service, lying in the hospital with second-degree burns and smoke inhalation that might very well kill him.

FBI Special Agent Nathan Carlisle stepped up beside her. "Are you all right?" His compassionate green eyes nearly destroyed what was left of her composure. She wasn't supposed to cry on the job.

"No." Maybe she couldn't cry, but she could be honest. Nathan and his partner, Andrew Ross, had been called in because burning a

285

church was considered a hate crime. She wouldn't be able to prove that, of course, until the suspect was caught, but might as well bring in the FBI right from the start. ATF was involved along with the Lake City Police Department.

He placed a hand on her shoulder. "I'm sorry. I mean it, Jesslyn." His kind eyes said he really did. "Thanks."

"Do you need to sit this one out?" he asked, his voice low. "I'm sure another marshal wouldn't mind taking this off your hands."

She shook her head. "No way. This one's personal." Which meant she probably *should* sit it out, but . . . nope. Not unless she was forced to.

"I don't blame you. I'd feel the same way."

She'd met Nathan a few months ago when he was in Lake City for a vacation and visiting his family. His office was in Charlotte, North Carolina. He and Detective James Cross were good friends, and James had invited Nathan to hang out with them when he wasn't with family. Which had been pretty frequently now that she thought about it. Whatever that story was, she'd grown fond of Nathan in record time. Too fond?

But she *was* honored she got to work with him—with all of them. And go to church with most of them.

Until now.

"A building isn't the church," he said.

She slanted him a glance. "You're a mind reader now?"

"Not exactly, but I read facial expressions pretty well."

"I'll save you the effort. The person who did it either didn't know Mr. Christie was there working, in spite of the vehicle parked right beside the back entrance, or he—or she—didn't care. Either way, a good man is in the hospital, and while I'm upset about the damage to the church, I'm more upset about Mr. Christie." And she wanted to talk to him when he woke up. If he woke up. It was possible he'd seen the arsonist. But she'd have to get in line. Nathan and Andrew would be the ones doing the questioning.

"Of course." Nathan paused. "Can I ask what you saw that makes you say it was arson?"

"Fires usually burn upward and outward. They create a V-shaped pattern." She pointed to the smoldering, blackened structure. "There are multiple V-shaped patterns in there. So what would you deduce from that?"

"Multiple starting points," he said.

"Give the man an A." She sighed. "And the detection dog alerted to an accelerant. Which could mean nothing more than someone stored cleaning products together, but you don't store those in the pulpit, Pastor Graham's office, the kitchen, and the nursery."

He winced. "Someone deliberately burned the nursery?"

"They did."

"That's a special kind of evil," he muttered.

"Part of me wants to take it as a message of some sort. Another part, the rational part, knows it was just a good place to make sure the fire spread hot and fast since it was next to the kitchen—in which all of the gas burners had been turned on." She shrugged. "Whoever did this was determined this building was going to burn to the ground. But here's the kicker. What's interesting is the purple stains."

"Why is that interesting?"

"They indicate a specific kind of accelerant. One that's homemade and easy to make, relatively safe to handle . . ." She shrugged. "But I'll know more once I talk to Marissa at the lab."

"You think this is a one and done?" Nathan asked.

"If it's a hate crime and they simply wanted to burn the church down to make a point, then yeah. If it's more than that . . . you investigate and figure that part out."

"You don't think this is the end of it, do you?"

She raised a brow at him. "What do you think?"

He shook his head. "I know what I hope. Unfortunately, it's not what I think."

"Same."

She stood for another moment, processing.

"How do you do it?" Nathan asked, breaking into her thoughts.

"Do what?"

"Your job. James told me about your house burning down when you were a child and losing your family. I can't imagine. And then you have to face fire every day." He shuddered. "I hate fire. Don't even like bonfires."

She couldn't believe he brought it up. Her past wasn't a secret, but it did seem to be a taboo topic for almost everyone around her. "Even though it was almost twenty-five years ago, I'll admit, it's not easy," she said. "But I wasn't there when it happened, so all I have is my imagination as to how everything went."

"Sometimes imagination is worse than the actual thing."

"True." She cut him a glance. "And mine is an educated imagination. I've studied the notes. I know exactly what happened. I just don't know who did it." She nodded to the church. "But this? This isn't easy, but it's not hard either. It's my job, my passion. One I chose as an attempt to honor my family. An arsonist killed them and was never caught. I can't describe what that feels like. I never want another child or family member to go through that." She blew out a low breath. "So, while each fire triggers memories and regrets, it also reminds me of why I do what I do."

"Makes sense." He went silent for a moment, and Jesslyn waited for him to get around to asking whatever he was thinking about asking. "I caught the interview you did a couple of days ago about your family's death. The plea to help catch the arsonist before the twenty-fifth anniversary of the fire."

"You saw that, huh?"

"You did a great job. Your love for them and your passion for justice came through loud and clear—especially your intent to keep looking until you find the person who killed them."

"Oh. Yes. I probably should have toned that down a bit."

It had been the first time she'd publicly spoken out about her family's deaths, and the surge of anger and grief that had swept over her caused her to lose a fraction of control over her emotions. She'd jabbed her finger at the camera. "If you're alive, I just want you to know that I'm still searching. You killed my family twenty-five years ago. They didn't deserve that and neither did I. I hope you can't forget that night. I hope it lives with you and torments you each and every hour of each and every day. You may think you've gotten away with it and that people have forgotten, but I'm here to say you haven't and people haven't. In fact, I have a plan to make sure everyone remembers that night. Remembers my parents for all the good they did before their premature deaths. I'll remind the world that my sisters never got to grow up. They will be remembered while you remain in the shadows, always looking over your shoulder wondering when I'm going to catch up with you. Because I will, and that's a promise I intend to keep."

Jesslyn swallowed against the sudden surge of emotion and looked Nathan in the eye.

He offered her a gentle smile. "No, I don't think you needed to tone it down. It was raw and honest, and people will admire you for what you're doing."

"Thank you," she whispered, then cleared her throat. "I just don't want my family forgotten. They deserve more."

"Absolutely."

"I meant what I said. I plan to find him one day. As long as he's still alive, I'll find him."

"What if he's dead?"

She hesitated. "I've thought about that and feel like I'd know."

"How?"

She sighed. "Truly, I have no idea. I'm probably just lying to myself about that in my desperate desire to see someone pay for their murders. It just tears me up inside to think of him getting away with it. Maybe even laughing about it all these years."

His eyes lingered on her, studying her. Dissecting her?

She snagged his gaze. "What?"

"The more I talk to you, the more you intrigue me."

Okay, that was bold. "Hm."

"Too blunt?"

"No." Too perceptive, maybe. She'd have to remember that if she wanted to hide her feelings from him. But right now, she didn't. "You know my story. What's yours?"

He raised a brow. "I have a feeling I'm missing a few details."

"Not many." Okay, maybe a few.

"Jess?"

She turned to see Pastor Chuck Graham walking toward her, sorrow in his blue eyes. She looked at Nathan. "Excuse me a minute?"

"Of course."

She hugged the seventy-two-year-old man who looked like he'd aged another few years overnight. "I'm sorry, Chuck."

He pressed fingers to his lips. "Just . . . why?"

"I don't know. Only God and the arsonist know the answer to that. So, unless one of them talks . . ."

Chuck blinked back tears and nodded. "Well, this won't stop us. We'll just rebuild and find a place to meet in the interim."

Jesslyn nodded. "Absolutely."

Other church members had started to gather outside the perimeter of the crime scene tape, and Chuck walked over to them, his shoulders held straight, chin lifted high. When he reached the group, they hugged, shoulder to shoulder, then started to pray. Jesslyn ground her molars and swept her gaze around the onlookers. Sometimes arsonists liked to watch the fallout of their work, but no one in particular stood out to her.

Then again, whoever was responsible wouldn't be wearing a sign labeled "I did it."

"You think he's here?" Nathan asked, his voice low.

She spun to face him. "You really need to stop doing that. It's unnerving."

His lips twisted into an amused smile that sent her heart racing down a path like it hadn't done since . . . ever.

All righty then.

"You're an investigator," he said. "It's not hard for another cop to tell what you're thinking." His gaze slid from hers and scanned the crowd just like she had. "We'll get some video footage and pictures, but I don't think he's here. At least not in view."

"Well, he doesn't have to be." She pointed to the TV crew camped out to the side, cameras rolling. A helicopter buzzed overhead with more cameras. "He can sit at home and watch the whole thing from the comfort of his recliner."

AFTER ALL THIS TIME with the department, this was the first time Nathan had gotten to work with Jesslyn, and he had to admit, watching her in action was downright impressive. He'd heard there wasn't anything she didn't know about fires and accelerants, but hearing her talk about purple stains and what they meant was fascinating.

Hanging out with her at a friend's lake house was very different from sharing a crime scene with her. While reserved by nature, at the lake house she was relaxed and witty when she decided to speak. Here, she was intense, focused, and dead serious.

Impressive.

Admirable.

Attractive.

Okay, maybe that last one wasn't exactly wise, but the truth was, he'd been interested in Jesslyn long before today. The moment he met her, he'd decided he wanted to get to know her better. Which was why he'd kept his distance. He had issues. Burdens he'd never share. Which meant he'd keep his attraction tucked away in that part of his heart he'd slammed shut years ago. Not even his partner, Andrew, knew he and Jesslyn had a whole lot in common when it came to their growing-up years. That they'd both lost people they loved to a fire. While Jesslyn seemed to race toward it, he avoided it at all costs. Fire terrified him, and he wanted no part of it. Investigating it was fine. Just don't ask him to get close to it.

Andrew had no idea of any of that, but they'd only been working together for a few months. They were still building that bond most partners grew into. And while he'd die for the man if it came down to it, he wasn't ready to share his deepest, darkest secrets. That kind of trust took time, and he was in no hurry to move it along. Thankfully, Andrew didn't seem to care and tended to mind his own business. But the potential was there and that was all that mattered for now.

Nathan transferred his thoughts to the woman beside him and gave her a sidelong glance. She continued to stand silent and still, her eyes on the scene, giving no indication she was aware of his presence.

Another reason to keep his interest in her six feet under. She might not appreciate it, and they had to work together.

Andrew headed toward them, and Nathan cleared his throat. "I'll call you if I have any questions," he told Jesslyn.

"Of course." She finally turned to him and offered him a slight smile. "It was good to see you, in spite of the circumstances."

He really needed his heart not to do that thing it did every time she barely smiled at him. Andrew stopped to talk to one of the other firefighters, giving Nathan a few more precious seconds alone with Jesslyn. "You too. I'll be in touch."

She nodded and the smile slid away. Then she took a deep breath and picked up her helmet. "I've got a report to write. I'll see you guys later."

"Later."

She walked away, straightening her shoulders and lifting her chin, preparing herself for battle. Because that's what the investigation was going to be. A battle to find the arsonist before he struck again. Because they both knew the odds were that he would. They'd have to tell every church in the vicinity to be on alert.

On that cheerful thought, he turned to his smirking partner, who'd snuck up on him. "What?"

"Why don't you just ask her out already?"

So much for Andrew minding his own business. But Nathan heard the friendliness behind the mild teasing. "Why would I do that?"

"Because you want to?"

Nathan sighed. He really did, but . . . "I can't."

"Can't or won't?"

"Both."

Andrew's smirk turned into a frown, but Nathan ignored him and headed for his department-issued Dodge Charger. While he liked the vehicle, he much preferred his Rhino XT—despite the ribbing he got from fellow officers for having such an expensive ride. But his brother-in-law, Kip Hart, was a personal injury lawyer and had presented him the vehicle as a Christmas present. Nate had tried to refuse, but the pleading look on his sister Carly's face had him caving—with the caveat that when his twelve-year-old-nephew was old enough to drive, Nathan could gift it back.

"We'll cross that bridge when we come to it," Carly said.

And now, Nathan had two more years of driving the cool SUV before he had to figure something out. In the meantime, he had an arsonist to find and a woman to put out of his head.

As soon as he climbed into the driver's seat, his phone rang and he answered it with a quick swipe of the screen before he registered the name. *Rats.* "Hey."

"Wait, is this a recording?" Eli, Nathan's oldest brother and all-around know-it-all, teased.

"Stuff it, bro. I've got reports to write. What's up?"

"Ah, you didn't check your caller ID before answering, huh?"

"Eli . . ."

"I know you avoid me until you just can't anymore."

"Only because you annoy me." Saying the words without heat didn't make them any less true. Some days he wished he'd taken an assignment on the other side of the country.

"Why do you think that is, Natty?"

"It's Nathan." *Natty* was in the past, when life was fun and innocence still existed. But Eli would call him whatever name he wanted to because he was Eli. And Eli only cared about himself, in spite of his profession. Always had, always would. "Tell me what you want or I'm hanging up." His brother the psychiatrist. Always trying to psychoanalyze him. Did Eli truly not understand how obnoxious he was? It wasn't the first time Nathan had wondered that and definitely wouldn't be the last. He probably should just flat-out ask the guy but was afraid of the lecture he'd get in return.

"Fine," Eli said, "but one day you're going to need to stop taking your anger at yourself out on others. It's way past time you forgave yourself for—"

Nathan hung up.

Ten seconds later, his phone buzzed again and he let it go to voicemail. In his rearview mirror, he could see Jesslyn standing beside her car, on the phone. He watched her, wishing once more things could be different. That he could be different. That his past was different. She turned and caught his eye before he could look away, freezing him on the spot. He lifted his hand in what he hoped was a casual wave and drove out of the parking lot.

ACKNOWLEDGMENTS

Many thanks to all who had input into the story. Thank you to my crimescenewriter loop with all the professional law enforcement peeps who are more than willing to offer help and insight into the professions they love. If you're a writer, this is a must-have resource for your research toolbox. ☺

Thank you to Retired FBI Special Agents Wayne Smith and Dru Wells for all the help you give on each and every story. If there's something wrong, it's not because of them! ☺

Thank you to my family who offer unconditional love and support that allows me to write my stories. I couldn't do this without you.

Thank you to Revell and the amazing publishing team. Most especially to Barb Barnes who can't officially retire until I do! Thank you to the beta readers who catch mistakes that slip through! They're tricky little ninjas, but you rarely allow one to escape.

Thank you to the beloved readers who clamor for more stories. I'm so blessed that you love my books and I don't take you for granted. Thank you, thank you, thank you.

Thank you, as always, to Dr. Jan Kneeland who answers texts like, "I need to shoot someone, but I don't want them to die. What's a good place on the body for a bullet?" She's finally learned to roll with it. Ha!

Thank you to my brainstorming buddies who never fail to offer multiple solutions to escape every corner I write myself into. #pantser problems

Lynette Eason is the *USA Today* bestselling author of *Double Take*, as well as the Extreme Measures, Danger Never Sleeps, Blue Justice, Women of Justice, Deadly Reunions, Hidden Identity, and Elite Guardians series. She is the winner of three ACFW Carol Awards, the Selah Award, and the Inspirational Reader's Choice Award, among others. She is a graduate of the University of South Carolina and has a master's degree in education from Converse College. Eason lives in South Carolina with her husband. They have two adult children. Learn more at LynetteEason.com.

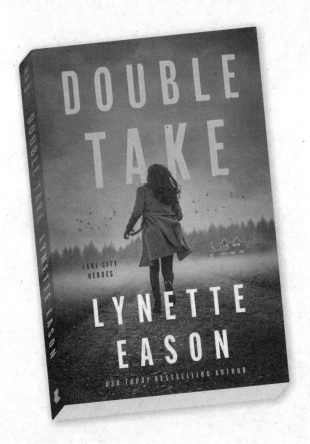

Find **HIGH-OCTANE THRILLS** in the
DANGER NEVER SLEEPS Series

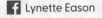 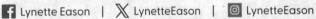